A sound in the distan
tension his thoughts
him. "What was that?" Scott asked softly,
but he knew.

"Sounds like an engine..." Dorian was backing up inside the cave as she spoke. Scott dropped to his stomach, sliding toward the edge of the small clearing of land in front of the cave. Hoping that the landscaping of desert brush would hide him from whoever might be driving down below, he peered into a vastness that angled downward for hundreds of yards.

"What do you see?" Dorian's voice had lowered, sounding strangely vulnerable to him.

Was she hoping for rescue?

As he sought out the source of the engine that was echoing in the canyon below, Scott found himself feeding on that supposed hope. He'd found his kidnapper, was on the brink of taking down the ring—everything was finally aligning...

"Get down!" He spat the words, his thoughts interrupted by the sight of the sun glinting off metal.

Dear Reader,

Welcome to Sierra's Web! The nationally renowned firm of experts, college friends bound by tragedy, are all working on this one. This story has been germinating inside me for a couple of years. I saw it. I felt it. And finally, it came to life! Having been in there so long, it took a lot of me with it!

As you run for your life, you're getting my firsthand knowledge of sights and sounds in the mountain range that I look at every single day as I write. The Superstition Mountains, on the east side of the Phoenix Valley, are massive and hold lore and life and all kinds of magic. I've climbed to the top of the highest peak. I've been in the middle of the range with no cell service. I've visited a little town similar to the one in this book. I've stood at a mountain wall and tried to read centuries-old hieroglyphics. Right here in my Arizona mountains.

And a reunion—I had one of those, too. With my very first boyfriend. The first boy I'd ever kissed. Almost thirty years after our last young kiss. He looked me up on the internet just eighteen months after I'd driven by his town without stopping. A detour I took while on book tour. Thinking about him. We've been married almost seventeen years and love is still our driver. And my message? Believe in happily-ever-after. And most critically, believe in love.

Tara Taylor Quinn

A HIGH-STAKES REUNION

TARA TAYLOR QUINN

HARLEQUIN

ROMANTIC
SUSPENSE

HARLEQUIN®
ROMANTIC SUSPENSE™

Recycling programs for this product may not exist in your area.

ISBN-13: 978-1-335-59403-7

A High-Stakes Reunion

Copyright © 2024 by TTQ Books LLC

For questions and comments about the quality of this book, please contact us at CustomerService@Harlequin.com.

TM and ® are trademarks of Harlequin Enterprises ULC.

Harlequin Enterprises ULC
22 Adelaide St. West, 41st Floor
Toronto, Ontario M5H 4E3, Canada
www.Harlequin.com

Printed in Lithuania

MIX
Paper | Supporting responsible forestry
FSC® C021394

A *USA TODAY* bestselling author of over one hundred novels in twenty languages, **Tara Taylor Quinn** has sold more than seven million copies. Known for her intense emotional fiction, Ms. Quinn's novels have received critical acclaim in the UK and most recently from Harvard. She is the recipient of the Readers' Choice Award and has appeared often on local and national TV, including *CBS Sunday Morning*.

For TTQ offers, news and contests, visit www.tarataylorquinn.com!

Books by Tara Taylor Quinn

Harlequin Romantic Suspense

Sierra's Web

Tracking His Secret Child
Cold Case Sheriff
The Bounty Hunter's Baby Search
On the Run with His Bodyguard
Not Without Her Child
A Firefighter's Hidden Truth
Last Chance Investigation
Danger on the River
Deadly Mountain Rescue
A High-Stakes Reunion

The Coltons of Owl Creek

Colton Threat Unleashed

The Coltons of New York

Protecting Colton's Baby

Visit the Author Profile page at Harlequin.com for more titles.

To Tim—I am so thankful for our reunion, and you.
I loved you then, now and forever. Tara Lee Barney

Chapter 1

He was stealing his newborn! Dr. Dorian Lowell ignored the pounding of her heart as she raced through the darkness toward the gray-hooded, hunched over man hurrying from the small stucco birthing center. Her frantic steps silenced by the grass, she ran full tilt toward the old red truck parked in a corner of the lot. The two-hour-old boy needed constant medical attention. He'd die within hours without it.

She'd seen Jeremy, the estranged father, pull in and head into the birthing center moments before. Had warned Security.

He was almost at his truck, not running like she was, but moving at a good clip, head down, shielding the newborn he held in both arms, upright against his chest.

If she screamed for help, it was unlikely anyone would hear her.

If she ran for help, he'd get away.

That baby's only hope lay with Dorian rescuing him before his father got to the truck.

Breath constricted by the panic tightening her chest, she crossed onto the pavement just steps away from the young, slim-framed man, hoping to reason with him. They'd all had a rough day, and he was overwrought.

As soon as he heard her steps, he jerked, straightening, and pinned her with a glare that was menacing in the moonlight. His eyes. She didn't recognize them. Two sharp pinpoints of warning…

It wasn't Jeremy! And in her peripheral vision, she noticed a second truck—Jeremy's truck—parked down a couple of spaces in the lot.

Too late to stop her forward motion, she upped her momentum toward the tiny baby boy the stranger held, her self-defense class of long ago taking over as she kneed the kidnapper, grabbing for the baby—not Jeremy's baby—at the same time.

Her blow was strong enough to make the hard-looking man loosen his grip for the split second she'd needed. With the blue bundle wrapped in one arm, she raised her other hand to the man's face, ramming her palm into the base of his nose. She felt a crack as he backhanded her upside the head, and, dizzy, stumbling briefly, she ran.

A shot rang out behind her.

Swerving in between cars, she just kept running.

FBI Agent Scott Michaels broke all speed limits as he raced across a desert highway to the small birthing center in Las Sendas, Arizona, forty miles southeast of Phoenix. Every second counted when it meant the kidnapper had another second to get away from him.

Six months of trying to track a series of newborn kidnappings, to find anything that linked them—other than the MO, a message board on the dark web and a hunch—and he might have just found his first real lead. The first kidnapping gone wrong.

A mistake made.

He had an eyewitness. A renowned physician who'd been leaving the facility late that night due to a complicated birth that had nearly killed both mother and child.

A heroic doctor, from what he'd heard. The woman had single-handedly saved another newborn male child.

There was already a BOLO out on the old red pickup she'd described with the California plate, and if there really was a God out there, someone would locate the vehicle.

It could crack the case that had been haunting him for months.

For a split second, just after Scott had turned onto the road that would lead him from the highway into the small town, he thought his non-prayer had been answered. At the first intersection, still on the outskirts of civilization, he saw a truck. Old. Beat up, just like the witness had described.

But as he drew closer, his heart accepted what he'd expected to see. The truck, while old, was black, not red. And not only was the guy behind the wheel not exhibiting any evidence of being in a hurry, he was wearing a white shirt, not the gray hoodie the witness had described. And a cowboy hat, which he tilted toward Scott, waving him to pass through the intersection without stopping.

Giving Scott a clear view of the Arizona plate. Not California like the doctor had reported.

Still, didn't mean someone else couldn't find the red truck. A few minutes later, with adrenaline pumping hard, he pulled into the birthing center parking lot, which was ablaze with red flashing lights. Showing his badge, he was inside within a minute, and being directed to the room where the doctor was waiting for him.

Each minute that passed was another opportunity for the kidnapper to get to another newborn.

Because there'd be another baby stolen that night.

The ring Scott's gut told him was behind the kidnappings had an order to fill and had just lost the merchandise. He'd seen the sale pop up on the dark web that morning…

Grim-faced and determined, he knocked on the door he'd been shown, and opened it before the feminine "Come in" had even been completed.

Opened it and stood there…staring.

"Dorian…" He couldn't remember her last name. It would have changed anyway.

But he remembered her. Far too vividly.

"Scott?" Open-mouthed, with a reddening bruise marking the left side of her face from the ear down the jaw, she stared at him. In wrinkled purple scrubs, with her red hair up in a bun, she didn't look like she'd aged at all in the fourteen years since he'd had her in class.

And…very briefly…in his arms.

"You aren't in the army," she said.

And she wasn't wearing a wedding ring.

"I was. Trained in law enforcement, made rank of sergeant, but wanted to fight crime on a broader scale." None of her business. Just as his plans in the past hadn't been. But that hadn't stopped him from sharing them with her. And then regretting having done so.

"You saved a baby's life tonight," she blurted, blushing. He remembered that about her, too. The way her fair skin turned red anytime she said anything that made her uncomfortable. "Or rather, your training did. I used what you taught me."

He'd been waiting to deploy, had been filling the time teaching a summer self-defense class at the community college. And she'd been…engaged.

To a guy who'd grown up with her, knowing her family.

By then, he'd already learned a hard lesson about him being on the outside looking into that kind of life. So he'd paid careful attention to avoid pursuing the instant attraction he'd had for her. One that had seemed to be returned, and on a level beyond the physical.

As if he really knew anything about living life on that level.

The younger version of the successful doctor had been impressively alert during his class, and he witnessed the exact same focus and attention to detail, the same ability to remember things, as she answered his questions about the thwarted kidnapping. She was able to describe her kidnapper, not only the size and build that closely matched the father she'd first taken him for, but the shape of his jaw, and the soullessly evil look in his eyes. She was certain she'd never seen him before. She'd already talked to the police, had sat with a local officer who'd responded to the scene and was also a sketch artist, but Scott needed other details. The kind you couldn't draw.

"Did he speak?" he asked. "Did he have an accent? Sound educated?"

"All I heard was a string of common swear words when I kneed him. No accent, but he slurred his *s*'s, like he had a tooth missing. And… I think he smokes. His voice had that raspy sound…"

If he could form a mental picture, he'd have more of an idea of where to look first.

"And he smelled like manure," she said. "And maybe hay. You know…like a farm…"

Bingo. Standing, he thanked her, looked her in the eye, and when he started to linger there, to smile his gratitude, he caught himself and immediately reached for his wallet, looking inside for one of his cards. Handing it to her, he told her to call him immediately if she thought of anything else, and, with a last directive to take care of herself, to follow police orders for her own protection, he turned to the door. He needed to get out of the small space.

Away from reminders of the things he wouldn't ever again let himself want.

But he looked back. Saw her watching him.

As if, for a second, she was remembering, too…

He refused to go back. Looked at her and said, "It looks like you might have a black eye by tomorrow." In a few more minutes it would already be tomorrow.

And he had an urgent job to do.

Find the kidnapper.

For three reasons now.

To save the babies yet to be taken. To find the ones who'd already been sold. And to make the fiend pay for that bruise filling up the side of Dorian's face.

What kind of weird fate brought Scott Michaels to investigate a thwarted kidnapping in Arizona? All the years Dorian and Sierra's Web—the firm of experts she and her friends had started—had been working with law enforcement, and he suddenly shows up at a crime scene?

It had to be some kind of warning sent by fate, issued to validate the choices she'd made so long ago. Reminding her why she'd made them.

With so many of the Sierra's Web partner experts finding love and settling down—with her own kidnapping the previous year still challenging her—maybe she'd been experiencing some weakening in her resolve to stay single.

Distracted by her initial reaction to seeing the man again, Dorian instinctively put on her professional face as Chief Ramsey came in to tell her that he would assign someone to escort her to wherever she was going as soon as she was ready.

"That's not necessary," she told him, emphatically certain of that fact. The bruise to her head, while painful when touched, and ugly looking, had been superficial as she'd had the advantage of being the aggressor in the second that the blow had been thrown. She'd been cut, right at the edge of her jaw, the result of the kidnapper's gloved hand jamming her earring into her skin, but overall, she was fine.

And she absolutely did not need one of Las Sendas' already overtasked police officers to follow her the two miles between the birthing center and the room that had been rented for her in the lovely old historic hotel downtown. All the Las Sendas law enforcers had been called in to work the attempted kidnapping, and they all needed to continue doing so.

She'd never forgive herself if they lost the guy because they'd pulled someone off the case to babysit her.

"This is the kind of thing Sierra's Web handles every day," she said, collecting the bag she'd dropped as she'd come out of the employee entrance at the side of the building and had seen the kidnapper leaving with the baby. "You've already seen how we work. Glen, our forensics and science guy, will probably be at the hotel by the time I get there. I'll be right back here in the morning, checking in on the patient I was here to assist with, and will be hanging around in Las Sendas as long as my partners think I can be of help to find the kidnapper."

"Still, this guy doesn't know you can't positively ID him," the chief said, but Dorian could tell the man was eager to keep his officers on the kidnapper's trail, as he should be. Major crime didn't happen in Las Sendas, which was one of the reasons the small town had been chosen to house the prototype birthing center.

"It's more likely he's going to be getting as far away

from here as he can, rather than hanging around for me,"
she reminded him, to assuage any guilt he might be harboring, as he walked her out to her car. After twelve years of
being the medical expert on cases with her partners, many
of them criminal cases, she knew the drill.

A thorough glance around the busy parking lot convinced them both that she was fine to walk to her vehicle.
She saw him already heading to his squad car as she pulled
out of the parking lot, shakier than she'd wanted the chief
to know but eager to get to Glen.

Hudson Warner, Sierra's Web technical expert, was up
and already working on the dark web site Scott Michaels
had mentioned.

After giving Glen whatever he needed, Dorian was going
to take a hot bath and put the night behind her. Or at least sit
up with her newly-purchased-in-the-past-year handgun at her
side for protection and watch old sitcoms until the sun rose.

She'd been abducted off a hiking trail sixteen months
ago because she'd been unprepared. She was not going
to let the fiend who'd taken her rob her of peace of mind.

Make her afraid to live her life.

When the idea of living life brought thoughts of Scott
Michaels to mind as she drove, she allowed them to distract her. The self-defense instructor, former army sergeant
turned FBI agent, had no idea that he'd brought a completely different moment to a horrible night. Seeing him
again…she had no idea how she felt about that.

Had mixed emotions to the point of being slightly sick
to her stomach.

She'd hurt a man she'd loved because of Scott. Had first
started to lose her ability to trust herself because of him.

And yet…still got warm inside, just seeing his face
again.

Her whole life, Dorian had been wise beyond her years, able to see clearly and make successful decisions, to remain practical in times of crisis, to be an asset to her family and those around her. She'd chosen her best friend, a man she'd known since she was born, to be her life's partner.

And then she'd met Scott, and, if not for the man's inner strength, she might actually have found herself in bed with him…

Turning the corner onto the road that led to Main Street, she saw an old pickup stopped at an adjacent corner ahead and for a second, her heart leaped to her throat, constricting her air. Then she got close enough to see that the truck was black, not red. And when she caught a glimpse of the cowboy hat the guy was wearing, she sat back in her seat, admonishing herself for being so jumpy, even as she gave herself some slack.

She'd been kidnapped and held for days. Not something she'd get over in a matter of months. Maybe not even years. And yet, when the baby had been at risk, she'd run straight into danger.

Still, she avoided looking at the driver as she passed the truck. Until her peripheral vision caught movement and she turned to see him staring right at her.

Her stomach jumped up to choke her.

She knew those eyes.

Gunning the gas, Dorian kept both hands glued to the wheel, her focus fully on the road in front of her. Reminding herself that if she didn't turn up at her hotel in the next ten minutes, her partners would have experts on the ground, looking for her.

The truck gained on her, coming up on her right, blocking her from making the turn onto Main Street.

Forcing her to continue straight on a deserted road that led toward the mountain.

Forcing her into darkness. Any second, it was going to run her off the road. No time for expert help.

She was going to die.

The thought was clear.

Suddenly it was as though she was in an operating room, looking at a patient who was coding. No panic. It was her job to stay calm. Aware. To make the best decision.

Letting go of the wheel with one hand, she reached into the pocket along the thigh of her scrubs, retrieving the card Scott Michaels had given her and, pushing her hands-free calling button on the steering wheel, rattled off the number on the card. Her partners would look for her, too late. But the next baby could still be saved. She had to let the agent know where his kidnapper was. She had to prevent other babies from being hurt.

"He's on my bumper," she blurted into the phone as soon as she heard the click that told her he'd picked up. "Black truck. Hampton Road." She pulled in a breath, maybe her last. "East." Another attempt to get air. "Past last turnoff…"

The truck's headlights reflected off her rearview mirror, blinding her, and then, with a jolt from behind, a crunch, her chin hit the steering wheel. She felt the sting, the split, felt a swoosh of air on an open wound. Moisture. Blood.

"What's going on?" Scott's urgent tone kept her gaze focused on the road. That was all. Blood. Pain. The road.

"Dorian! Talk to me."

"I'm…"

Another jolt. To the rear driver's side of her car.

Then, with a huge bump, the sharp explosion of the air bag against her upper body, she went careening off the road.

Chapter 2

Scott heard the crunch of metal. What sounded like hissing. "Dorian!"

Thug. Thuuggg. Flesh hitting flesh? Or something else?

His blood ran cold.

"Dorian!" Throat tight, entire body on red alert, he squealed to a stop in the middle of a deserted country road just east of town. GPS had mapped out local farms for him. He'd been on his way to the second one when his phone had rung.

"Dorian!" He called again and heard only hissing. They were still connected. He couldn't let go of that thin thread, of whatever clues she could give him.

Of the hope that she'd let him know she was okay.

Black truck?

At the sound of a grunt, he hollered. "Dorian!"

A groan was his only response. The sound of a car door opening.

And the line went dead.

Had she crawled out? Managed to escape? He wanted to believe she'd be fine.

But he didn't.

Dialing Chief Ramsey, the man with jurisdiction on a local incident, Scott relayed what he knew, including Dorian's description of the black truck.

Birthing center surveillance tapes had shown that Dorian had been correct, in that the truck used in the kidnapping was red. He told Ramsey about the black truck he'd passed on his way into town, a good hour after the attempted kidnapping. Ramsey let him know that a patrol car was close to Dorian's location and would be there in less than a minute.

As soon as the chief hung up, Scott dialed Hudson Warner, the tech expert Dorian had put him in touch with from her firm. He gave Hudson all the information he had, including the fact that he'd been on the lookout for a red pickup truck from the second he'd left the center's parking lot that night and hadn't seen even a newer model one. Warner was giving him Glen River's number, the partner who was just arriving in Las Sendas, but Scott disconnected midconversation when Ramsey's call came in.

"We've got her car," Ramsey's voice came over the line. "There's no sign of a truck and no sign of her, either."

"Trace her phone. She was just talking to me..."

"It's sitting here on the seat. Along with her bag. Handgun still inside it. Tells us she likely didn't have a chance to fight back. He can't have gone far, Agent Michaels. Either back toward town, and we'll have him, or he's got less than a minute on us heading out of town. That's a five-mile stretch with no turnoffs and I've got a car waiting for him on the other side. State police are here, too. We'll get him."

Scott wanted to believe the man. Wanted to believe that with her twelve years with her firm, Dorian, while a medical expert, not law enforcement, at least knew how to handle a fiend long enough for someone to get to her.

He wanted to follow protocol and let others do their jobs. But the kidnapper was his jurisdiction. And whether anyone else thought so or not, so was Dorian. His entire adult life, the only thing that gave him peace inside was giving his all to get justice for good people, and something was telling him she was one of the best human beings he'd ever known.

He'd seen it in her in the past—her faithfulness to her fiancé, her regard for her parents, the way she helped others in class—and it had been evidenced that night, too. She'd risked her life for that baby.

And had succeeded in saving it...

He hadn't even been all that surprised when he'd heard that she was a partner in Sierra's Web. While he'd never worked with the nationally renowned firm based right there in Phoenix, he'd definitely heard of them.

Her smartwatch...

She'd looked at her watch to read a text while he'd been questioning her. She'd answered the text on her watch, punching quickly, as though with practice, on the tiny screen, while her phone had been sitting right there. He'd asked why...

Her watch had its own separately designated line—with a number given out only to key medical personnel so that she could be reached anytime, day or night, no matter where she was.

Driving toward Hampton Road, following his GPS, Scott put in another call to Hudson Warner, telling him to ping Dorian's smartwatch. Because the watch was for Dorian's non-Sierra's-Web-related medical work, Hudson didn't know the number. But assured Scott he'd find it and get back with him.

Until then, Scott was going to drive every mile with hay in the vicinity. He'd walk every field if that was what it took. He wasn't stopping until Dorian had been found.

The kidnapper had her. It was the only logical explanation. She'd said he was behind her, as though he'd know exactly what she'd meant. She'd called him, and that night's case was the only reason she'd have done so.

Did the man sitting in wait for Dorian, taking her hostage, mean that he'd be too occupied to kidnap another baby that night?

Or was there more than one baby snatcher on the payroll?

Was Scott really after an entire kidnapping ring? Or just a single, severely demented man who'd managed to amass millions while keeping law enforcement completely in the dark?

Or was Scott wrong that the kidnappings were even related?

All questions that ate at him, insidiously, as he peered through the darkness, looking for a hint of fair skin. Keeping his foot on the gas pedal pressed down to the floor, he felt the tension grow in him, laced with fear, with every mile he traveled without success.

He was heading farther out of town. Ramsey, Sierra's Web, they'd cover the obvious. He was going for hay and manure in the same place.

Warner might or might not be able to help, but that watch, the number, gave Scott hope.

He had to save Dorian.

And somehow be able to use the night's horror to finally take down whoever it was who'd been terrorizing parents in several states for more than six months.

He had to do it or die trying.

She wasn't going to just let herself die. Hurting everywhere, Dorian promised herself that she would hang on long enough to help her partners, to help Scott Michaels, find the kidnapper of babies. She had to pay attention.

To note every detail.

She'd been unconscious when her abductor had pulled her out of the car but figured she couldn't have been out for more than a minute or two, if that, as she'd felt him yank her arms back and bind her wrists with some kind of twine that still bit into her with a nasty sting.

The ride on the floor of the truck, behind the seat, had been excruciating, to her head, her arms, her face, but thankfully hadn't lasted long. Had the truck been black? Not red? That didn't make sense, did it?

And then she'd been hauled from the truck and dumped in what she'd figured out was a lean-to, or maybe a barn that had partially fallen. She had a ceiling overhead, and at least two walls, maybe three, but could see sky and outdoors when she opened her eyes. Which wasn't often.

The guy—the kidnapper, she was pretty certain, judging by the same manure-type smell she'd noticed in the parking lot of the birthing center earlier that night—hadn't checked to see if she'd regained consciousness. He'd just hauled her up, carried her to the inch or two of hay upon which she lay and dropped her there.

As far as she could tell, there were no animals anywhere around. At least not the kind that lived in barns and ate hay.

Anything else—the bobcats, coyotes and other natural life that were known to roam during the hot Arizona nights, looking for water—were out of her control and therefore, not worth worrying about.

With resolve firmed, she wiped away the sweat beading on her forehead by rubbing her face against the shoulders of her scrubs. And cringed when the bruised side of her face made contact with shoulder bone.

She was pretty sure her chin had stopped bleeding, but with her hands tied together behind her, she couldn't do more than touch her chin to her chest for evaluation. Her injured skin stuck more than slid as it made contact. Her blood was coagulating, and she took that as a good sign.

In her mind, she talked to Sierra, the friend they'd all lost in college, the reason Sierra's Web had been formed. And to her parents, who'd died in a car accident five years before. Told herself they were all watching over her. She had to believe that, because the thought of their love, something she'd known through tangible action on earth, gave her strength during those weak moments in the dark.

Strength of mind would see her through. And she fought to hold on to it by every means she had.

Focusing on the doing, rather than the fearing—as her parents had always taught her to do, and Sierra had done—she took stock of her surroundings.

Figuring it would serve her better to have her abductor think she was unconscious, she continued to remain completely still—other than the few hurried shoulder wipes and chin checks she administered whenever she heard her kidnapper's footsteps crunching gravel in a way that told her he was moving away, not approaching. Figuring, at those times, he had his back to her.

How long had she been there?

Twenty minutes? An hour?

How did she tell?

Feeling panic start to rise up in her again—far too reminiscent of the year before—she chanced another glance, her gaze staring toward her feet as she lay in the fetal position, and noticed nothing that would indicate time passage.

Using the previous year's captivity as knowledge to her benefit, she reminded herself that not everyone kidnapped to kill.

That her friends, her partners, were the best in the business and could succeed where others didn't.

That she had to do all she could to help them.

And that Scott Michaels was on the case, too. Maybe another expert on the ground. Right there in Las Sendas.

She was hot. But in that part of Arizona, nights only cooled to the high eighties. It had easily hit one hundred five in Phoenix and Las Sendas the day before, and would that day, too, she was sure. Once the sun came up. Even in the shade, she wouldn't maintain lucidity more than a day or two without water.

But there was hope.

A vision of Scott Michaels as he'd come in the door that night—Agent Michaels—flashed before her mind's eye, and she calmed. He'd been on the phone with her. Had heard the abduction. Knew where she'd been… Would call Hud…

Sierra? Mom? Steer me.

The kidnapper had driven over rough terrain to get her to her current prison. He'd gone off road.

Would anyone look where no roads led?

Did her smartwatch still have coverage? Scott knew she had it…

Thank God a text had come in while she'd been in the interview with him.

She could still hardly believe he'd been there at all, that Scott Michaels had been the FBI agent to walk through that door…

When weakness threatened, she let her mind stay on the image of the handsome self-defense instructor turned FBI agent, as she'd first known him fourteen years before. Tall, over six feet, muscled and lean, lithe like a tiger she'd once thought…his dark hair had been shorter then, military cut, but those blue eyes…they'd seemed almost like magic orbs to her younger self, reaching inside her as though to speak without words.

It had been the same that night, too. His hair was longer; there was bristle on his once clean-shaven face, and more lines around those eyes, but the way she'd felt during that brief second he'd met her gaze…almost as if they were meant to know each other…

She'd probably imagined it. Or was imagining it as she lay there, but for the moment, she wasn't sure she cared. That look, it lit her up and she needed all the light she could get at the moment.

If thinking about Scott Michaels was what it took to keep her inner fires burning long enough to figure out a plan of escape, then she'd willingly imagine away…

"I got it all worked out…" The words came to her from a distance, but grew louder, as though the speaker was coming toward her. Same smoker's voice. "We sell her. She'll be worth something. Kind of like bonus pay…"

Sell her?

Worth something?

Acid burned her stomach. She tried to draw in a deep, calming breath, but the pressure in her chest stopped the flow midstream.

Trying to find coherent thought, she flashed back to Scott. The baby-kidnapping ring he'd been trying to break into, to uncover and obliterate…

That was why he'd been there, at the center, in jeans and a dark T-shirt. He'd heard about the kidnapping and had come running. She'd been his first real lead. Was the only person alive that he knew who'd actually seen the kidnapper.

"I know. It's three hours to the border. All we gotta do is get her out of the country, and no one will know we ran into trouble. I'll get another baby and deliver it as planned—don't you worry about that." The voice came with confidence. There was no discernable accent. And the *s*'s still hissed. Paying close attention, then, she listened for anything that set the man apart, any identifier she could give Scott or her partners when she saw them again.

Because as long as she was alive, she had to believe she would see them again.

It was that or panic about the "sell her" part.

Her abductor sounded more educated than not. What else had Scott asked her?

The pauses in between conversation…she never heard replies. Was her abductor on the phone? Hud could trace that…

"Yeah, man, I swear, no one else saw me. We're cool. And about to make a little bit extra on the side…"

Man. The kidnapper was talking to another man. And it sounded like it was just the two of them in on the deal…

And then there was silence. Either the conversation ended, or her captor walked out of hearing range, on grass maybe? She hadn't heard the gravel crunch.

Didn't much matter. If the pair were planning to deliver a baby as planned, most likely that meant the next day, and they still had a three-hour trip, two ways, to make her gone, first—she didn't have until morning, or even enough time to wait for Scott, or anyone else, to find her.

She had to stop wallowing in emotion, rise above and do something. Almost as if her mother was right there on the hay speaking to her, Dorian felt her backbone stiffen.

She needed a plan. A way to take the kidnapper by surprise again, to attack and give herself enough time to get away, while possibly even having to do it all with her hands still tied behind her back.

No panic. Only thought that led to action.

Her legs had always been strong. And were uninjured. They were tied, too, but more loosely. The guy had made a mistake. Not noticing that she'd pulled her knees apart as he'd tied, keeping her ankle bones slightly separated.

Kicking off her shoes, she rubbed her ankles and toes, getting her socks down and away, which provided a little more give in the ties. Then, over the space of some painful minutes, she used dance lessons she remembered from grade school, got one foot turned in to the other, and into a ballet point, allowing the arch of one foot to slide along, and over, the protruding ankle bone of the other. With some severe muscle pain, turning the foot more, she pulled first the heel, at ankle height on the other foot, free of the tie and quickly got her arch and toes through. With one flick, she slid her other foot out of the rope's circle. Then, drawing from everything Scott had taught in self-defense class, she considered various kicks, to various body parts, that, if landed with accuracy, would allow a relatively small person to overtake a much larger one.

She practiced the kicks, uncaring if her captor noticed the movement. She didn't have all night. While she worked her legs, she started in on the ties at her wrist, too, with a vengeance. No matter what it took, she had to get her hands through those ties. She might do irreparable bodily damage, but she'd rather lose her skin, her normally shaped bones, than her life.

Or to have another baby lose theirs.

She had to get free. There was just no other choice now.

If she didn't, not only was another baby going to be kidnapped yet that night, but if the kidnappers got away, their business could continue in the future, too. She could not allow herself to be shipped off, or die, and let that happen.

Her parents hadn't raised her to allow such a thing.

Promising herself that she wouldn't fail, promising Sierra that she wouldn't fail again, Dorian gave everything she had left to keeping her word.

Chapter 3

Scott knew better than to let Dorian, or any woman, call out to him in a personal capacity.

His need to find the doctor was wholly professional. Her life mattered to all those she helped in the course of her work.

And she was the lead to his kidnapper.

Finding the man could put an end to a horrific six months of baby thefts.

Chief Ramsey's ability to organize both his men and the visiting law enforcement was impressive. Within an hour they'd combed every inch of the Las Sendas roadway, and, as Sierra's Web private investigators arrived, had started on four-wheeling paths through the desert as well.

With everyone else covering the grids Ramsey laid out, Scott stayed on his own course, searching out farms in the area—or any place where there might be manure or hay. Hudson Warner had experts on the computer, scouring hay sales, hayseed sales and vendors that had anything to do with hay, cows or manure used to fertilize ground. Didn't matter that it was the middle of the night. Warner had told him—it was what family did.

Dorian was family to her partners. The man didn't discuss his partner with Scott at all.

Didn't surprise him a bit.

And though he wanted to know more about the woman, he didn't ask. Not a surprise, either.

As he searched, he told himself he couldn't possibly hear Dorian's silent call. Just as he hadn't really sensed an affinity with her when she'd been in his class all those years ago. The way he remembered it had been like she'd needed something from him. And could give him something he'd needed in return. But he didn't trust the impression a bit. Back then, he'd still been in the early stages of accepting that he would always be the guy with a past good people didn't want to associate with. Born of parents that good women wouldn't want genetically attached to their own kids.

Had Dorian really been able to sense him back then, she'd have seen how lost he'd been, not some guy she'd be drawn to.

He hadn't become someone worthy of respect until after they'd parted, when the army filled the parental role he'd been missing all his life. And later, the FBI serving as his adult family had enabled him to give the world the best version of himself—finding justice for good people on a much bigger scale than policing in the army had allowed.

Somewhere along the way, long after knowing Dorian, he'd finally learned how to like himself.

A part of him wanted Dorian to know that. For no good reason.

They were ridiculous thoughts to thwart the frustration wrought by the unending stillness in the darkness surrounding him. Thoughts that kept hope on the table that he'd find her alive.

Determination filled him as he drove along dirt paths that served as roads, seeing nothing but the black shroud of night. What good was all his work if he couldn't save innocent babies who still had a chance to know the unconditional love of decent parents?

If he couldn't save the woman who'd brought him a touch of softness when he'd needed it most? Even if she hadn't known it.

Dorian. She wasn't Lily. He didn't even, for one second, think any differently. But she was like Lily in that she'd been raised by ethical, loving parents who'd instilled in her a sense of service and decency. Of accountability.

She'd been raised in a world where good won.

His heart had been broken when he'd learned the truth about his own place in that world. But he'd become a man through it. A man who didn't have to hide from himself or hide himself from anyone else.

A man who'd found real peace—and acceptance from others—with who he was.

He would not let a soulless kidnapper stop him. There had to be more to life than that. More to his life.

Rage gnawed at him as he bumped along, bottoming out his SUV, scraping metal against desert rock. He was an able-bodied strong man, ready and willing to help, but he wasn't finding the woman in need.

Or protecting the babies who would soon be stolen if he didn't find the woman.

This kidnapper, this monster, had become so much more than a case. Over the months of failure to save newborns, of meeting with grieving families, Scott's work to capture the kidnapper had become personal.

And now the man was imprisoning the vision of an angel from Scott's past.

Bile rose in Scott's chest. The phone rang. Distracting him from emotions that did not serve him, or anyone, well.

Hudson Warner.

The tech expert had been able to identify the number registered to Dorian's smartwatch. It hadn't pinged for over an hour, but the last known location was south of Las Sendas, at an abandoned homestead out in the desert.

He'd already sent the location to Scott's phone. And was alerting other law enforcement as well. The closest team was still almost an hour out.

Hanging up without wasting a second on thanks or goodbyes, Scott touched his screen a couple of times and tore out for the location of the watch—just five minutes away from where he was.

Because he'd been out looking for hay. In areas that weren't already being searched.

He saw the half-fallen barn before he was close enough for his engine to be heard. And pulled off the road and down into a ditch the second he determined that if he went any farther, rounded one more corner, he could be easily detected by anyone at the barn watching the road.

After checking his gun, and the knife encased securely in his sock, he turned off the internal light so it wouldn't flash when he opened the door and slid out.

Precious minutes passed as Scott traversed rocky desert ground on foot, using the tall saguaro cacti, desert trees and scattered tall bushes as coverage. And then, as he lay on the ground, crawling through open space on his belly— trying not to think about the snakes that traveled the same hard desert ground in the same way—he saw it.

An old truck.

Black, not red.

And…the guy in the white shirt and cowboy hat. He couldn't make out any distinguishing characteristics. The moon's glow only gave so much. But the guy was leaning against the hood of his truck, one foot up on the bumper behind him, looking outward, as though waiting for someone. His jaw was moving. Could be talking on the phone.

As Scott crawled, more slowly, watching that the head didn't turn in his direction, he saw the guy spit.

Chewing tobacco. Not phone call.

Something one did while waiting?

On what? A phone call? Others to arrive?

Or was he just a guy who happened to cross Scott's path for a second time, who also just hung out chewing in the middle of the night?

There was no sign of Dorian. Didn't mean she wasn't there.

But it could mean that.

Could be this wasn't his guy. Her phone had pinged in the area and his gut was telling him he'd found his man. Cowboy hat and all.

Would have been nice if he'd listened to his gut when he'd first seen the guy back on the way into Las Sendas. He could have prevented Dorian from being traumatized further.

Maybe even prevented her death.

He couldn't think like that. Moved forward. She was alive. She had to be. She wouldn't go without one hell of a fight. And he'd given her some skills…

About a hundred yards from the barn, he saw movement. Legs held up in the air, wearing something loose enough to be scrubs, seemingly running wild.

He couldn't make out much else. Just the legs moving intermittently through the moonlight, but, heart pounding, he knew it was her. Pulling out his phone, he texted an SOS to Warner and then, upping his pace, knowing that the kidnapper could decide to get back to his prey at any second, he pulled out his gun and crept forward.

He couldn't shoot the guy, not yet, not until he knew

there was no one else on the property. If someone was in that barn, keeping watch on Dorian, the second his shot rang out she could be as good as dead.

Based on the crash he'd heard, and the scene Ramsey had described, she had to be in pain—a lot of it, judging by how she was thrashing—while the guy outside stood there and chewed.

One hundred yards became one hundred feet. Scott felt like he'd won the lottery when Dorian raised her scratched and bruised head in his direction. Her mouth dropped open. He could see her teeth in the moonlight.

He told himself she smiled as he continued forward with excruciating but necessary slowness, watching her for any sign she might give him as to what he might be crawling into.

A phone rang and he froze, not sure if it had come from the area of the truck, or through the opened barn. Since she'd turned her head in his direction, Dorian hadn't moved.

Was someone there, then? Guarding her?

He heard a voice, male. Couldn't make out the words. But he heard running, in his direction, had his gun ready. He wouldn't shoot unless he had no choice, to shoot or die, not until he could get a look inside the barn and be able to take out anyone in there, as well, before they could hurt Dorian.

Help would be on the way soon.

"What the…" He heard the words, the smoky voice, as, with horror, he watched the guy who'd been leaning on the truck reach Dorian, a gun to her head as he hauled her up and pushed her forward.

She didn't make a sound, or move her head, as though she knew not to give him away, and he stood, too, knowing he couldn't let the man take her again. The call...had it been a go-ahead the guy had been waiting for?

Go ahead to where?

For what?

It wasn't going to happen; whatever it was. He couldn't let it.

Where was Ramsey? Warner's guys? Anyone?

The guy moved quickly, and Scott had to be careful not to be seen—by Dorian's captor, or by anyone who might still be in the barn. Or on the property.

That missing red truck bothered him.

Keeping himself in shadows, he made it to a tall, three foot round cactus by the rear passenger side wheel of the truck, while the kidnapper opened the driver's door, pulled the seat back and shoved Dorian into the storage space behind it.

She fought back, kicking him, fighting for all she was worth, but within seconds was inside with the seat slamming back in place, holding her prisoner. Hoping that her continued ruckus had the attention of her captor, and anyone else in the vicinity, Scott ducked and made it to the side of the truck, then slid like a snake over the side of the bed, straining his arm muscles as he carefully held his weight, lowering himself slowly down, fitting around the junk inside, without giving himself away.

The engine started. The truck burst forward, even before he heard the door shut.

Dorian had angered her captor.

But she'd also given Scott the chance to get in the bed of the truck.

Smart lady.

With his mind on Dorian, willing her to be strong awhile

longer, he prepared himself to be ready for whatever was going to happen next.

He had his goals. Save Dorian.

And stop the kidnappers from stealing even one more newborn baby away from their parents.

Nothing else mattered.

The drive was longer, bumpier, more excruciating than before as her captor, with an arm along the back of the seat, had a gun on her this time as he drove. He'd been in a hurry, clearly agitated, and hadn't taken the time to re-tie her legs. Somehow, she had to use that lapse to her advantage.

Lying up against the back of the truck, she felt a thump as they hit the next set of rocky terrain on their route. A thump that came from the bed of the truck, not from tires beneath the truck. Something she hoped the driver couldn't discern.

Scott Michaels. *Agent* Scott Michaels.

He was back there.

He had to be.

Dare she believe it?

Since it gave her strength in the moment, she could.

She had to do whatever was necessary to hang on. To keep sharp and do, not feel. To focus enough to be ready for whatever came next.

To be able to help Scott and her partners. Not hinder them. To prevent more families with newborn babies from being obliterated by grief. To save the babies from…who knew what?

Scott thought they were being sold.

To whom?

Dare she hope that those little ones who'd already fallen to that fate, those Scott hadn't been able to save, were at least being loved by people so desperate to have a family that they'd broken the law to do it?

Or…better for the babies, but not the parents…what if the people buying the babies didn't know the babies were stolen? What if they thought they were part of a legal adoption?

She'd read about that…

Her heart cried out at the thought. There were no winners in a situation like that. Even the buyers were victims.

The only way to prevent the pain was to stop the kidnappers.

At any cost.

She slid more heavily against the back of the truck as the vehicle started up an incline. Imagining Scott right behind her, pretending that he'd found a way to lodge his body up against the front of the bed of the truck, she told herself that they could share strength through the metal separating them.

An hour passed. Maybe more. Driving up rough terrain. Unpaved roads. In captivity she'd been in the desert, at the base of the mountain range. If they were now up in the miles and miles of uninhabited mountains…

She held her head up from the hard floor as best she could while they bumped along, and still, she gained new bruises, flying up and landing on her shoulder as they hit a particularly bad rough patch.

Had Scott's body done the same? Risen up? Enough to be visible in the rearview mirror?

She feared the worst when the truck came to a sudden stop.

Scott was in the truck—and had been discovered.

Her heart beating a rapid tattoo, she was slow to distinguish another roar drawing close—an off-road vehicle approaching?

The "man" on the other end of the phone.

The accomplice.

Shaking, she braced herself. A woman with her hands tied behind her back against two men? She reminded herself she was prepared to do whatever she possibly could…

And then the truck door opened.

It had lightened outside. Dawn was coming. And her captor wasn't reaching for her.

"Did you get rid of the red truck?" The smokey toned voice sounded conciliatory. Not at all commanding. Which sent shards of fear through her. If her kidnapper wasn't the dominant one, what more did they have in store?

"Of course. It's at the bottom of Canyon Lake." The voice, male, more menacing than her captor's had been, came closer. "You fool!" The voice continued, near the truck.

"No, look, man."

A latch sounded and the seat back slid away from her a split second before her almost numbed, tied-back arm was yanked, practically from its socket. "Try anything and you're dead." The voice was harsh, but no more than a whisper right up to her ear, as her abductor hauled her out of the truck.

She had to do something. Might only have that moment.

Shaking, filled with fear, head aching and body weary, she stood there. Was she going to fail? Again?

Where was Scott? She'd wanted him to be in the truck, but she had no proof.

She'd seen him, though. Back at the lean-to.

Odd that of all the FBI agents who could have walked in the door the night before, it had been him…

There was more to be done…

Swear words flew around her as the men argued about

her, the man who'd taken her jerking her shoulder every time he responded to his angry partner.

The other man was older, bigger, bearded, but spoke like he was educated. Scott had asked her about that. To pay attention to such things…

"You've lost sight of one very clear point," the newcomer finally bit out, all volume gone from his voice. "You aren't being paid to think for yourself, to decide a new plan. The general wants a baby. Period. We aren't some sleazy operation here. We aren't low-life human traffickers…" The bigger man reached under his shirt.

A gun appeared in his hand, and before Dorian even registered what was happening, a shot rang out.

Chapter 4

As if in slow motion, Dorian stared at the still pointed gun as, at her side, her captor fell to the ground. The partner had shot her captor and she was next, his gun was pointed straight at her. Her gaze glued on that gun, the finger on the trigger, she saw it start to move, and then suddenly, leaving her standing there, the big man darted to the front of the truck.

Before she could move, Scott, a pointed gun in one hand, grabbed her arm with the other, pulling her with him.

She heard another shot. From beside her. Scott's gun.

Then one from farther away as he shoved her into the killer's four-wheeler. Instinctively, she dove across the seat so Scott could get in beside her, behind the wheel.

"Stay down." Scott's voice was almost unrecognizable to her in its anger. And urgency. On the floor, she felt the rumble as the vehicle started up.

With his gun still pointed, Scott drove with one hand, propelling them forward so abruptly she hit her head under the dash.

More shots sounded. From next to her, and in the distance. She heard the ping of metal against metal, just to her right, before they bounced painfully around the corner of a mountain peak, and then another. Winding around a dangerous cliff that, from her perspective on the floor, seemed too narrow for the vehicle to sustain them for long.

If they went careening over…

When she grew light-headed, she told herself to breathe. Kept her head down. And held on to the metal bracing the seat.

Scott had found her. Her partners, law enforcement wouldn't be far behind. Right? Even up there?

She just had to hold on.

And maybe pray a little.

Was that how Sierra had felt, right before she'd been killed? Like, if she just stayed strong, and prayed, right would win? Justice would be served?

If Dorian had only paid more attention to the last visit her friend had made to the clinic…had asked why Sierra had been there. She'd known Sierra wasn't due for any checkups. Had seen no sign of illness…

Sierra had been such a private person. Dorian had let emotion—her love and respect for the woman—cloud her judgment…

"We've lost him for now." Scott's voice called her back. Her gaze shot up to him. He'd slowed, was perusing the area as he drove, frowning, clearly worried.

While they turned and bumped over the rough terrain, and with her arms still wrenched behind her, Dorian got herself up onto the seat.

Scott gave her a quick glance, shoved his gun under his thigh on the seat, reached toward his foot, pulled a knife out and, barking at her to turn, cut the twine digging into the base of her hands.

"Did you hit him?" she asked above the rumble, refusing to wince as she moved her freed shoulders, flooding with gratitude for the man at her side.

"I don't think so. Not enough, at any rate. Maybe in the leg as he was jumping in the truck. He was still shooting after we'd rounded the mountain."

They'd managed to get away.

But only for the moment.

The man behind them wasn't going to quit looking for them. He couldn't. He knew they'd seen him. And that he'd pay with his life if they managed to make it back to civilization.

Scott's theory…kidnapping babies…multiple babies… he'd been right. There was some kind of horrible business being run right there in Arizona.

And a general was behind it all, pulling the strings. An army general? Some diabolical fiend who'd only served criminal endeavors and just fancied himself with the title? Or just a guy whose luck was about to run out?

"You okay?" he asked.

"Of course." Pain didn't count. Physiologically, every-thing was in working order. Inside…she feared she'd never be okay again. But that was emotion talking.

She couldn't trust it.

She had to fight the feeling…to do whatever it took to stay alive. "How about you?"

"I'm fine," Scott said, his gaze directed ahead of them, over the land they traveled—a flat, rocky prairie-type area, acres big, on a small mountain peak swallowed up by a huge range. The Superstitions. She'd been gazing at them with awe all the years she'd been in and out of Phoenix.

She'd had no idea there was an entire world up there, hidden behind the highest cliffs.

"Thank you."

Scott had risked his own life to save hers. He'd earned her undying gratitude.

While his driving wasn't as frantic, the FBI agent was still moving at a good clip. She thought maybe he nodded. "Don't thank me yet. We've slowed the guy down, for now, but he clearly knows these mountains. Far better than we do." He reached into his pocket and handed her his phone.

"Speed Dial, 2," he said. "Hudson Warner said he'd be tracking my phone. Hopefully we won't have long to wait, but just in case..."

With frantic fingers, Dorian got his phone on. Dialed 2.

Nothing happened.

Glancing at the top bar, heart sinking, she had to tell him, "We have no service." And had no idea how long they'd been without it.

Then she told him the rest, too, about the phone conversation she'd heard outside the barn before Scott had arrived. The part about selling her and still taking another baby to deliver on time, too. His lips tightened, but his gaze didn't leave the road for even a second.

She could feel his frustration.

Tried to fend off her own desperation.

Another baby's life was going to be on the line within hours.

Their lives were in immediate danger.

And they were on their own.

He was out of bullets. He'd driven them to a spot where driving was no longer possible unless he turned around. Something he couldn't afford to do.

Pulling to a stop at the edge of the clearing he'd been winding through, Scott turned to Dorian. The reddened bruise on the far side of her jaw fueled his anger anew. "I can't promise to get you out of this," he told her, right up front.

Without breaking eye contact with him, she nodded.

Didn't even blink. "I know. But I can promise to do every-thing in my power to help you try," she said back, giving him a surge of…something that had no place in his life.

Warmth.

Like he'd fallen into the middle of some damned Christ-mas movie.

And so, to get them back into the real world, he just laid it right out for her.

"My cylinder's empty. We can't go back down the way we came. Not without risking a death trap. And, for the same reason, we have to ditch the four-wheeler. Makes too much noise. For all I know, he's got a tracker on it."

"Our best bet for staying alive is to go farther into the mountains, which we can only do on foot," she said, with another nod.

Like they were out having a cup of coffee.

Lily would have burst into tears when the first bullet rang out. And he wouldn't have blamed her.

Trying not to admire Dorian, he continued. "Good news is, we have the best of the best looking for us, aware that we're out here, and that the kidnapper is, too."

"My kidnapper," she told him. "No one else knows for sure yet, that you found your guy."

"Our guy." The correction came before he'd had a chance to analyze the words and hold them back.

Reminding him of his runaway mouth with Dorian in the past.

"You took him on single-handedly last night and won," he added, just to make sure that she understood he wasn't pairing the two of them up for any other reason.

And ignoring the part where the guy ended up kidnap-ping her later.

She didn't even glance his way. "It's hot, even up here

in the mountains, dry as hell. It's past time for breakfast and we have no food with us. Nor have we slept. Of more concern, we're out in the desert without water."

The doctor had spoken. Dire facts.

And yet, they were the exact impetus he needed. Rather than taking on whatever sick dudes were in his very near future in that first moment, he could leave them to the very near future where they belonged.

"I hope to have us out of here before we get too hungry." He held on to the possibility even though, realistically, he knew that they were going to have to find something to eat in the mountainous wilderness. He had a knife. Would have to catch and kill something. If he was lucky, a fish in a mountain stream.

Still, not an activity he wanted to think about.

"How are you feeling? Do you have a headache? Did he hurt you…otherwise?" His jaw clenched. He had to know.

"No headache. Just achy and sore, but nothing that's going to slow me down."

He held her gaze for long seconds, assessing her words, and, with a nod, trusting her to tell him the truth, he got back on track.

Opening the glove box, looking under the seat beneath him, he came up with a first aid kit, a flare and a couple of sticks of gum. Ripping one in half, he put one section in his mouth and gave her the other.

Dorian followed his example on her side of the vehicle and found a partially crushed, half-empty bottle of water.

"And a phone!" she told him, with an actual grin, as she held both up.

The smile left her face as quickly as it had come. But in that second…

He'd recognized the woman in his memory from the past. The one who'd put her arms around him…held him close…

They had his phone, too. And no service. But they could turn one off, saving battery, and have it later for a flashlight or compass as needed. And once Scott got them to safety, that phone she'd found could prove invaluable to his case. The near future, not the now.

After they'd both sniffed and then poured sips of water down their throats, careful not to touch their mouths to the bottle, Scott stripped off the button-down shirt that was part of his normal work attire, leaving him in a T-shirt more suited to hot mountain days. Wrapping their small pile of supplies in the fabric, he secured it all with careful folds and tied sleeves and slung it over his shoulder.

"We need to get to a water source," he told her abruptly, jumping out of the vehicle. Because while he wanted to hope they'd be out of the mountain before lunch, he had no guarantee of that, and survival came first. "There are streams running throughout these mountains. Our first goal is to find one."

She was right beside him before he'd taken more than two steps. "Sierra's Web just had a case in another mountain range not all that far from here," she told him, "It involved a missing child, and then a couple of law enforcement officers who were being stalked. I ended up on scene, to treat the female officer after several attempts had been made on her life. They stayed alive over the space of a couple of days by hiding in natural caves grooved out of the sides of the mountains—just like the Native American tribes lived in centuries ago…"

He didn't remember her as a talker. Figured she was more nervous than she was letting on.

And turned out, maybe he was, too, because, as they started to walk, to hike, he asked for more details of the previous case. Of which there were plenty. He was identifying with every one of them.

Right up until she said, "The two officers, they're both thriving. And getting married. To each other."

At that, Scott turned his back and started to climb the mountain in front of him.

Dorian hadn't known that a phone's compass still worked without service. Thankfully, Scott had and was using his app to keep them from wandering in circles as they climbed up and away from the four-wheeler and then farther into the rocky denseness.

"We need to step carefully, making the least amount of movement, and try to stay covered from view. My thought is to go up and then, on higher ground, head back in the direction we came," he said maybe an hour after they'd headed out on foot, as she kept pace right behind him. Turned out her rubber-soled work shoes were better for more than foot comfort during long hours of standing. They had good traction on the slippery rock face, too.

"I like that," she told him. "The closer we can stay to the area where your phone last pinged, the quicker my friends are going to get to us."

"The FBI and state and local law enforcement will be on the trail, too," he reminded her, with a quick glance back at her. Her heart lifted a second when she saw the almost grin on his face. It was more a light in his eyes than an actual turn up of the lips. But she recognized it.

Or thought she did.

Her mind had to be playing tricks on her. A coping

mechanism. No way she'd remember a glint in someone's eye from fourteen years ago.

She was a scientist of the human body. Knew better.

"I'm also hoping, with the higher elevation, we can spot the killer, be able to keep an eye on him."

Killer.

She'd been standing right there. Held captive by a man, hurt by him. As he was shot to death right beside her.

If not for Scott, she'd have been next.

She shook her head.

Dug her foot harder into the mountainside. "Hopefully we'll be able to hear him if he's still in the truck," she said aloud. Shivering, but pressing on, too.

It was what she knew. The doing. What she trusted.

Her mind.

Her Sierra's Web partners.

And…maybe, Scott Michaels, too?

Only because he'd saved her life.

Her thoughts bounced a bit as she walked. And then, as she nearly impaled herself on the sharp needles of a pear-shaped pad of prickly pear cactus, her mind was suddenly clear. "Hey, hang on," she said. "Give me your knife."

Without question, Scott reached under his pant leg and pulled out the blade she'd seen him grab earlier.

"Have you ever eaten prickly pear?" she asked him, squatting down by the massive plant as she carefully removed the pad that had almost caught her.

"I've had a prickly pear margarita."

She nodded. So had she. "We're lucky this is the time of year everything's blooming," she continued, acting as though she knew exactly what she was doing. "We aren't going to starve out here."

While she worked on the pad, she reached up for a red

berry at the top of the plant. "Start with that," she told him, handing Scott the piece of fruit while she went back to work.

"We can eat cholla and barrel cactus, too." She'd never had them. Or prickly pear, either, for that matter. She broke away the first piece of fruit from the pad, handed that to him as well. "That's high in antioxidants, fiber, minerals and vitamins," she told him, working on a piece for herself. "And, according to one of our nation's most respected health clinics, it's good for treating cholesterol, diabetes—" she got her own piece free "—and hangovers, among other things."

Standing, she turned, her piece of fruit almost to her mouth, to see Scott standing there, a berry in one hand, the piece of fruit she'd handed him in the other, staring at her.

"What?"

He shook his head. Took a bite of the fruit, and, eyebrows raised, said, "It's sweet." Then took another bite.

"My stomach's growling and I was just remembering an article I read in a professional magazine a year or so ago. Certain cactus fruit is becoming quite the star in a lot of different cuisines. Sought after in fine dining venues for salads, among other things. This is one of them. As opposed to the Agave...there, certain parts could kill you," she told him then, standing there in her dirty scrubs, with juice dripping out of the corner of her mouth.

Only to look up and see him staring at her again.

Self-consciously wiping her mouth, she continued to eat. But when she glanced over a third time, to see his attention more on her than the meal she'd provided, she refrained from taking the bite that she'd had on the way to her mouth. "What?" she asked again.

"I just...remember you."

The words hit her hard. Where she couldn't afford to be

touched. Until they'd found the kidnapper—the killer—until they'd saved whatever babies they could, and gotten themselves to safety, there could be no consideration for matters of the heart.

And afterward…well…maybe they could be friends. Like she was with Hud and Glen and Winchester, Sierra's Web's financial expert partner…

"You were the best student I ever had. The way you took everything in, processed, produced…"

Yep, he had her pegged. "My parents raised me to be an asset to society, not a drain on it," she told him then, thinking they'd be done with it.

"I can't think of many people I know who wouldn't be panicking right about now."

If he didn't quit talking, she might start doing that.

"To what end? If I give in to desperation, I weaken my chances of succeeding." She was spouting pep talks from her youth. Heard her dad's words. Her mother's. Silently thankful that they were watching over her.

And she was desperately fighting Scott Michaels's effect on her, too. The man had ruined her life once—albeit unknowingly—by engaging emotions that were counterproductive. She could not allow him to do so again.

She wouldn't break another heart.

Or, if she had any way to prevent it, lose another life.

No matter what it cost her.

Chapter 5

He'd been on the hunt before. In life-threatening situations.

Alone, and not.

But Scott had never been on a job with a genius woman doctor who exuded caring and compassion, while she calmly solved a basic survival problem. Nourishment. Before it had even become a problem.

Not only was she finding nutrients to sustain them, by knowing which plants were safe to eat, she managed to get juice for them to drink as well. With his help, once he caught on to the process.

They ate, filled their squashed water bottle, drank, filled it again.

And moved on.

Up.

He'd known there were edible plants on the mountain. He hadn't known which ones. And hadn't wasted a lot of time worrying about it, either, planning to find a stream and fish. Figuring he could use the flare to start a small fire for cooking.

There'd been no sign of the kidnapper. He wanted to hope that he'd hit the guy well enough that he'd gone back to whatever hole he'd climbed out of for treatment. Scott allowed himself various moments over the next hour where he went with the thought.

But knew he couldn't let his guard down. The guy, or someone else who worked with the general, would be on their trail.

Other than some basic warnings as he foraged the terrain and prepared Dorian to do so behind him, he walked in silence.

Was mostly thankful that she did as well.

Even while he wondered what she was thinking.

It had been that way in class, too. It was like the woman had a treasure trove going on in that mind of hers, one filled with jewels that he had to have.

Fanciful.

Ridiculous.

Reminiscent of the foolish kid he'd been in high school, thinking he'd found a woman, and through her an extended family, who fully accepted him despite the baggage he carried.

At that thought, he glanced at his phone, and stopped.

They'd been hiking well over an hour.

"By my rough estimate, we've reached about where we were when the black truck first started up the mountain road, just at a much higher elevation."

The black truck. Driven by a man now dead.

Shot right in front of her. Holding her tightly enough that she'd have felt the push back of the blast. And she hadn't said a word.

Or shed a tear that he'd seen.

He'd seen her shaking a time or two, though.

Dorian caught up to him. Stopped, looking over the ridge in front of them. He'd been leading them back to the outside of the mountain range but wasn't so sure that had been the best idea.

"Should we head down? Try to get to a road before dark

and hopefully flag someone for help? Or, best case miraculous scenario, run into someone looking for us?"

He'd had the thought. Before he'd realized how long it was going to take them to reach their current point. He shook his head. "It's going to be scorching in another hour or so," he told her, assessing the steep slide of rocks directly beneath them. "And the more we move on the outer mountain face, the more easily we'll be seen. By our own people, yes, but by anyone out to attack us, too." He'd been fairly certain the kidnapper would have shown himself by then. Even just with the sound of his engine. Yeah, the guy had had a body to dispose of, but no way he was just going to let them walk out of there and identify him.

Not with a "General" involved.

More likely, he, or someone else, was hunting them. "Depending on his scope, and weapon, we'd be an easy take down without ever knowing he was there…" He said the words aloud because Dorian needed the information.

"We can't stay up here forever, hoping someone on our side finds us," she shot back, sounding a little cranky.

Lessening his tension just a notch for a second or two.

"Agreed. But we have no way of knowing if we've been followed. We head down now, and we could easily become target practice. We wouldn't have much hope of surviving."

"It could be the same if we continue forward," the good doctor pointed out with the practicality he'd admired in her in the past. "For all we know, he drove back to take care of the body he left behind and headed straight up from there."

Scott had been on the lookout for that possibility. And yet, every time he'd searched down the mountain during their trek, there'd been no sign of life, of movement of any kind. And that made him nervous, too.

"Which is why I think we should head from here farther

into the range but keep the same coordinates as well as we can. Find one of those caves you talked about. And take turns getting some sleep…"

An hour before, the possibility of such a plan had been last case scenario. He'd had time to think. To assess.

To come to terms with the situation.

"And move at nightfall," she finished his sentence for him. Frowning. Deeply.

"Which means we have little chance of preventing another kidnapping to fill today's order," he admitted what he figured they were both thinking.

"Unless someone on the ground, any of the teams involved at this point, are able to do so." Her words were soft. Gentle.

A reminder that there was always hope.

"I'm hoping my phone will at least ping to the location where he shot his partner," Scott said, thinking out loud. Welcoming the presence of a sounding board he trusted. "Even if he got back to the body before anyone found it, my agents will scour every inch of the ground. If the guy left one spot of blood, one footprint…"

"My partners will analyze every speck of earth, trace a piece of rubber, or even a tread, to a tire, to a service center, if that's what it takes. And hopefully get an identity on at least one of them."

Right. Sierra's Web. A firm of experts known to law enforcement all over the country.

How had a medical doctor become part of such an organization?

Instead of asking, he said, "Hopefully they'll have blood to analyze." Her personal life couldn't be his business then, any more than it could have been in the past.

Except…now that they would most likely have been pronounced as officially missing…and were planning to spend time alone in a cave, followed by a nighttime climb down the mountain…

"What about your husband? It's not my place to ask, but I'm assuming he's a member of Sierra's Web as well?"

It would explain her association with the firm.

She turned away. Was glancing toward the mountain range interior, or what was visible of it from their vantage point. "I'm not married. Look over there, on the other side of that ravine…just below the second overhang from the top…"

His gaze followed her pointed finger.

She wasn't married.

After a couple of seconds, he picked out the solid rock inset on the mountainside. Whether a cave that actually led into the mountain itself, or just a massive overhang that gave the appearance of one, she'd found decent shelter that should give them enough coverage to protect themselves, while still allowing a view of the immediate surroundings without them being seen.

In other words, about as safe a resting spot as they were going to get.

She wasn't married.

"Stay behind me," he said. "I'm going to hug the mountain as much as I can and single file, we'll be less visible."

He'd been hiking that way anyway. And she'd been staying in his path. There'd been no reason for him to reiterate.

Except to point himself to the track upon which he must stay. The job. Getting her to safety and then himself back on the killer's trail. The reminder set him immediately straight.

Scott set off, all instincts honed, determined to keep them that way.

And leave the fact that Dorian wasn't married to the ether.

* * *

Dorian didn't ask Scott if he was married. His personal state was none of her business. He'd said in the past that he had no intention of marrying or raising a family. And she'd noticed no wedding ring. But then many of the doctors with whom she associated didn't wear them, either. All the handwashing…

And she put her curiosity about his current matrimonial state down to a normal interest after reacquainting with someone one knew in the past. When the silence got to be too much as they hiked, when it started to allow her mind to feed her reasonable fears, she asked Scott what she could about his life. His most recent cases. His most memorable ones.

Because, alone with her unforgettable self-defense instructor for the first time in years, her thoughts kept returning to him. And every time they did, she knew a moment's respite from the dark weight boring down on her.

She found out the man specialized in kidnapping cases. Heard about a domestic situation. Something she could, unfortunately, relate to as she'd been called in on a few such situations that had ended up requiring specialized medical care.

Her foot slid out from under her, wrenching her hip. Catching herself on a boulder protruding from the ground, bruising the underside of her forearm, she slowed for a step. But didn't call out. Wouldn't slow him down. Kept her gaze focused on the cave she'd found, instead. The place they were going.

She didn't question him any time their destination was out of sight, either. Trusting him and his compass to get them to the natural rock room that would, hopefully, allow them some rest.

She'd been up twenty-four hours. Assumed he had, too. And he hadn't spent a few of them lying in hay, as she had. His body had had no chance to rest.

Not that she could convince herself that any second of her time in that broken down barn had been restful.

Still, as more than an hour passed and they finally reached their destination with no sign or sound of other human habitation, she wasn't sure she wanted to sleep there. Ever.

They both checked out the covered alcove, one at a time as the other kept watch, and determined that it would work well. It went farther back into the mountain than she'd figured, and with a shiver, she insisted that she'd take the first watch while Scott slept.

Hoping that they'd be rescued before she had to take her own turn. Looking at the back of that cave, seeing the darkness, had reminded her of the year before. The disturbed man who'd taken her because desperation had driven him over the edge.

When Scott shook his head, insisting that he'd keep an eye out, needing to get a significant lay of the land immediately surrounding them, she stood strong.

"You're physically much stronger than I am," she pointed out, a bit relieved at how normal her voice sounded. "And while I have had self-defense training from one of the best, it stands to reason that my trainer would still be better equipped than I. If it comes to a hand-to-hand battle with this guy, you have the better chance at success. We need you rested."

Straightening her spine, shoulders back, she prepared for argument. She was not ready to walk back into that dark hole and close her eyes.

No amount of fatigue was going to force its way past her current tension and allow her to sleep.

"Give me an hour."

Open-mouthed, Dorian watched Scott's back as he moved farther into the alcove, and then, she spun around, before he'd settled in, and determined the least risky vantage points for her to hold to keep the agent safe as he slept.

Chapter 6

Scott woke with a rock painfully digging into his hip. Holding a complete stillness he'd learned in the army, he listened, sniffed, and slowly came back to where he was.

With whom.

And sat straight up. The sun had risen high in the sky and was already on its slow way down. No way he'd only been asleep an hour.

Dorian wasn't in sight. His gaze shot around the cave as, moving like a panther, he stood. There was no sign of her.

Or of a struggle.

Fearing that the killer had her captive just outside the opening, waiting for Scott to appear so that he could take down both of them at once, Scott slid his knife out of its holster, and, holding it straight out in front of him, slowly advanced.

One flick of his wrist and he could take the killer out. As long as Dorian wasn't between Scott and the guy's jugular.

Keeping his back to the wall, he slid slowly along the side of the cave that gave him the biggest view of the exterior ground. And had taken only a few steps when he saw her.

Dorian was standing, her back and one hand against the side of the mountain, studying the terrain lower down, eating some kind of fruit.

Relief made him weak for the second it took him to pull out his phone and glance at the time.

"You let me sleep three hours." His tone was accusatory. Hell yes, it was. He'd trusted her to...

"You're the one who's most likely going to be called upon to keep us alive," she stated softly, with total calm. And then, still standing watch, her gaze making the rounds, she finished off the fruit and reached into the front chest pocket of her scrubs.

"You need to look at this," she told him, handing him the phone she'd retrieved from the four-wheeler they'd stolen from her kidnapper's killer.

"It's a burner. There's no owner information listed, just text messages. But he's going to be beyond murderous when he finds out it's missing and figures out we have it."

He took the phone. Quickly pushed the screen enough times to get to the messaging app.

Read.

And, with energy pushing at his skin, felt the weight of worlds on his shoulders when he looked back at her.

"We can't go back yet," she said. "Even if it was safe to do so."

"I can't get you any further into this."

But she was right. In his hand, he was holding possibly the best chance he was ever going to get of stopping something bigger than even he'd imagined it could be.

How many babies had already been ripped from their biological families? He had no way of knowing, but judging on the months that had passed, he figured in the double digits.

And how many more would there be in the months or years to come if Scott didn't succeed before worry that they'd been compromised caused the general to order the operation to simply pack up and disappear?

To continue their work elsewhere?

Location didn't matter to them.

Only secrecy did.

"I'm guessing the red dots might designate birthing clinics all over the Southwest," Dorian said, glancing at his screen, as he studied some kind of map.

Could be that. Or locations where potential drop-offs had been identified.

She reached over and, with one finger, scrolled to another image. "I think these might be customers," she said, looking at the list of lowercase letters that spelled nothing.

"They're all in sets of two," Scott agreed. "Like initials."

But none of it was as immediately compelling, igniting a fire within him, as the first message he'd read. "Someone was told to be at the mission at ten tonight," he said, looking at the doctor in her thin dirty scrubs.

And seeing a breath of fresh air.

Even as tension pressed the breath from his lungs.

"I think the mission is here, in these mountains," she told him. "I was kind of following our coordinates as we hiked, when I could see your phone. And if you scroll back a couple of months' worth of messages, you get almost the same altitude we were at when we first started hiking, but quite a bit east. Doesn't mean it's here. But the men were here. At a clearly predetermined meeting spot."

He liked where she was heading with the theory, but maybe because it gave him a chance to end the sixth-month nightmare? "They'd need to meet someplace close to pass off the baby," he agreed. "My guess is these high desert mountains were a meeting place for the kidnapper, and the middleman who was clearly his boss."

She nodded. "But wouldn't it make more sense, then, for the kidnapper to get the hell out of town? As in, drive across flat desert, in any direction, and meet up at any number of deserted areas where no one would ever see them? Where there's no chance of security cameras? Think about it… Why do you think we hear about bodies being found in the desert? Because it stretches for miles and miles, uninhabited land in every direction after you leave the Phoenix valley…"

Her passion grabbed him.

Her words were what hit him hardest.

They freed him from whatever stupor seemed to have slowed him since her return into his life. Allowed him to go with his gut.

"The mission is in these mountains," he said to her. "As you say, any direction away from the valley on land is filled with miles and miles of area where illicit activity could thrive. But that's not where they headed. And in the mountains, with the difficulty of traversing the terrain…"

She nodded. "I took a course on Arizona history when Sierra's Web first settled on Phoenix for our corporate headquarters. There was a ton of activity in these mountains during the gold mining days. And still believed to be a lot of gold up here. To the point that prospectors arrive here every year, hoping to find some. Which is totally beside the point except that there were some areas where miners clustered. They became like rustic camping towns. Some even built buildings…"

He'd been nodding while she was speaking. "There's actually one down by the east valley," he said. "It's like four or five roughly built buildings that are now a restaurant, shop and a one-room museum…" He was talking about a place he'd visited years before, but, in his mind's eye, was envisioning what could be a secret hideout. Something crafted from the remnants of a broken down, abandoned settlement. "There'd be some kind of path or trail from the place, out of the mountain," he said then, looking again at the coordinates on his phone.

Was he wrong to be thinking about testing his hunch?

Alone with an expert physician who had her own work to get back to?

Alive.

"We can't go back," she said then, as though following his thoughts.

"No, but if we head toward this place, if it really exists, right here in these mountains, then we're walking straight into the fire." He'd be putting her life in further danger.

"There's a baby drop-off at ten. Obviously, there were other newborn options on the kidnapper's list, which makes sense, and would also be something his killer would know..."

Her points were spot-on. This wasn't her first criminal hunt.

She took a step closer to him. "For all we know, he's already got a second infant...which, according to that—" she pointed to the phone screen "—will be delivered to the mission at ten."

Yeah, he got that. And knew, if he was on his own, he'd already be heading toward the coordinates of what they'd both figured could be the mission.

"So if we hit it tonight, after dark..."

She wasn't going to give him a chance to protect her.

And for what?

Their theories were all based on supposition. Fanciful, wishful thinking even. And yet, he and the men and women with whom he worked had solved more cases than not based on just such mental deductions. Evidence was gathered… as he'd been doing for six months. Theories established. They followed them as far as they could until new evidence appeared.

As it had the night before with the botched kidnapping that fit the method of operation Scott had already established.

Dorian finding the phone…

Even that made sense. The man he'd shot at had planned to kill off his problems and depart the way he'd arrived—in a four-wheeler that could travel off road in the desert, leaving little to no tracks on the hard ground, no trace.

He'd have succeeded, too, if not for Scott hot on the trail, and in the bed of that beat-up old black truck.

The killer would have had his phone safely stowed, in the event his kidnapper put up a fight…but the killer ran into law enforcement out looking for a kidnapper.

Because, as far as Scott knew, he and Dorian were the only two living people who knew that the kidnapper was dead. And that they were on the trail of his killer.

And so there he stood…with evidence shining up at him.

If he was with another agent, staring at that phone, there'd be no question that they'd follow their hunches. Climbing into danger, when necessary, was the job they'd signed on to do.

Being wrong was always better than not checking out every possibility.

He still didn't like it. His gut was in flux. Telling him unequivocally that he had to get to those coordinates that night. At the same time, it was warning him that he had to put the current life in his hands before the six-month long case. How could he find a way to get Dorian into protective custody, and then make it back up the mountain undetected? There might not be enough hours to do one, let alone both.

A sound in the distance interrupted the tension his thoughts were sending through him. "What was that?" he asked softly, but he knew.

"Sounds like an engine…" Dorian was backing up inside the cave as she spoke. Scott dropped to his stomach, sliding toward the edge of the small clearing of land in front of the cave. Hoping that the landscaping of desert brush would hide him from whoever might be driving down below, he peered into a vastness that angled downward for hundreds of yards.

"What do you see?" Dorian's voice had lowered, sounding strangely vulnerable to him.

Was she hoping for rescue?

As he sought out the source of the engine that was echoing in the canyon below, Scott found himself feeding on that supposed hope. He'd found his kidnapper, was on the brink of taking down the ring—everything was finally aligning…

"Get down!" He spat the words, his thoughts interrupted by the sight of the sun glinting off metal. "It's the black truck. He's back and he's coming in our direction," he added, not moving as he kept watch.

"He can't make it up here in that vehicle." Dorian's tone was calmer than not, stating what they both already knew.

"No. But it's imperative that we not give him any clues as to which direction to head up to find us," he bit out, barely allowing his chin to move against the earth as he spoke. "Are you on the ground?" He didn't chance a turn around to look.

"Yes. Flat. Sideways across the opening, just beyond the cave entrance, so I can see you."

Why that mattered—to her or to him—he couldn't worry about. The important fact was that her choices gave him confidence that she could act in a way that would help him help her. She was down. Inside. Just as he'd asked.

And was keeping a watchful eye outside, too.

Like a fellow agent, watching his back.

As he was still processing the thought, the sound faded in the distance. He'd lost sight of the truck. "He's made a turn away from us," he said, still perusing the landscape with total focus.

"I can't hear the engine. Are you sure he hasn't stopped, and is on foot?"

"Positive, for now," he told her, rolling away from the edge of the cliff to sit up between a desert bush and the cave. Still out of sight, just in case. Yet with the mountain at his back and a complete view around them. "Over there, I could still hear the truck, heard the engine sound fade away. Not shut off."

He heard movement, turned to see Dorian sitting upright, cross-legged, at the entrance to the cave.

"We're safe for now," he said, not allowing his gaze to linger on the captivating redhead. "Get some rest. You're going to need it later."

He had rudimentary charts to study, with only a small phone screen on which to do it. The killer's burner. It was smaller and cheaper than Scott's department issue, but it had 90 percent charge. Scott's, which was much more valuable to him for many reasons, being tracked by his peers, for one, was down to 75 percent. While it was offline, and couldn't be traced, he had it off to conserve energy.

He might only get one shot at reaching the mission, when the time came. He had to be as clear about where to head as he could be. Comparing coordinates he'd been following while they were hiking that day to the few he saw on various screens, he caught movement to his left. Glanced over to see Dorian still sitting upright in the middle of the cave opening.

"You've got to sleep," he told her. "Whether we head to the mission, or back down, I'm going to need you to be able to climb, to hike, as quickly as you did this morning."

She didn't look his way. Just kept staring straight out, into the vastness beyond, as though seeing something besides the desert mountain-scape.

"I'm relaxed," she told him. "And therefore, getting more rest than I would if I close my eyes right now."

The slightly lowering sun was shining into the cave's opening, alighting her face with a glow that was so perfect it seemed staged for the screen. He wanted to believe she was some kind of angel who could make the impossible possible.

But he didn't have that luxury.

"Close them anyway," he told her, purposely lacing his tone with authority. "That way you at least have a chance of drifting off."

If she didn't get some sleep, she was going to be a hindrance. He'd deal with it. Just wasn't as confident he could get her back without detection if he had to carry her.

Which could mean holing them up in another cave somewhere for God knew how long. He'd fail to save the baby due to be transported that night and could lose his chance at breaking up the kidnapping operation.

He could lose Dorian, too.

She had to sleep.

No other option.

He held his strong stance for several minutes. Giving her a chance to comply.

After a length of complete silence coming from the cave, gratified, he turned, ready to smile at the sleeping woman.

And saw her sitting upright, just as she had been.

Staring right at him.

Chapter 7

"Why?" The word came at Dorian laced with some frustration.

"Why what?" she asked, calm as ever. But she knew.

"You're a doctor. You of all people know the importance of rest to the human body's ability to perform. We have no idea what's ahead. But we can count on there being a bit of physical exertion involved."

He was right, of course. Saying things she'd been sitting there telling herself. Apparently, stating the obvious was the only way she and Scott Michaels could communicate.

She had to sleep. Her emotions, her one weakness, were getting the better of her.

And she knew how to lessen their ability to debilitate her. Medically, psychologically, her brain knew the answer.

Sitting there in silence wasn't it. She was only feeding the fear.

"Sixteen months ago, I was out hiking with a friend... Camelback Mountain, you know it?"

She glanced at him, wanting to find something in common, to talk about hikes they might both have taken. And rave about the view from the top of Camelback.

To make small talk to distract herself...

He stared out at the view. "I've seen it from a distance.

Have flown over it. Never hiked it." He didn't sound in the mood to rave about gorgeous landscaping.

"We'd just come back down, were in the small parking alcove getting into our separate cars, and an arm went around my neck from behind. I was shoved into the back of my own car." She relayed the facts like a tale she was telling.

Might interest him, might not. No matter to her, either way.

Inside, she quaked. Every nerve on edge, she stared out at the mountains, the huge drop just in front of them.

Wanted to run and had nowhere safe to go...

A hand touched her arm and she jumped, hitting her head, and screamed.

The hand covered her mouth. Trapped the sound inside her.

Shaking, feeling her accelerated heartrate pounding in her chest, Dorian barely heard the voice.

"Shhh. It's Scott. You're okay." *Scott.*

Oh, God. What had she done?

Reacting so foolishly to a simple touch.

"I'm going to move my hand now. Just stay quiet."

She nodded. Embarrassed. Ashamed. Stared down, studying the hard rock and dirt surrounding them as though there'd be some cure there.

For her fear.

And her humiliation.

Warm fingers beneath her chin lifted her face, and she made herself find the courage to look up at the man who'd just witnessed something none of her partners—her best friends—had ever seen.

"I apologize," she said, pulling on every resource she had to bring out the doctor in her. "I thought talking about it would ease the paralyzing effect it was having on me. I miscalculated."

She'd put herself in counseling immediately after she'd been rescued. Had followed all protocols and been cleared months ago to end her sessions.

Standing beside her, he held a hand out, as though to pull her to her feet. She stood on her own. She would not continue to appear weak. But that hand, the warmth…just as she was wishing she'd grabbed hold when she'd had the opportunity, those fingers wrapped gently around her arm, just above the elbow, and she walked with him the couple of feet to the rock wall against which he'd been sitting. Slid down with him behind the six-foot-tall desert bush through which he'd broken viewing windows.

"It would help me to have the basics," he said. "We don't know what we might be facing over the next hours, and I need to be prepared for any triggers…"

His words were wholly professional. His tone sounded anything but.

The combination reached her in a way nothing else had. She was a professional. Her counselor, her workmates had all dealt with her on that level. And she was a human being who'd suffered serious emotional and mental trauma. Her friends and partners had met her there.

Somehow Scott Michaels seemed to reach out to both versions at once.

"He wasn't after me," she established right away. "He was after my friend. Other than keeping me locked up for days— and demanding some medical care—he provided food and left me alone. I was able to secure his cell phone long enough to send a couple of messages to my friend's cell phone. In a code we'd established when we were kids…" The most important part of the story at the moment. She'd be of use to him, not a hindrance.

"My team got to me, and then to my friend's deranged client just in time to save my friend's life."

"So last night…"

His words trailed off. Leaving her wondering if he was thinking about the way she'd risked her life again, to rescue that newborn baby. Or if she'd maybe lost her hold on reality a bit, having been cooped up in that barn.

"I was doing alright until I walked into the back of that cave." She told him what she figured he most needed to know.

The man lifted his arm, opening up his chest to her. "Put your head here," he told her, his tone more of a command than not. Still, he kindly said, "You need to sleep, and I can provide the security to allow you to relax."

He wasn't looking at her, but rather, was clearly focused on his watch duties. His gaze sharp, moving from one area to the next, resting long enough to make mental notes and then moving on. He didn't issue the invitation a second time. Just sat there with his arm up against the wall behind them.

Because she was exhausted, because she knew he was right and she could be the cause of a failure that ruined many lives if she didn't rest, Dorian slowly leaned over, giving more and more of her weight to the rock hard, but warm, strong and strangely comforting torso that had been offered up as her pillow.

The rise and fall of his breathing rocked her gently. The steady beat of his heart was womb-like. And when she closed her eyes, Dorian tried to focus on a mental vision of the organs in his chest, how they moved as they did their jobs. She tried to see blood being pumped and floating through veins. Instead, she floated back fourteen years.

Remembering a gorgeous and passionate self-defense instructor—one who exuded a compassion, a knowing that was deeper than normal—showing her how to keep herself safe…

He was sitting on the hardest case of his life. The hardest seat his butt had ever propped on for hours unending, too.

Both cheeks were asleep. He figured the condition was for the best, as the discomfort and numbness were constant reminders to the front part of him that kept wanting to jump into life. Every single time the woman sleeping soundly on his chest stirred at all.

She'd been kidnapped the previous year…

He just couldn't get past it. Couldn't find a way to settle the wrath that her words had instilled in him. That she'd been held for days…

And had had the wherewithal to get a phone and help save herself. Remembering a code from her childhood…

He'd never met a woman anything at all like her.

Intelligent way beyond his means, he was sure, but he'd been up against that before. He liked having someone on his team who could fill in his blanks. Who knew what he did not.

Dorian wasn't on his team.

They were just two people stuck in the mountains and running for their lives. Who also happened to both have risked their lives to save babies.

Maybe a team.

A very momentary one. Soon to dissipate. He'd head back to his office in Nevada. She to her probably luxurious home somewhere in the Phoenix valley.

Yeah, he liked that part. Them living a full state away from each other. Gave some distance for security purposes. No chance in running into her again once their short acquaintance concluded.

Scott tensed, hearing an engine again. For the third time. Not the truck. It was louder. Not as smooth. Had the killer found his four-wheeler?

Had the good guys found them?

In time for him to get to the supposed mission farther in the range? If he never solved another case, he had to get this one. Only the worst kind of fiend preyed on newborn babies.

The sound was still in the distance. But heading in their direction?

Pulling out his phone, he turned on the camera, focused it in the direction of the sound, in the gulley far below him, zoomed in as far as he could go...

"It's the four-wheeler we were in." Dorian hadn't moved, had given no indication that she was awake, but her words were clear.

And accurate.

He lowered his phone, not wanting even a glint of sun through the brush catching his lens, signaling their whereabouts.

"Move slowly," he told her. "Keep low. And get into the cave."

A few minutes later, when the distant sound of the engine stopped abruptly, he followed her inside. Gave her his guess as to the longitude and latitude of where the four-wheeler had quit running.

"He's at least two hours out," he added, "and that's assuming he spotted movement up here and is heading straight this way."

Dorian glanced at her watch. "It's another hour or so until dusk."

Sitting beside her, a foot of hard rock ground separating them, Scott kept his gaze outward as he nodded. "I'd say we go now, anyway, get that much of a lead on him, but he's armed and has proven that he'll shoot. I'm guessing at anything that moves at this point."

She didn't respond verbally. If she nodded, he didn't see.

"If you're still up for it, I think, once dusk hits, our safest bet is to head toward the mission," he said then. "If we're lucky, we save the baby. At the very least, we might find an actual settlement, with people who could help us get out of here. We can't go back the way we came. Not for now, at any rate."

He was thinking out loud.

And warning her at the same time.

He could be putting her life at more risk.

She was in trouble regardless.

The guy was clearly after them.

What he needed to get a picture of was her ability to hang tight in the face of more danger. They had to address the fact that she was not only a victim of a kidnapping the night before, but that the event had triggered trauma from the previous year. It he didn't stay on top of her emotional state, he could lose her.

"How's your friend doing? The one who was hiking with you last year?" From what he'd gleaned, the nameless woman had nearly been killed. Approaching the topic through the suffering of a third party sometimes made conversation less threatening in the moment.

"Good," Dorian said, her voice sounding so normal, filled with strength, that Scott turned to look at her. And breathed easier when she met his gaze head-on.

"She moved to Phoenix, opened a law office that is already thriving due to the numbers of clients that stayed with her in spite of the distance and is engaged to the lead detective from her case."

He glanced outward long enough for a perimeter check

but didn't stop his gaze from returning to her brown eyes. "Sounds like she's a lot like you."

She shrugged. "We were best friends when we were little. Lived next door to each other. Unfortunately, I was just a kid and couldn't be there for her when she needed me most. She pushed me away, and I let her…"

There was more there. He heard messages between the words. But didn't pursue them.

"You think you're going to be okay, moving on out of here?" he asked bluntly.

"I know I am. I fall apart when I have nothing else to do," she told him, head-on. "Never when I'm active. Just keep me busy, Agent Michaels, and you'll have a soldier worthy of your lead."

He felt like a grin should be attached to the words.

There wasn't one.

She'd lost some of his confidence. The truth hit Dorian harder than it should have. Than it would have had he been anyone but Scott Michaels.

The man who'd been her secret shame.

Two families that had been close friends for decades had been irrevocably changed by Dorian's secret, but hotly burning, attraction to the man when she'd been engaged to someone else. Her parents, while disappointed and worried about her, had stood by her when she broke up with her childhood sweetheart a month before the wedding. Brent's family, while polite on the surface, had not done so. Feelings had been too strong to ignore, drawing a line between sides, and eventually the families had drifted apart.

"Are you married?" she asked then, to keep her mind active, while her body couldn't be. And to get her head straight where the FBI agent was concerned. They had far more pressing matters than her heart issues would ever be.

And another woman's husband…that was the immediate shut down she needed.

"Nope."

Oh.

"My job consumes me night and day, a lot of the time. If a case comes up, I'm gone. Period. Doesn't matter if it's a holiday or I have reservations for a week of survival training…case comes first."

If he was giving her warning, she heard it loud and clear. If he wasn't…his life just seemed…like hers.

Which gave her the reassurance she'd needed. And another boost of strength as her heart settled back down beneath the blow of disappointment.

She glanced back out at the walls of rock and natural growth surrounding them in the distance. Was finding her vibe.

And then he sent, "You divorced?" at her, pulling her gaze back to him.

He didn't blink. His blue eyes, always seeming so intense to her, didn't waver.

She did.

The question was fair; her mind rallied. He'd found out she was engaged when they'd known each other in the past. She'd had tears in her eyes when she'd announced the news as she'd pulled herself away from him.

In the present day, just hours before, she'd told him she wasn't married.

Besides, she'd opened herself to his question when she'd asked about his marital status.

So she gave him the one word. "No."

That was all.

Chapter 8

With every muscle taut, his insides tied up in knots, Scott made himself sit in that cave for another half hour. It was just the possible culmination of a case that had been eating at him for months—the fact that he finally had a tangible lead—that was playing with him.

Not the woman sitting next to him.

It was only the forced downtime, the fact that they were trapped together with no outside world contact, that had his thoughts, his senses seemingly consumed with her.

"I come from bad stock." He heard the words come out of his mouth. Wasn't feeling any inclination to take it back, even recognizing the lack of a reason to share.

From the day he'd left for boot camp, he'd never mentioned his past.

The point had been to leave it behind.

Funny how he'd taken it with him, within him, every single day since.

"Excuse me?"

"Just…those who knew me back then tended to shy away when they found out my background. I wasn't a great kid growing up."

"Why are you telling me this?"

God only knew.

He looked over at her. "Just don't want you thinking I'm someone I'm not." Solid truth.

"Can I trust you with my life?"

"Absolutely."

"Then we have nothing more to say on the matter."

Good. He nodded.

Feeling like more of a fool than he'd felt in decades.

Because he wanted to say more.

"Time to get going," he said instead, standing.

To get back to the task at hand. To living the life he'd chosen for himself.

Focusing on the greatest thing in it—the career he'd built.

To that end, he headed out of the cave, staying low long enough to get a lay of the land, to see gray and shadow where once there'd been sun.

He heard movement behind him.

Knew Dorian was there.

"If you're capable, we need to head straight up and over," he said, taking in the steep climb, the best natural handholds and steps along the way.

"I'm capable."

"Then let's get to it."

He took the first steps.

And didn't look back.

They'd been climbing for a while. Used to working long, strenuous hours during medical emergencies—sometimes going a full twenty-four without sleep—the physical challenge wasn't the problem.

Spending every second worried about the possibility of a bullet flying out of nowhere and into your back was taking its toll on her mind.

Darkness was starting to fall. But not enough to make their movements invisible.

The only thing that seemed to calm her was focusing on the cute butt in front of her. Or rather, the enigmatic man to whom it belonged.

He was clearly an expert at what he did. As a co-owner of a firm of experts that employed hundreds of the best of the best in a wide range of fields, Dorian appreciated and respected his expertise.

But she wasn't in awe of it. In her world, he was one of many.

Normal.

So why did the man stand out so much? Seem so remarkable to her?

Other than a brief stop for a meal of fruit and cactus juice, he hadn't slowed his pace since they'd started out. Turned his phone on occasionally to check coordinates, but even then, kept walking.

"How much battery do you have left?" she asked after the third time he'd checked, as they changed course a bit. Heading more east than north.

"Fifty percent."

"We've still got eighty-five on the other phone." The killer's phone.

"And every time we turn it on, we risk him locating us."

"It's a burner."

"And if he has the IP address, and someone in his organization with clout, they could be tracking it."

"Someone with clout?"

"We could be dealing with a cartel."

Her heart thudded. She'd wondered, of course. "Clearly there's a hierarchy," she agreed, glad to be talking at least.

And because the conversation kept her mind occupied,

and fear at bay, she spent the next hour asking him more about various cases he'd worked. Finding common denominators with some of Sierra's Web's cases. Talking business.

"Wait, you're in the Las Vegas office now, you said?" she asked as they clawed their way up a steep incline by grabbing hold of plant roots.

"Yeah." He'd been checking each root before using it for weight-bearing, as though he knew that with the rocky ground, a lot of plants were ones that could survive with minimal roots and pulled out of the ground easily.

Darkness had descended upon them in earnest, but, rather than feeling safer Dorian felt more exposed. The moon's glow, up on the mountain, felt like a spotlight to her.

"We had a case there last year. Another stolen baby case, actually," She kept up the shop talk, finding energy, a semblance of goodness, in the similarities in their worlds.

Their life experiences.

As though they were connected that way somehow.

"The bounty hunter that helped a woman find her dead sister's baby," he said then, as though he'd known all along about Sierra's Web's Nevada case, and found the coincidence no big deal. "I didn't work the case, but I heard about it. Partially because of the way it all played out. The people involved."

He turned then. Met her gaze for the first time in hours. Even in the shadows, she could feel the force of that look. "I haven't ever worked directly with Sierra's Web, but I know of your firm, Dorian. I just didn't know you were a part of it."

She wanted him to feel as though their nearly conjoined lives meant something to him. To find something meaningful in the way they'd wound back into each other's lives.

Because she did?

He'd swung back to the next foothold, pulled himself up. And, as he'd been doing since they set out, he waited for her to occupy the space he'd just vacated, before moving on.

"They didn't even know for sure there was a baby," she told him.

Just as he didn't know for sure there was a mission. Or what the word represented in the cryptic messages. He was assuming a building of some kind.

He also had no way of assuring that they were actually heading toward it.

His comment earlier, him coming from bad stock, she couldn't get it out of her head. Because she couldn't figure out why he'd made it at all.

Had he been warning her that they might fail?

"This case…it's important to you." She was guessing, but pretty sure she was right. And suddenly had something that captured her full focus. As though it mattered more than any possible ill that could befall them.

Any trap into which they might be hiking.

"They all are."

"But this one's different." For such a confident, dedicated, successful man, he seemed off his mark.

As she was.

It took one to know one.

Words from someplace in her childhood psyche came back to her.

"Babies taken from loving parents…to end up being raised God knows how…" He'd started and then stopped.

As though any further words would make him sick to his stomach. Or fill with a rage he didn't need blocking his focus.

As though his words, his understanding, wasn't just business. It was personal.

And suddenly she got it. "Because you were raised without loving parents and your whole life has been affected by it."

His foot slipped. For a second, as he hung by his hands on a couple of roots, Dorian couldn't breathe.

His foot lifted to another, wider, rock jutting from the mountainside. He moved silently from there, to the next less treacherous yards along a ridge.

And Dorian, following right behind him, decided she'd said enough.

He had to get the woman out of his life. It was like she exuded some invisible, lethal callout to him that made no sense and had no good purpose.

She was wickedly smart.

Challenged him to be his best, for sure.

He'd had a lieutenant in the army who'd done the same.

But he'd never lost his focus or found himself pouring his sorry heart out to the guy.

As he turned to check on her, as he'd been doing, mostly surreptitiously, careful not to catch her eye, he felt another power pulling at him.

Mostly in the groin area.

Even in dirty, wrinkled two-day-old scrubs, lit only by the moon's glow, with her long red hair falling out of the ponytail she'd rebanded after she'd awoken, the woman was like a siren straight to his libido.

He'd been turned on before.

Pretty regularly since he'd hit puberty.

Some guys were wired that way.

He'd never ever had trouble turning away from the sensation. It was all part of being responsible with his sexuality. You learned to control those impulses. To divert them.

Self-control had never been an issue for him. Not even as a little guy. He might want something to eat, but he'd never cried out for food. Or anything else.

Not that he could remember.

He'd learned to ignore the hunger pains.

And so many other things.

So why in the hell was this one woman so hard to ignore?

One more step up and he'd reached the top of the highest ridge he'd been able to see while climbing. Expected to be met with another, taller mountain to climb ahead of him. Maybe after a bit of downward sloping. Hopefully at least a small valley with a mountain stream.

He made the last move and found himself on a piece of flat ground that reached for an acre, as best he could tell. Couldn't see much out beyond it around the entire perimeter. Thought he saw the shadow of a higher peak in the distance to the east.

Figured the perimeter was surrounded by ways down off the peak.

And turned immediately to give Dorian a hand up to flat ground.

"This is probably overkill, but I need you to drop down to your belly," he told her, watched as she did so, and then followed her down.

She was looking at him, her eyes glistening in the moonlight. Not with tears. He saw readiness there. Much like he'd seen in Afghanistan when he and a comrade were on their bellies at night in a war zone.

He'd known he was up for the task ahead of him then.

Hoped to God he could get the job done that night.

Because he had a woman on top of a mountain peak at least a mile straight up, in the dark, with a killer at their backs.

"Watch for rattlesnake holes," he told her. "They're one part of desert wildlife that are not usually out at night, and only attack when threatened, but if one is partially out of its hole asleep…"

He left the rest hanging there.

"I'm aware of the desert night life," she told him then, her expression serious. Mouth completely straight. "Mountain lion, bobcat, coyote, javelina, possibly bear…"

She knew the dangers.

Was prepared for possible hardship ahead.

Could he possibly have just read that last message from eyeball glints in the darkness?

Blinking, Scott looked straight ahead to the east. His coordinates—which could be no more than numbers on a chart that had absolutely nothing to do with kidnapping, babies, rings, killers or a mission—were pointing him in that direction. "We're headed there." He nodded straight. "Since we have no way of knowing what's just beyond the ridge, we're playing it safest by staying low."

If she nodded, he didn't see it. He'd already started to belly crawl. Heard her moving closely beside him.

He liked that. Her staying close.

Wanted to turn on his phone's flashlight but didn't dare. And kept watch on the ground he shimmied over, taking in the area she'd been occupying, too.

They made it to the ridge in minutes, with her head to his shoulder, half a crawl behind.

Motioning for her to stay back, he gave a last push of his foot.

Suspending his head out over solid ground.

And saw lights.

Chapter 9

Dorian waited for Scott's okay before scooting forward that last push to see the view just over the edge. His silence wasn't good.

If the killer was right there, pointing a gun at Scott, he'd have Dorian soon enough, anyway. If it was some form of wildlife, she might be just the distraction Scott needed to act.

After seconds of wondering what he was facing, figuring that if he was in trouble, she had to know in time to try to help, she joined him.

"Lights…" She hissed the word. Excited.

And scared, too.

"I can't tell what they're from." Scott's voice came softly. "If someone's down there with a telescope, they're going to see us descend."

"What if it's someone who could help?"

He came immediately back with, "What if it's the mission?"

She looked at him. Caught him watching her.

"We have to take the chance," she said, believing that if he was alone, he'd have already descended. "Either way. We have a chance to save a kidnapped newborn. Or we save ourselves and then get to work on finding the killer and figuring out what he's involved with. This is what Sierra's Web does every day. I swear to you—we'll find these people."

"I'm going to find them," Scott said, his tone sounding deadly. And then, with a nod, he added, "And would very much appreciate any help Sierra's Web can give me, if it comes to that."

He was already lowering himself to a piece of ground jutting out just below the ridge. Reached a hand up to help her down, too.

"It's not going to be very dignified, but I think the best way to do this is to sit on our butts and slide as much of the way as we can. Greatly decreases the risk of falling, and will also, I hope, help shield us from prying eyes."

"We could pass for animals, at least on first glance, if someone saw movement," she added, agreeing with him again.

So many times over the past twenty-four hours.

It had to mean something.

She didn't know what.

But she liked it. Being with someone who read circumstances as she did.

Which her partners did pretty much all the time...so why should Scott stand out?

Because he wasn't one of the six friends she trusted unconditionally? The six people in the world she considered family?

She brushed her thoughts aside. "We should each take some sips of juice," she said aloud. At her insistence, they had refilled their bottle every time they opened a cactus for pieces of fruit.

He slid the shirt-made small supply pack down his arm, opened it up. Gave her the first drink. And split another half a piece of gum with her. Which left them a half.

If they were lucky, and the lights below meant some kind of friendly civilization, they could each frame a quarter of that last half as a reminder of their strength, perseverance and—hopefully—victory.

Until the killer was found, and his organization exposed, Dorian wasn't going to be celebrating anything.

But to be most effective, she needed the help of her partners.

Scott, on the other hand, seemed perfectly capable of taking down an entire fleet of kidnappers, if that's what it took.

The way down was much speedier than the trip up the other side of the mountain peak had been. The lower they went, the more careful they became. Staying behind brush as much as possible. Traveling in one motion when they could.

When Scott suggested that Dorian straddle his backside, she did so. And through the tension of possible death, maybe even somewhat because of the heightened negative emotions at battle within her, she felt warmth pool in her crotch as she scooted behind him, opened her legs and wrapped them outside of his, as, with hands on the ground, she pushed herself up against him.

His hands grabbed her ankles, wrapping them around him, leaving the side of one foot touching his groin.

Which kind of felt…hard.

Before she could react, he was moving, using his feet to steady them as he lowered them down a steep, slippery rock incline. Still with her hands behind her, she tried to keep her butt lifted off the ground as much as possible, to carry her own weight.

What she wanted to do was wrap her arms around the man's chest, close her eyes and hold on.

She wanted to pretend that they were on some kind of pleasure jaunt.

And for a second, there in the dark, on her way down

into possible hell, she let herself imagine what such a sexy foray with Scott might look like.

Painted a vivid video in her mind.

And returned to the hot, dark, dangerous present with a jolt when Scott said, "It's some kind of settlement, for sure."

Glancing over his shoulder, she couldn't see much.

What looked like single lights scattered about.

But then she glanced at the screen he held, his phone's camera zoomed in. Things were blurry, but as he scanned the area below, she could see what appeared to be various buildings, scattered pretty far apart. Homesteads? Part of a mission? The pinpricks of lights appeared to be security lights, or widely scattered streetlights of some kind. They were too far up to be able to see more than roofs. Any lights that might be on inside buildings weren't visible from their vantage point.

There was a line running between buildings…what looked like…

"Is that a road?" she whispered rather than spoke, for no logical reason. They'd spoken seconds before.

Just…they couldn't get that close and be discovered.

"A dirt one, probably," he said. "It's too jagged to be paved. We need to get closer." With that, he patted her ankles locked in front of him, as though giving warning to hold on, and scooted down farther. Sliding some, on smooth rock, bruising her butt muscles when the terrain got rough.

Dorian held on. Kept watch as best she could in the moonlight.

Glancing at Scott's phone whenever he turned it on, she kept apprised of the area they were approaching. And of the time, too.

"It's an hour until drop-off time," she said aloud when

he came to a stop behind a tall, fully flowered Mexican red bird of paradise. They weren't going to make it.

Saying nothing, Scott unhooked her feet at his groin. Nodding to the right.

Another cave, more of a deep culvert, but large enough to obscure them from view. She had to move, lead the way.

Staying concealed behind brush, she went first. Crawled to the back of the culvert, behind a jutting rock face, and stood. Glad for the privacy. The hint of protection.

Not afraid of being trapped.

Her body was sore. Nothing that hinted at anything other than normal wear for the day she'd had, following the previous night.

Was it only twenty-four hours since she'd taken on a kidnapper and saved a baby?

Would she have done so had she known she was going after an actual criminal, rather than the distraught father she'd thought she'd been dealing with?

Scott, moving surreptitiously behind the desert plants immediately surrounding the culvert—reminding her of a soldier in a war movie—was using his phone to surveil the buildings that were still at least half a mile away.

The man was thorough. Diligent.

His dress pants were ripped in the back, halfway down the thigh, to the knee.

Her own clothes, while definitely ripe and wrinkled, were holding up well.

Scott turned then, ducking down as he entered the seven-foot-high opening—to stay behind brush to block any possible view of him, she figured.

"There's what appears to be a small town down there. Or at least a settlement of homes, which isn't all that uncommon out in rural desert areas."

She nodded. Could think of three of them off the top of her head.

"I counted at least ten homesteads…scattered throughout what I'm guessing are a couple of miles. There's one bigger building, a standalone, at the far north edge of the clearing. The road ends there. From what I can see, there's what appears to be a paved road heading east, toward the Globe-Miami area, a few miles up the dirt road. Hard to tell in the dark. But what I believe is paved road has reflectors along it, which I saw when a vehicle's headlights hit them."

His grave expression met her gaze then.

"You saw a vehicle." She said the words. Didn't ask them. Confirming what she knew she'd just heard. Taking a deep breath. "Coming or going?"

"Coming. A dark truck. Same size and style as the killer's. Doesn't mean it's the same one. No way for me to distinguish from here, but…" He came toward her, held out his phone.

Showed her a photo he'd taken.

Her chest tightened and she felt her pulse start to race. He'd caught the driver's side.

"It's got that broken running board," she said, forcing calming through a throat thick with tension. "I was staring at it when the kidnapper was shot…"

Adrenaline raced through her.

Accompanied by dread.

They were on the right path.

But would the two of them be able to survive against a possible operation of many?

"We need help." Scott put it right out there. "I still have no phone service. We're too deep into the mountains. I doubt there will be service down below, but I have to get down there and try…"

He didn't want to leave her.

And could not risk taking her down with him.

Most particularly since she'd just identified the killer's truck. A man above the kidnapper in the hierarchy. One who'd shot the baby snatcher for not following the general's orders.

"Put the burner phone on Airplane mode for now. Try to rest. Set an alarm for three a.m. If I'm not back, you sneak the rest of the way down this mountain range, on your belly if you have to, follow that road out of town to the blacktop and, once daylight hits, flag down a female motorist with kids to help you. If you can be patient for a police car to come along, do so. Do not turn on the service on that phone unless it's a matter of life and death. You could lead the killer straight to you. As you're moving, keep an eye out for places to hide in case you have to make a run for it. Rock is best. It's bulletproof."

He wasn't sugar coating a single word. He wouldn't insult her by doing so.

Every bit of information and training he could give her was one more chance to save her life. He took the bottle of cactus juice out of his shirt pack but kept the first aid kit. He'd be out among cactus, she was trapped in a cave, so the juice was a given.

And because he'd be out, and was less medically skilled, the first aid kit seemed like a given for him.

He unstrapped the knife holder on his ankle. Laid it down on the cement of the culvert, knife still inside.

"No!" Dorian's eyes were wide, the whites seeming to pop at him, as he looked up at her. "That's your only protection. You can't go down there, face off with who knows how many criminals might be down there, without any weapon at all. That's suicide. And…and…just plain not smart. If I do my job right, in the worst-case scenario that you don't get back to me, I won't need a weapon."

"You'll need to cut fruit. To eat and drink."

She shook her head again. "I'll use a rock. Lord knows my butt found enough sharp ones on the way down the hill."

The change in her tone of voice, the attempt at levity, the sense of control, had him staring at her. Hard.

He'd never not wanted to leave someone as badly as he didn't want to leave her.

And strongly disliked the idea of leaving her unarmed. If she got caught…

"Obviously, as a medical expert, I'm good with a knife," she said then, sounding almost as though she was teasing him. "But if it's me and either of the guys I've been up against in the past day, chances are good they'd be able disarm me and use the knife against me. At least good enough that I don't want to take that chance."

"I trained you better than that." His words held more than was professional, too. Completely inappropriate and out of place.

As their gazes met, he wasn't sorry for the exchange.

"I need you to get back up here, Scott," she said then. "We know the men you're going down after are armed and prepared to kill. Please take the knife. Give yourself the best chance."

Because she was right, he picked up his knife. Strapped it back in place.

"I'm trained to kill with a single throw of the blade," he told her then. Thinking about her alone in the culvert in the dark, worrying.

She nodded. Came forward, as though to see him off.

He put up a hand to stop her, stepping forward, not wanting her even a little visible inside the hole where he was leaving her.

With her forward movement, his hand landed half on her breast. Her momentum continued, all happening in a split second, and Scott found himself keeping his hand over her heart as her arms came around him and held on.

"Stay safe," she told him, looking up at him. "And, Scott…for the past…" She covered his lips with her own.

Dorian lay on the floor of the culvert, allowing her to be safe, and to follow Scott's descent down the mountain with the burner phone's camera. Five minutes apart from him and she could still feel the warmth coursing through her from a kiss she'd owed him for fourteen years.

Finishing something she never should have started.

She'd meant to give him something to live for—not in an egotistical sense, just a positive, life-affirming pleasant activity. Or so she'd wanted to believe.

Maybe she just needed to know what kissing him full on felt like. In case she never got another chance to find out.

But as she lay on the ground, following his nearly indiscernible trek, she worried that she'd distracted him at the worst possible moment.

The most incredibly selfish thing she could have done.

Because she was Dorian Lowell—the woman who hurt others when she let her emotions rule her head.

Even for a split second.

The thought propelled another.

She had to see him again. To apologize.

Over the next bit, while she lay there on the warm, hard earth, her eyes adjusting to the darkness, Dorian made a deal with whatever fates might be willing to listen.

She asked for the babies' safety, first and foremost. And then, for mental guidance, for the clarity to know, not to feel, and the strength to act on the knowledge. And most importantly, she swore that she would work harder, do more, for the rest of her life, if she and Scott could have just one more minute together.

To make things right with a proper goodbye.

She couldn't lose him like she'd lost Sierra.

A spirit could only take so much.

Or so she reasoned.

She got no response.

Until…not quite an hour after Scott had left…she heard a very clear sound.

Gunfire.

Chapter 10

He was hit.

And he had no time to tend to the wound.

Surprised at how little the initial strike hurt, Scott stayed low, moving through the brush on the edge of a clearing behind the big building. Made it to his safe place. Feeling the warmth pooling on his thigh, midway to the knee, sticking his pants to his skin, he took note, and, reaching down in the cement confines of his storm drain, pulled his knife from its sheath.

He'd seen a dark shroud-covered figure with something in their arms, hurrying into the back of the building.

Ten o'clock sharp.

Had missed the lookout camouflaged as a totem pole in the dark.

There'd been no sound of an engine approaching. Or leaving.

No moving vehicles that he was aware of.

He'd been made.

At least as an unfriendly on the grounds.

Probably not as an FBI agent.

There was no reason for the killer to think that Scott, or Dorian, had had any idea about the mission, or that they'd found its location.

He'd know they had his cell phone, though. He'd have

figured that when he got back to the four-wheeler and found it gone.

At the moment, Scott had three choices. Continue forth, hoping that he could evade a single lookout long enough to avoid getting caught.

Head back up the mountain to Dorian.

Or give himself up for the purpose of taking down the enemy. And saving at least one newborn's life.

He hadn't seen an actual child, but the figure with the bundle…at the exact time that had been indicated…

No way that had been a coincidence.

And as long as he was alive, and able to move, Scott couldn't leave that baby at risk without giving his life to save it.

The choice was just that clear.

That simple.

And that hard.

He'd been training for just such a moment his entire life. Self-defense. Knife throwing. The army. Numbers of bodies weren't as important as finesse. Skills. Awareness.

And he had an advantage. He knew where they were. They had no idea he'd pushed himself feet first into a drainage pipe—had had it scoped out since he'd reached the clearing.

The pipe was there to divert water coming down the mountains after snow, or during a storm, from getting to the building. He'd seen several like them in the desert mountain communities surrounding Las Vegas.

At the moment, it was also serving as a decent pressure point to stem the flow of blood from his wound.

Three men, that he'd counted, had converged on the grounds after he'd been shot. All armed. One with a rifle, two with handguns.

There was no telling how many more were out there that he couldn't see.

Or who might be watching from a window in the building.

The drop-off was at ten.

Was there a pickup that night, too?

Unless the next drop-off, elsewhere, wasn't until morning? And the mission was a pit stop, much like a middleman, to throw law enforcement off the track?

That could mean Scott had all night to try to save that child.

Time to assess.

To plan.

To lull the killer and his kidnappers into a false sense of security.

Let them start to hope that they'd scared him off.

Or killed him.

Either way, it was best for him if they believed he was no longer their problem.

Scott had a lot of experience dealing with the lowlifes who preyed on others for personal gain. Guys like them would rather leave a body to the coyotes and other desert life that would consume it, than have any chance of evidence being found on their person.

Or in their immediate surroundings.

The smell of blood would attract desert prey.

His tight cement casing would diminish the scent.

And he had his knife poised in front of him, ready to slash anything that tried to reach in and get him.

Human or otherwise.

Unless he heard a vehicle approach, he had some time.

Would wait them out.

Maybe he'd get lucky and find out more about what he was up against.

He just had to hope that the damage to his leg was superficial enough that he didn't bleed to death.

Dorian was partway down the mountain before fear for her own life, as well as Scott's, started to kick in.

The emotion didn't slow her down.

She used it to her advantage. Let it heighten her senses. She stayed low. Kept her camera on Zoom at all times, surveying the entire perimeter before her.

She listened acutely.

And she fought back panic. She would not let her nerves prompt any mistakes. Or stop her from trying to save Scott's life.

There could be any number of reasons for someone to have fired a gun in a remote desert town. A coyote in the yard, for one. If there were farm animals down there, which she suspected based on some of the outbuildings, coyotes trying to get livestock at night was a real concern.

She'd seen a man killed early that morning.

While standing next to the same truck that was parked down below.

Scott didn't have a gun.

She might be his only chance.

To do what, she didn't know.

She was a doctor. She saved lives.

Who better to tend to a gunshot wound?

That part was all worked out.

The rest of it…finding Scott…getting to him without getting herself killed…those problems were left for the future.

She had to take one step at a time.

And the plan in mind was to get down to the clearing without being seen.

Period.

Nothing else mattered in her current timeframe.

She needed all senses tuned to the goal.

A slight breeze blew as she got closer to the valley, chilling the skin on her arms after a day of intense heat.

Dorian allowed that natural shiver. Disavowing any fright that could possibly be attached to it.

She was actually experiencing some positive feedback from her emotional cortex, an appropriately working limbic system. Until she saw shadows moving around the building Scott had scoped out as the place the killer had called the mission.

Men, she concluded, based on their heights and bone and muscle mass. Three of them. All armed.

She was going to get herself killed without helping a damned thing.

Which was exactly what Scott had been trying to avoid when he'd told her to stay put.

She had to figure a way to be of use. She'd die if she had to, but the death needed to accomplish something good.

The thought was strong. Pushing her to do more. Do better.

Sierra's death had led to the arrest of a killer who'd preyed on others before her. And to the end of an illegal gambling operation that had hurt hundreds, if not thousands of families.

She owed it to Sierra, to Brent's family, to her partners, even to her friend Faith who was happily engaged back in Phoenix, to learn from her failures—turn them into victories. To make the pain that they'd suffered because of her serve some good purpose.

To somehow make sure that Scott exposed his kidnapping ring, that no more babies were stolen and that those who had been taken were found.

Her whole life had prepared her for this second meeting with Scott Michaels.

She'd come full circle.

Keep an eye out for places to hide.

His words came back to her, as the various instructions he'd left her with had been repeating themselves in her mind ever since his departure.

She was afraid to use her phone that low down, particularly with men on the lookout. Worried that she might give off even a small moonlit reflection from the camera lens, she perused the area closest to her, and farther away, too. She couldn't make another move until she had a hiding place in mind.

Rock.

Bulletproof.

If Scott followed his own rules, and with her limited knowledge of him she thought he would, he'd have had a place scoped out.

Dare she hope he'd made it there?

Was he in hiding?

Frozen with knowledge, and no incoming revelations, Dorian lay supine in a mass of desert brush at the base of the mountain for several minutes.

Wasting time.

Wasting time!

Though her eyes had adjusted well to the dark, she couldn't find any rocks in her immediate vicinity large enough, or enough of an outcropping of them, to provide shelter. Hadn't seen any since she'd left the culvert.

Her heart thumped hard when she heard shouting down below. A male voice. Not close enough for any identifiers.

She couldn't make out the words.

Stared hard, looking for any sign of Scott. Of an injured body.

And blinked when a floodlight suddenly shone from close to the building directly east of her.

They were looking for someone!

Her?

Scott?

She wanted to hope he was who they were looking for. Meaning that Scott had escaped them? Would men be out patrolling if they already had their prey?

They knew she'd be able to identify the kidnapper. And the killer.

That she'd been with Scott.

They could have him, or have killed him, and be hunting her.

Or had those men over there merely heard the same gunshot she had and were out looking for the source?

The light was moving slowly over the complex surrounding the big building. Hovering near the brush farther east of her, not toward her—yet. She had time to find a better hiding place. A minute, maybe. Her blue scrubs would be a dead giveaway.

Could get her killed.

After taking them off, she lay on top of them, scooting herself into the brush. Feeling scratches on her skin.

Welcoming them as a sign that she was acting, not panicking. Doing. And through the bottom branches she peered out.

Her view much better from there, she followed the light as it traveled.

And found the hiding place as the beam traveled over it.

A cement drainage pipe.

Unless someone shot directly into the opening, or threw a bomb or something, a body inside would be fully protected.

Could Scott be in there? Dare she hope?

The beam of light seemed to hover for a second, but as she held her breath, the light moved on past. Straight toward her.

Burying her head, face down, with her arms over her hair, Dorian breathed in dirt.

And waited.

The woman had kissed him.

Why in the hell had she done that? Bringing an element to their association that had no good outcome.

Opening the can of worms they'd been managing to keep sealed tight.

Lying in his cement confines, trying to keep himself from likening his current habitat to the casket he'd very nearly been headed toward, Scott let his mind wander where it needed to stay alert.

He wasn't just thinking. He was listening. Watching.

He'd thought, half an hour before, that he was a goner as a searchlight had come at him, hovering, before moving on. He'd backed farther into the pipe before the light had hit. And had been ready ever since, knife in hand, to fight whoever came at him.

And he'd been thankful ever since that he'd left Dorian safely up in the culvert. And still hoped to get back to her before the three in the morning deadline he'd given her.

If nothing else, he had to make damned sure that she didn't climb down straight into the fire of armed guards. Even if it meant making himself an easy target to distract them.

At least they were in the open now. Had they been patrolling as they currently were as he'd drawn closer to the settlement, he'd never have approached.

Were the guards there on his account?

Why had the light passed so long after he'd been shot at?

Maybe they weren't there for him at all.

The floodlight had been a clear check of the perimeter. Making certain that all was well before someone else arrived?

Was a baby switch going to be happening soon?

Was he being too conservative, waiting as he was?

No way he was going to just lie there, keeping himself safe, if a baby was about to be passed over to a new handler and taken away to a location he might never find.

He couldn't be so close and fail that newborn child.

The bleeding had stopped on his leg. At least with the pressure on it.

He'd pulled the shirt pack off his shoulder when he'd settled into the culvert. Had been using it as a cushion for his head much of the time.

Grabbing it up, he bit into the fabric along the bottom edge and tore it. Then, bumping his elbows against the inner wall of his very temporary housing, he ripped the strip along the entire length of the shirt.

Holding it, he slowly pulled his leg away from where he'd been pressing it against the cement. Winced as pain shot so sharply up to his groin and down to his foot that he almost cried out. And with a deep breath, looped the strip of shirt under his leg with the one arm that could reach. He wrapped it around, and pulled one end up to his other hand. From there, he held on, gritted his teeth and tied.

Tight.

Tighter than he'd thought he'd be able to take.

The fabric would loosen some as he walked.

Giving himself no more time for feeling the pain, he used his feet to push his body forward, to the end of the drainpipe, and slowly, watching everywhere he could see, he put his head outside into the warm night air.

The three guards were still in the yard.

Talking to each other.

Planning an attack? Had they seen him?

One laughed.

Another lit up a smoke.

And Scott belly crawled his way out of his cement holding cell, rolling slowly down a slight incline away from the building and the men supposedly guarding it.

His leg throbbed and stung, but he wouldn't let the bullet wound slow him down.

He couldn't.

Lives were depending on him.

He couldn't let Dorian's last touch be a kiss goodbye.

Chapter 11

Maybe it was overkill, but Dorian didn't put her clothes back on until she'd dampened them with cactus juice and then rubbed them in desert dirt and growth. Multiple times. The filth went against every grain of decency she had.

In a profession where she washed her hands and arms for long periods of time multiple times a day, she was loath to even touch the slightly camouflaged material, let alone dress her body with it. But dirt was better than death.

She couldn't let light blue apparel be a walking warning to bad guys in the dark.

Not that she walked toward her goal.

When her camera picked up a lit cigarette in the mouth of a gunman, while those she'd seen earlier were clustered together, she decided she'd just been given her best chance to move. Belly crawling, she rubbed her elbows raw, heading toward the cement drainpipe mostly buried beneath ground. Occasionally, when she had enough cover to allow the faster progress, she raised up to travel on hands and knees. With every single move she made, she was looking out for pools of fresh blood, for tamped-down brush or earth from recent occupation. For any sign of Scott at all.

She'd reached the back side of the drainage ditch. Glanced inside.

And froze.

Scott wasn't there. And she prayed to God he hadn't been.

A line of what looked like fresh blood streaked from the opening into the darkness.

Meaning that if Scott had been there, he was no more. Had he been in the pipe when he'd been shot?

And hauled out to God only knew where?

Cursing the darkness that shrouded much of the ground around her, she looked for more blood. To no avail.

But just because she couldn't see any, didn't mean it wasn't there.

If that streak was blood at all, she reminded herself, with a calming, steady, professional breath.

And if it was, it might not be human. The reminder piled on top of the previous one.

Giving herself a second to get out of the limbic system and into the cerebrum, she focused not on what had been, but on what she would do next.

She had to go with worst-case scenario. Scott could be incapacitated. Either from a hit, or capture.

Which meant she was on her own.

Did she do as he'd suggested, wait until early morning, and head toward blacktop? Save herself?

Or did she try to save a baby that had possibly been delivered on schedule at ten o'clock? Right about the time that she'd heard shots being fired.

Chances were good that Scott had been taken out. The timing…

Meant nothing, for the moment. If there was a baby, if, if, if…

Scott believed that he'd stumbled upon a link in a baby theft chain. Could she just slink away without at least trying to collect further evidence?

Without trying to find him?

If he was alive, and in need of medical attention…

If there was a kidnapped newborn within her reach…

The question wasn't whether she saved herself or not. It was how she was going to be of service in her current situation.

Doing what she could to find Scott.

And, if she couldn't save the baby, then at least she could gather information and stay alive long enough to deliver it to the authorities.

She had a phone with a camera.

Needed daylight to snap a picture without risking immediate detection.

What would Scott do?

The question came. Followed by an immediate answer. He'd stay low. Keep himself covered. And get closer.

Easier thought than done. But Dorian didn't let herself consider the difficulties in her path, except to find ways to counteract them as best she could.

Moving slowly in the darkness, she searched for her next hiding place. Someplace closer to the building. No lights shone from within it that she could see.

Did that mean the place was unoccupied? That no baby had been delivered?

They could have the wrong building. The wrong settlement.

The *mission* could have been a code word for anything.

But the black truck. She'd seen it.

The killer, who'd been higher up in the chain than the kidnapper he'd shot point-blank, had been at the building earlier that evening.

Or at least his truck—something associated with him—had been.

And it hit her.

The truck had been parked beside a trash bin. A large one, with a wooden closure built around it.

To keep wildlife out, she assumed.

The door to the closure had been ajar in the photo.

Could it still be open?

And could she get inside?

Both the truck and the trash bin had been on the opposite side of the building from the mountain.

Which meant that she could get to them without passing the armed men clustered together in the yard.

Almost as though they were waiting on something. Rather than patrolling as she'd originally thought.

If she could get to the trash enclosure, and just huddle, she might see another vehicle arrive. Be able, from within the shelter, to get a photo. Maybe even of a license plate.

Thoughts solidified, Dorian crawled, on her belly and her hands and knees. She listened intently, still watching the ground for any sign that Scott might have been there before her.

Parts of her journey took her out of sight of the men in the yard, but as soon as they came back into view, she froze until she could make sure there'd been no obvious change in their positions. Still three of them. One still smoking.

As she drew closer, she heard the soft rumble of their voices.

And changed course. A bed of bougainvillea plants covered almost one whole side of the building. Their flowering growth was thick, completely covering the stucco structure they grew against, and reached six feet tall. They were closer than the trash bin. And would be covered in thorns.

No place anyone would think to look for a lurker.

Approaching the building from the back, she was up on

her feet for the thirty seconds it took her to reach the cement base of the mission—if that's what it was—and dive for the ground. She'd risked motion detector lights but hadn't seen any telltale metal hoods anywhere.

Out in the desert as they were, motion lights would be on almost constantly during the night as wildlife hunted and wandered freely.

Taking just a second to catch her breath, to remain motionless while she listened for any fallout from her action, Dorian belly crawled at top speed to the corner of the building, and then around it, to slide under the hearty plants.

She felt the scrapes of thorns on her forearms. Her face. But pressed forward. Stopping only when she reached the far end of their growth. On the opposite corner of the structure.

The men had moved closer to the mission. Were just feet away.

If they saw her, she was dead.

Lowering her face to the ground, she let her hair fall around her, concealing skin, and took a minute to catch her breath.

She had to reverse course. Belly crawl backward.

But she didn't dare move lest she make a sound, alerting them to her presence.

Heard someone telling an off-color joke. Followed by laughter.

Which broke off midstream.

What were they doing? Heading toward her?

She couldn't move to get a look.

But if she didn't…was there already a gun pointed at her?

"Looks like the mission has changed."

She knew that voice!

Oh, God, she knew that voice.

It didn't sound closer. If anything, it sounded farther away. Someone just approaching?

"We popped a coyote," the joke-telling voice said. "No reason to call a halt…"

"Straight from the general," the killer's voice cut off the other man.

"You all clear out first. Now. I'll follow with Zellow and the merchandise. Head to plan B…"

The voices faded, as Dorian's heart rate grew louder. Pounding through her head.

They popped a coyote?

Did that mean Scott was okay?

And nearby?

What would he want her to do?

How could she help?

By not distracting him.

He'd needed to know she was safely up in the culvert so that he could do his job.

He'd want her to just stay put. To wait until the killer's truck headed out so she'd be safe.

And just let the baby be taken to plan B?

If Scott wasn't close enough to hear what she'd just heard, he'd have no way of knowing what was going down.

An engine fired up in the distance, the sound growing dimmer.

The three heading out first?

Or had they left on foot? Hiking back to transportation hidden farther up the road, too far for her to have heard?

How in the hell did she know?

Wait…was that…?

Yes, the newborn's whimper was unmistakable. Most particularly as it grew more strident.

Suddenly, it didn't matter what she knew, or didn't know.

Scrambling out from the sharp branches covering her, Dorian saw a shrouded figure holding a bundle.

Then, filled with horror, she noticed the killer standing beside his truck, gun pointing straight at Scott Michaels.

"Who are you?" The killer, gun aimed at Scott's head, bit out the question, loud enough to be heard over the baby's wail. The hunched, shrouded figure at his side didn't move. Doing nothing to attempt to quiet the clearly distressed newborn.

Scott was at death's door. He understood that.

But the killer needed something from him.

Needed to know who he was.

Was he someone who'd just stumbled onto the murder of a kidnapper, and interrupted the killing of his victim?

How had he come to be where he was when that had gone down?

Had he talked to anyone?

Killing Scott was not about one baby. One deal.

It was about saving an organization that was lining pockets far and wide.

Scott had to find a way of taking down two criminals at once—one whose shroud, denied Scott the chance to see what he was up against—and save that newborn's life.

On a leg weakened by pain and blood loss.

Knife ready, and with a silent, "Now," he lunged.

The gun went off, sending a bullet whizzing closely by Scott's right ear as his knife slid into flesh.

A shriek sounded right next to the killer…the shrouded man…was a woman.

Scott's arm withdrew in a flash as the bigger body fell too close for comfort, and in the next instant, he dove for the waist of the shrouded body, hoping to protect the bundle as he flew flesh into flesh.

He had the second shrouded body on the ground, saw the bundle roll from an arm to the ground, and, too late, saw the second gun pointed at his head.

And realized that he was lying on top of a man, not a woman. One who was going to kill him.

"No!" He recognized the female voice that came out of the darkness. Didn't compute it. But wasn't as surprised as he might have been when a soft-soled shoe landed on the throat directly in line with Scott's vision.

The gun at his head fell to the ground, as the hand holding it went limp.

By the time Scott was on his feet, Dorian had the baby in hand, was unwrapping the blanket enough to survey the tiny body.

She'd barely met his gaze, with a tense nod, when he heard the sound of an engine. Dorian's gaze shot to the road in tandem with his, and then, her eyes wide, filled with too much emotion, she said, "Someone's coming."

Headlights in the distance obscured the one lane road from view.

Scott grabbed a key ring from the killer's pocket and took Dorian's elbow. "Come on," he said, leading her toward the building. After unlocking the door, he ran the key ring back out, snatched his knife out of the killer's left side and followed Dorian inside, closing and locking the door behind him.

She came out of a doorway as soon as he entered, her finger in the quiet baby's mouth. "Find an attic, a cellar, anyplace we can hide," he told her.

She nodded toward her knuckle. "This isn't going to keep the little one quiet for long." She'd given Scott a long look, first. Had gone pale at the sight of the piece of shirt tied around his leg.

He glanced out a front window. The vehicle was getting closer. Only one, so far.

They didn't have long.

And she was right. Hiding wasn't a viable option.

He couldn't get back up to that culvert as quickly as Dorian could. He'd have to get her out of the vicinity and headed back up to safety.

While he deflected.

"There's a back door," he told her. "I'm right behind you. Head straight for the culvert."

For a split second, Dorian looked as though she might argue, but when a whimper sounded from the baby, she gave Scott one last emotional look and ran down the hall.

Chapter 12

With the baby in both arms, held to her chest, Dorian ran as fast and far as she could, keeping a watch on the approaching headlights.

And when they drew close enough for someone to get even a glimpse of her, she dropped to the ground. She unwrapped the baby long enough to fashion a sling out of the blanket, secure the baby inside and tie it around her, talking softy, lovingly, to the newborn as she did so.

It wasn't a mother's voice he might recognize after nine months hearing it through the womb. But it was better than no voice at all.

Scott wasn't right behind.

She'd known when she'd left that he wouldn't be.

But she prayed that he'd make it back to them.

There'd been a lot of blood around the swatch of material around his thigh.

She couldn't think about that at the moment.

With the baby tied to her chest, Dorian dropped to all fours and began her climb, staying hidden in the brush. Watching all around her for signs of wildlife that might think she was breakfast. The best defense from them was to make noise. To call out in a mean voice.

Neither of which she could do.

Pausing to fill both pockets of her scrub pants with handfuls of rocks—a spray she could throw if need be—she continued upward.

Not looking back.

She couldn't.

If she saw Scott in trouble, or anything that led her to believe he was…she'd slow her own progress.

And worsen the baby's chances of escaping further horror.

But she couldn't help listening.

For any approaching danger, yes. But without that distraction, she was left with a silence that could, at any moment, be filled with gunfire.

"We'll be there soon," she told the little one in her care. Whether by the grace of God, or the swaddling against her chest and swaying motion of movement, the baby was quiet. Breathing evenly.

She assumed, asleep.

Forty-five minutes after she'd last seen Scott, she was crawling into the culvert. Her hands and knees were bloody. She suspected her elbows were, too.

She was thirsty. And knew the baby would need sustenance.

They were safe for the moment.

Not facing madmen with guns.

But they had a long way to go before they made it out of danger alive.

She took off her shoes, used them as the base of a cradle, set side by side, more than a baby's length apart. And as she gathered twigs and branches long enough to fit over them, and then brush to top them with, she felt the prick of tears in her eyes.

Blinked them away.

Several times.

And finally, was able to untie the sling from around her, lay the still-sleeping baby in the makeshift bed and cover the newborn with the blanket.

From there, she allowed herself one glance, through the phone camera, down to the compound below.

And saw nothing but stillness.

Darkness.

The sun wouldn't be rising for another couple of hours yet.

Desperation rose up, pushing at her from the inside out, and Dorian stomped her stockinged foot. Self-pity weakened her.

Made her less effective.

She ventured a little farther down a ridge to find a prickly pear cactus and slammed a rock onto the lowest pad, breaking it off. Back at the culvert, she used another, sharper stone to cut through the skin.

She sucked the first piece of fruit that filled her fingers and she grabbed and pulled.

Ate the second one.

By that time, she was watching, almost constantly, the mountainside leading up from the buildings below.

Made herself focus on useful activity.

She could feed the baby from the water bottle—had long ago learned how to feed a baby without a teat or nipple available. On more than one occasion, she'd referred new mothers to a national website that gave step-by-step instructions with pictures.

Not all babies were able to suck.

And while she squeezed juice to fill the bottle, she thought about the rest of the digestion process. The juice could likely cause more stool. Looser stool.

She needed diapers.

Figured she could rip off the bottoms of her scrubs and fashion something that she could tie around the baby's bottom.

Children had been born and raised long before disposable diapers were invented.

Before stores were around to provide cloth ones.

And…one step at a time…she was doing it.

Doing—not giving in to the fright and despair hovering at her edges.

But her hands were less steady. Her head starting to hurt.

As she grew more and more desperate to know that Scott Michaels was okay.

And that he was coming for them.

Scott's head was spinning—with information, a need to reach his colleagues, and, he suspected, a need for rest and sustenance after his loss of blood—as he made the last turn in his climb up the mountain.

The short, ten-minute walk took him half an hour. That included a five-minute stop to cut food and drink for himself and then consume it.

As the adrenaline seeped out of him, he was finding himself only capable of doing one thing at time.

Half dragging his leg, as well as the bag he'd filled to bring up with him, he came over the crest that made him visible to the occupants of the culvert. And they to him.

Dawn would be breaking soon.

Another day during which he needed to accomplish so much.

Miracles.

A day for which he currently had no plan.

Get to the cave.

Period.

His thoughts ended there.

"Scott!" He heard Dorian's voice before he saw her burst from the culvert, no baby in hand.

His thoughts cleared. As did his vision.

"What happened?" he asked, as energy started slowly to surge through him. "Where's the baby?"

"He's asleep," she said.

"He?"

"I changed his diaper. And fed him."

She sounded…different. Surreal. And…different.

A note to her voice he didn't recognize.

"Come on—let's get you in here and let me get a look at that leg," she said then, as though she'd woken from a twelve-hour power nap. As far as he could calculate, she hadn't had more than an hour in the culvert.

She stood there, seeming to almost burst with a need to move, but didn't move away from the opening of the space to let him in.

Instead, she smiled at him. Touched his face.

If he wasn't so out of it, he wouldn't have thought there were tears in her eyes. But he was. So he did.

"You made it back."

He didn't miss the whispered words, sounding to his haywired brain as more of a prayer than a statement.

And then, "What's that?" as he dropped the strap of the satchel he'd confiscated, among many other things he'd taken that he knew were important, but didn't care much about at the moment.

He swayed.

Knew he had to lie down.

And was pretty sure that when he did, the good doctor kneeled down beside him and kissed his lips…

* * *

Dreams of Dorian…a younger Dorian…kissing him faded as Scott drifted into consciousness. He had no idea of how much time had passed. Where he was.

He started cataloging sensations even before he opened his eyes.

Hard ground.

Weight against him.

Leg throbbing.

He was alive.

Dorian!

He lay frozen, not wanting to alert anyone that he was awake. Not wanting to move in case the enemy didn't know he was there.

Had he made it to the culvert?

He'd been on his way.

Had stopped to eat.

Had been hurting. Badly. And feeling light-headed…

His lids shot open. Rock faced him from above. To the left, more rock.

And to the right…

Dorian?

Her eyes closed as her head rested on his shoulder, facing him.

So, he was still asleep then.

Still dreaming.

Except that…his leg was throbbing.

As was the arm on which the doctor lay.

And…there it was again…a whimper.

The sound that had awoken him.

The baby!

He'd made it back to Dorian!

He drew in air. Deeply. Held it there. Savoring.

He'd made it back to the culvert.

And Dorian and the baby were there.

The whimper came again and the weight against the right side of his body disappeared in a flash. Scott closed his eyes, needing a moment.

Dorian had lain with him?

Slept with her head on his shoulder?

Had anything else happened that he needed to know about?

Anything he'd done?

Didn't seem possible.

Not with the struggle he'd been having just to put one foot in front of the other before he'd lost consciousness.

He'd made it back.

The last thing he'd asked of himself.

And there was so much more to do.

Sitting up slowly, he expected dizziness. Had none.

Saw that his head had been lying on a pillow of leaves.

And that his body had been so cushioned as well.

Had he fallen on them?

Shaking his head, he turned around, looking farther into the culvert, and saw Dorian, with the baby in her arms, holding the water bottle to his lips.

His.

Had he dreamed she'd told him the baby was a boy?

Dorian wasn't looking at the baby.

She was staring at him.

Getting his bearings seemed pertinent. "What time is it?"

"Eleven."

Light flooded the culvert.

Eleven in the morning?

He'd slept for five or six hours?

And she'd slept with him.

At least for part of the time.

Pulling his legs up, he meant to stand—to head outside and take care of necessary business. Felt the pull on his lower thigh and saw the bare skin down to his ankle.

The bandage.

Glanced back at Dorian.

"I figured, since I had no anesthetic, the best time to take care of it was when you were passed out."

He shook his head. Felt a smile coming on for no good reason and held it back.

"You took care of it." Statement. Not question.

His mind calculated that it could only have been a little more than twelve hours since he'd told her he saw a vehicle in the compound.

It had turned out to be the killer's black truck.

Chuck McKellips, he now knew.

Right.

He knew a lot.

Details from the night before flooded down on him, and Scott stood up. Feeling ridiculously naked in his pants with one leg cut off.

"Where's the bag I brought?"

She nodded toward the leaves his head had been lying on. The satchel had been used as the base for the pillow.

As he glanced down, his eye caught an image off to the left, behind where he'd been lying. Back by a make-shift cradle.

Spread out, like medical tools on a tray ready for surgery, were all the items he'd retrieved from the mission before he'd headed back up the hill.

Grabbing the jeans and shirt that were going to be too large for him, he headed outside without another word.

Chapter 13

Scott was dressed in jeans that had to be rolled up at the cuffs and belted at the waist when he returned. Dorian, who'd finished feeding the baby and was waiting for her own turn outside, couldn't seem to stop looking at the man.

They were on the edge of a danger she'd never dreamed of—not even with all the tough spots her partners had been in over the years, with her own kidnapping the year before. She was facing down an organization that had power and money far beyond what she had expected.

Ripping apart untold lives as they walked in shadows, stealing newborns from their families.

She and Scott were two normal human beings without special powers against the evilest of powers.

A trapped duo.

One of them was injured.

And the other was caring for a baby.

"You found the clothes I brought you," he said, nodding toward the dark beige elastic-waisted pants and pullover top she'd donned after feeding the baby from the ready-made and still sealed formula bottles he'd had in that satchel. Along with a stash of tiny disposable diapers.

She stared at him, trying to rid herself of the woman who'd given in to temptation and lain down with her head on this unconscious man's chest and had actually slept. Dorian nodded and walked out.

Keeping low, noticing no activity down below at all, and seeing no vehicles, she quickly took care of business and headed straight back to the culvert.

Scott had wanted her on the paved road by dawn.

But with the quiet below, they should be able to head out. Get the baby to safety. And hopefully prevent yet another kidnapping at some other, as yet unknown birthing center.

At the very least, birthing centers across the Southwest, and probably beyond, needed to be notified to beef up security, keep outside doors locked. Not allow anyone but immediate family inside only if their name was on a pre-arranged list and they showed ID.

The doctor in her was in full gear.

Couldn't be said for any of the rest of her.

Scott was sitting in the back of the culvert, right next to the sleeping baby, phone in hand, when she dipped into the cave.

"I need to check the wound," she told him. "You didn't happen to save the cutoff pants, did you, so you can stay covered up?"

Asinine. Completely ridiculous. She was a doctor. Saw nudity all the time.

Growing hot, she forced herself to look at him, knowing that she'd just given herself away.

She couldn't look at his nudity and promise to remain professional.

Where he was concerned, she'd been compromised.

"I did," he told her. "But only because I didn't want to leave them out where anyone could find them. When we leave here, we need to get rid of any sign of our habitation, while leaving enough debris scattered around to make it look as though no one has been here."

Okay, good. He was on track.

She reached for the first aid kit and medical supplies he'd brought back with him. Didn't ask questions, expecting him to head out and change.

Instead, he stood, unbuckled his belt, unhooked and unzipped the fly and let his pants drop.

Everything in her froze.

Heated up quick.

And she saw the shirt that more than covered his groin area.

Taking a deep breath, refusing to let herself panic over behavior so unlike her, she focused on what she did know.

"I specialized in children's medicine," she told him. "But knowing we were forming the firm, I also certified in several other specialties and do regular rotations with top doctors from all forms of medicine specialties, which is what allows me to keep expert status in the field…"

She was rambling. But it was working. Putting mental space between them. Allowing her to focus on the torn skin she'd managed to repair and, most importantly cleanse, very early that morning, sealing it with butterfly straps.

"How deep is the bullet?" He remained standing. She didn't suggest otherwise. If there'd been fresh blood, that would have been different.

"I got it out," she told him. "It was a flesh wound. Just nicked the muscle. It needs stitches, inside and surface, to heal without scarring, but the butterflies are sealing the wound tight enough to keep infection out. There's no oozing."

She'd prefer that he be on antibiotics. And stay off the leg as much as possible. The salve she'd found in the supplies had been enough for the moment.

Hopefully they'd get lucky.

She bandaged his wound securely, but as sparingly as she could, needing to reserve supplies in the case of infection, or reinjury.

Both of which were highly possible with the hiking they had ahead of them.

She busied herself with putting away the supplies as Scott pulled his pants up. Checked on the baby, who'd eaten well, twice, and was sleeping soundly.

"His mother's milk will be coming in," she said then, getting emotional when she shouldn't be, as she assessed the even breathing. A distraught new mother, mourning her missing baby, fearing for him, desperate to find him, didn't need to be dealing with breasts aching for a baby to feed.

She cared about her patients. Felt empathy for them.

But it didn't ever get personal.

"Come, sit." Scott patted the pallet she'd made for him to lie on. And then had shared with him.

For a second, she thought he meant to talk about that. To talk about them.

As if there was a them.

He'd woken up with her head on his chest.

And she had no good or professional explanation to give him.

She went forward anyway. Took the seat he'd proffered.

Awkward or not, painful as it could be, she had to own up to her actions.

They needed the air between them as clear as it could be if they were going to be a successful team.

He'd pulled out his phone. Turned it on. The first thing she checked was battery level. It was crucial that they have enough to make one call when they were within service.

His battery was almost full.

And it hit her.

He'd come back for her and the baby. Not because they were still on the run.

The supplies…the battery…

But his leg…

"We can't stay here," he said before she could find words to articulate pertinent thoughts within the flying and wayward ones inserting themselves into her head. "But before we go, you need to know everything I know. In case you have to leave me behind."

Her gaze shot to his face.

His gaze was glued firmly on his phone.

"The vehicle you saw last night was one of the guards we'd seen earlier, coming back to find out why McKellips didn't show up at plan B."

She studied his face, because what she was currently seeing on the phone screen that seemed to be mesmerizing him was just a bunch of groupings of letters, symbols and numbers that meant nothing to her. "McKellips?"

"Chuck McKellips is the man who killed your kidnapper."

"The man you knifed."

"I hit purposefully. Enough to disable him long enough for us to get away, but not hit any major organs."

She'd figured that much out when she'd seen the knife hit.

Just as she'd applied expert pressure to knock out the man who'd had the baby, but not to kill him.

When Scott hadn't come right behind her back up the mountain, she'd feared the unknown baby carrier had gotten him. "I thought I got you killed by not telling you that the second guy wouldn't be out all that long."

He shook his head. "It's not my first rodeo, Doc." There

was a hint of teasing in his tone, and he finally looked straight at her. Meeting her gaze.

She wasn't sure what he was telling her. Knew that she had so many things to say that she didn't want him to know.

Scott looked away first. And she felt like a failure for not having had enough of her own common sense about her to have already done so.

"They spread out to find us, two outside, one in. I managed to knock out the one inside, drag him out the back, leave him on a trail heading to the road and get back inside before the other two got back. Praying the entire time that they hadn't found you."

"I was on my belly," she told him. "Climbing straight up here." Because…it seemed appropriate, letting him know that he could rely on her to make smart choices. As long as they didn't involve her body close to his, apparently.

"I was hiding when McKellips came inside, and when he didn't find his underling there, he ran back out looking for him. He found him, and then took off up the road…"

As Scott had obviously planned. The man was good at reading his enemy. And playing him.

"I heard McKellips talking to the other guy outside a while later. They got the guy I konked into one of the vehicles and were both heading out."

"Did they say where they were going?"

Scott glanced her way again. His eyes weren't telling her anything she didn't understand. They were filled with warning.

"What?"

"They were going to find another baby to fill the order. It was due this morning at nine. At a place they call the grocery."

Mouth open, she stared at him. Wanting to grab up the

little one behind her and run as far and as fast as she could. "A store?"

Scott shook his head. "My guess is it's some kind of private residence." And then he added, "They don't know who I am. They think I'm some lowlife who was hanging around Duane's place…"

"Duane?"

Those blue eyes met hers again. Almost as though they were holding her somehow. "I'm assuming he was your kidnapper."

"They think you're a friend of his?"

"They suspect I was. Trying to get in on the cut. But Duane didn't know the drop-off points. He doesn't know anything. He was just some guy McKellips knew in the past and recruited to do a few kidnappings."

"They figure me for having the baby, thinking I'm going to hold it over them, at least get some money out of it. They're writing that one off. And you, too. They think you're as good as dead. That now that I have the kid, I'll get rid of you."

He was watching her the entire time he talked. She didn't blink. Just kept holding on to him eye to eye and listening.

"They're alerting the squadron, whoever the hell that is, and everyone will know by now that if either of us are seen, we're to be shot on the spot. They can't let the general get wind of the mess Duane made of things. And they can't risk losing the mission as a cog in the wheel. If it goes, so does their team. And the money's more than any of them will ever see again in their lifetimes."

Sick to her stomach, she still held his gaze. And nodded. "That much."

Sucking in his lips, he turned back to the phone.

"Not knowing who the squadron is makes our task much more difficult." She put the obvious on the table.

"I have reason to believe there might be law enforcement involved." He dropped the words quietly, staring at his phone again.

"Or that there could be," he corrected himself. "I heard McKellips refer to someone by a series of numerals. Sounded like a police badge number to me. A small operation out of a municipality not far from Globe. I worked with them once, a few years ago. Recognized the numbers."

The man was smart. Focused.

Things she currently felt lacking in herself.

She proved as much by asking, "I'm assuming there's no service in the valley?"

He shook his head. "I found an office in the building... the place looked like some community center from fifty years ago, mostly decrepit and filthy, but there was an office in the back. Powered by a generator. After the two left to kidnap another newborn, I put my phone on a charger lying on the desk and went through the place."

"The supplies..."

He nodded. "There was a closet with baby stuff. I grabbed what would fit. Our clothes were in plastic, shoved in a bottom drawer of an old dresser in a small janitor-type room. I'm pretty sure these guys didn't even know they were there..."

"They'll miss the power bars. The baby stuff..."

He shrugged. "They'll know I circled back, is all. What's going to piss them off the most are these..."

Pulling his gun from his holster, he opened it, showing her fresh rounds. "Some not so bright person left them in the back of the bottom desk drawer."

He'd used his knife to pick the lock.

"I've got a box of them," he told her. "They wouldn't fit in the satchel. I hid them just outside the culvert." He glanced at the wall as that slipped out.

Because she'd gone through his satchel. Knew what hadn't been in it.

And she frowned. "Why did you do that?"

He shook his head.

"Scott?"

His silence didn't fit the hours they had ahead of them. "We can't do this without complete truth. And trust." She told him what she'd already decided for herself if he asked about that head of hers on his shoulder.

Or the kiss which she'd given him when he left the night before.

"I was…not doing all that great," he told her. "I fell. The box slid a couple of feet. I somehow thought it was the bullets or me getting back to you and I chose me."

Oh.

Oh! Her heart leaped.

And she said, "Do you remember where they are?"

"Yep. Already found them." Lifting his pant legs, he showed her a pair of socks stuffed full of bullets. "I'm not going to be unarmed again."

She wanted to argue. To talk about his wound and the extra weight.

Didn't trust herself to get it right.

And Scott, who'd turned back to his phone, didn't seem open to anything she had to say on the matter.

They were just going to have to trust each other with some things left unsaid.

Chapter 14

Scott didn't admit to weakness. Ever. Just wasn't his MO.

Instead, he worked through it. Took care of what ailed him on his own and moved forward.

So what in the hell was he doing, giving Dorian even a hint of the hell he remembered as his last moments before unconsciousness the night before?

Scrolling with his thumb on his phone screen, he came up with an answer he could live with. Accuracy not confirmed.

She was his doctor, tending to the bullet wound he'd received in battle. She'd need to know details in order to diagnose him, in the event of possible complications.

And to that end, she was also his partner over the next hours. There were things she had to know.

Landing on the screenshot he needed first, he handed her his phone.

She took it. Gave a cursory glance at the sequences of letters, numbers and symbols and shook her head. "What is this?"

"Those are confirmation of previous kidnappings and deliveries of babies for illegal adoptions." He swallowed. "I know this because of a site I found on the dark web several months ago. Your Hudson was going to work on it the night you were kidnapped. Those markings are code for dates and times."

"I'm guessing the yin yang symbol means the deal was executed successfully?"

He nodded. And then, weighted with the same gravity that had hit him the night before, he pointed to the four different intricate symbols that separated date and time in every single line.

"Are you familiar with those?"

She nodded. "Ancient Chinese, right? Guardians of the directions?"

He nodded. "Dragon means east. Bird south. Tiger west. Turtle north."

"North is actually the Black Tortoise…" She stopped. Handed back his phone. "They've got at least four drop-off locations," she said then. "This place—" she nodded downward "—is only one of them."

"And we don't know if it's north, as in Northern Arizona, or west as in Western United States…"

"Could be south, because it's down in the valley…"

Once again, she was on track with him. "Exactly."

"We have no idea what kind of scope this organization spans…"

He nodded.

"Did you find anything on the general?"

He shook his head. "But it's clear that McKellips, who is one tough dude, is intimidated by him."

He felt her shiver. Struggled to resist the urge to put an arm around her. Pull her close to his warmth. Even if only to give her enough false assurance for a moment of respite.

Which made no sense.

He wasn't a coddler.

And she wouldn't appreciate being coddled.

After effects from the gunshot wasn't quite out of his system yet, apparently.

He still hadn't shaken the initial rush of pleasure he'd had, waking up with her head on his chest. And he damned well didn't have the wherewithal to deal with that.

He got it. She'd been exhausted. Had taken care of the baby, of him. Built a cradle, a pallet for him—all in the dark. Building a second pallet would have taken energy she couldn't afford to expel. And she'd only had one satchel to use for a pillow.

For all he knew, she'd lain her head there to keep track of his heartbeat and exhaustion had just overcome her.

It all made sense. Except the way he couldn't get past waking up with her there.

Dorian stood, almost as though she could sense his growing desire for her, his awareness of her at the very least. Went back to check on the baby.

Giving him a breather.

That didn't last long enough.

She was back, sitting beside him on the pallet. Handing him a power bar. Unwrapping one of her own.

"We're going to need every ounce of energy we can muster," she said then, as though she had a plan in mind for them to head into.

"The minute we step outside this culvert, we're hunted targets," he told her. He'd sworn to himself that he'd get her safely home.

He couldn't change the facts.

"Sounds like we're hunted no matter where we are."

Yep. She got the full picture. He'd known she would.

Finished his bar in less than a minute, and rose. "You ready?"

"Yeah." Her lips said one thing. The stark look in those brown eyes gave another reply.

"We have to head to the road," he told her. "Our chances of making it back over the mountain, and then down without being caught, are slim. McKellips clearly knows that side of the range. My guess is that he either lives there, or has a place in the area, at the very least. He'll probably have traps set…"

"We have to head to the road because with your leg, and a baby, our chances of making it back the way we came are lower."

His leg wasn't a consideration. He'd make it, either way. But the baby…with cries echoing through a canyon…

"We need to stay up high as much as possible, keep distance between us and anyone on the ground hunting and stay low in the brush, behind trees, at least until dark."

She nodded. Was already packing things back into the satchel, while he dismantled their pallet. Leaving some pieces strewn about, spreading others around the area outside the culvert.

"We have to stay out of sight of anyone who could be in the other buildings we saw scattered about the settlement area," he told her as he returned inside to see her zipping the bag. He was stating the obvious. Thinking out loud.

Needing to make certain they were completely united on what lay ahead.

Their lives, the baby's life, depended on them being so.

He glanced over at her. "But it stands to reason, with a road leading to blacktop, there could be other homesteads farther down."

"Our side of the mountain has them," Dorian offered. "Just randomly scattered…people wanting to live off the grid." She reached down, he expected for the baby, saw her take up the blanket instead.

Watched as she fashioned a sling, tied it around herself.

"Can you come here?" she asked then, and he wanted to hold back.

Him and Dorian…with a baby…saving it was one thing…the idea of returning him to his parents, a given.

But…

She was waiting. Ducking as the top of the culvert lowered the farther back he went, Scott ended up kneeling beside the woman.

"We need him freshly changed and fed," she said then. "He's going to cry when I wake and change him unless you can distract him with his bottle."

She handed the small container—one of the dozen he'd found—to him.

And he…

Didn't take it.

"I've, uh, never fed a…baby."

Dorian's hands froze, suspended above the infant, as she looked over at her companion.

And saw an expression of complete blankness on his face.

Something so simple, and he—the instructor, the soldier, the FBI agent in charge—was afraid to take a bottle?

Had no idea what to do? Not even enough to bluff his way through?

He had to take it on. They had no choice. And no time for a tender family moment.

"What if I wasn't here?" she challenged him. "You wouldn't just let this little one starve to death."

She could very well not be there by the next feeding.

He'd had the wherewithal to grab the formula and the diapers.

"You want to do the diaper change or the feeding?"

He took the bottle.

And when she nodded, nudged it toward the baby's lips. The little guy suckled, Scott's big hand suspended above that tiny mouth. Dorian's fingers shook a little as she got the summer weight sleeper down over the tiny, sporadically moving limbs.

She and Scott...the baby...her heart was reaching.

She couldn't let it.

Focused her mind on fluid-ounce consumption, keeping track of feeding times, noting the amount of urine in the diaper. The lack of solid waste. Got the job done.

And then almost wept when she glanced over and caught the expression on Scott Michaels's face. It was like a painting...the combination of awe, and peace amid days' growth of whiskers...

She wanted to just stand there, to watch...to share it with him.

But he looked up at her, brow raised, eyes steady. Had she imagined the expression?

Needing it for some reason.

"You ready to go?" he asked her, the words, so professional sounding, slamming into her. Knocking the nonsense out of her.

"Of course."

With the sling already secured around her, she reached for baby and bottle at the same time, sliding the arm with the baby inside the sling. Settling him there.

Like the professional she was.

Scott, the satchel slung over his shoulder, turned, as

though to check on her, to make certain she was right behind him.

And the sound of a dislodged rock, tumbling down the mountainside, echoed around them.

Scott wasn't gentle about getting himself and Dorian flattened against the wall. They were in place in that first second. Frozen. Listening.

When no other indication of an intruder came, he motioned her to stay still and made his way to the entrance of the culvert. Dipped his head out just enough to scan the area.

With his hand down at his thigh, he waved her closer to him. Buried his face in the side of her neck. "I need to get a look over that ledge," he whispered. And handed her his gun.

With a nod, she took it.

And he took the scent of her, the warmth of her soft skin, with him as he lowered himself to the ground, and snakelike, slid out of the culvert.

Heart pounding, he counted two vehicles down below, at the office building.

And saw two men climbing up toward the culvert.

Shoving himself backward, feet first, in the dirt, he stood inside the culvert. "We have to go now," he whispered, taking Dorian's arm. "They're still ten minutes down. The ledge will hide us from their view, but not for long."

She didn't speak, didn't ask questions, just followed behind him.

Stepping carefully.

So close Scott could feel her there.

Her warmth egged him on to be stronger. More focused. Wiser.

He let it.

Keeping their bodies against the side of the mountain, he led them around a wall of rock, staying parallel with the culvert's entrance. One slow, steady, quiet step at a time. Keeping watch in front of him, while he listened behind.

Ignoring the pain in his leg.

The fact that the baby could cry at any time.

With no idea how many people had come back in those two vehicles, he had to assume the area was filled with them.

Had to assume that McKellips had made his delivery that morning as well.

And had brought the squadron back to clean up their mess.

Which meant getting rid of all the evidence.

Human and otherwise.

Half an hour of silence, bodies almost touching, they moved forward slowly. Until Scott came to a halt. Bracing himself as Dorian stepped into him.

He pointed to another small cave, looked for her nod.

Got them there. And knelt to check the compass on his phone.

"We're parallel to where we were," he told her quietly.

"You think they saw us?"

He'd been wondering. "Either that, or in my pained state last night, I left some kind of trail." He'd been castigating himself silently. Just put it right out there.

"I should have stayed away," he told her. "If something happens to either one of you…"

"It would much more likely have happened already if not for the supplies you brought us." Dorian's tone was softer than normal. Warmer.

More personal.

"They know that we were there," she reminded him. "Makes sense they'd search every inch of land that served as possible escape routes."

He'd had that thought, too.

Which meant... "Another team could be heading up here. We have to keep moving. Even if it's in circles."

She nodded. "How's your leg?"

"Hurts like hell." There was no reason to deny the obvious. She'd just think him a liar.

"How much longer you think the baby's going to be asleep?" he countered back.

"We should get another hour, at least."

He nodded. Reached in the satchel for the full juice bottle. Handed it to her first. Sipped after her.

And liked the familiarity of having done so.

Chapter 15

Scott was looking a little flushed. Concerned, Dorian reached out to lay the back of her hand against his cheek and neck.

He stood completely still, staring at her, his jaw tight.

And she pulled her hand away. She shouldn't be doing that without a warning or explanation.

Touching him as though he was hers to touch.

"I'm sorry," she said. "I'm worried about infection."

His gaze dropping from hers, he turned and stepped just outside the small rock inlet, scanning their perimeter. Spent longer looking up at the climb atop the cave than eastward, toward the road. Or south, parallel to the way they'd been traveling.

"I'm going up," he told her, stepping back inside. "You and the baby can stay here, in the shade. I'll take my knife but leave the gun. I'm assuming you know how to shoot?"

She nodded. "All seven Sierra's Web partners took training and were certified shortly after opening our firm." She'd never shot anything but a target, though. And didn't want that to change.

Was about to tell him so but he continued. "There's a ledge about ten feet up, fronted with brush. It's as perfect a lookout as we're going to get. With the baby…" He glanced toward the sling tied to her chest and then away, shaking his head. "We can't hide three of us as easily as one. I need to see if I can figure out what we're up against. At least get an idea of numbers."

The plan made perfect sense. She liked most of it.

"Fine," she said, reaching for the tie on the sling. "But I'm going. You stay here with the baby."

His mouth dropped open as he stared at her.

As though she'd been speaking a foreign language.

His gaze moved to her fingers untying the sling. "Wait, what are you doing? No."

She didn't argue, just continued to implement her plan.

"You'll make him cry," he said then. "We need him quiet."

"If you'll come over here and let me get him tied to you, the chances of him staying asleep are excellent. The warmth and heartbeat emulate the mother's womb. Most any human would do." Not entirely factual, the any human part, but pretty close.

He didn't move.

"You're flushed, Scott. Whether you like it or not. You aren't superhuman. You had an untreated open flesh wound for hours and were climbing and sliding in dirt, among other things. An elevated temperature indicates infection. You need to stay out of the sun for a bit and rest your leg. I can carry one guy on this journey. I can't carry two."

With a nod he handed the gun to her.

She took it. Set it down while she stepped up to Scott, facing him. Thigh to thigh, and, holding the baby between them, his weight being supported by both of their chests, she transferred the sling ties from her hands to Scott's. Stood there, helping to hold the baby while he secured the infant against him.

When the newborn was settled and showing no signs of

waking, she picked the gun back up. Put it in the waistband of her pants and pulled her shirt down over it.

Glanced up to see Scott glancing at the strip of belly she'd just exposed.

As though he could find any part of her dirty, ponytailed hair, bruised jaw and unshowered body the least bit attractive.

"Keep your back covered at all times," he told her as she stepped up to the cave's entrance. Glancing back at him, she nodded.

And for a second or two, couldn't look away.

He didn't either.

It was as though he was urging her not to go.

But she had to.

And his silence told her that they both knew it.

The doc had told him to rest his leg.

He needed the baby to stay asleep.

Chomping to get his ass out of the cave and take on whoever was hunting them, Scott put his two most immediate challenges first, and, with the baby snuggled against him—curiously, not a horrible situation—he slid his back down the cave wall, as close to the entrance as he could get and remain in the shade, and sat.

Knife in one hand.

As a gatekeeper, his abilities were strictly limited, but he was at least able to see enough of the flat ground in the inlet outside the cave to keep watch from all approachable directions. And he was in a knife's throw distance if someone was unlucky enough to enter the area.

His leg throbbed. He hoped to God infection wasn't setting in.

And if it was, he'd have the good doc lance it and they'd move on.

There weren't any other options.

That throbbing, feeling as though it was in tandem with his heart, became like a metronome as he sat there. Counting beats until Dorian returned.

Senses acutely tuned, he listened for any movement of loose rock. The crack of a twig. A breath that didn't belong to him or the baby.

The hour was nearly up and Scott was standing, preparing to head up the mountain, baby and all, to find Dorian when she quietly appeared in his line of vision. She was on her belly, sliding over a ledge of rock at the edge of their little inlet clearing.

Her forearms were scraped. Bleeding lightly in a couple of places. Her elbows, too.

With her back flat against the mountain's rock wall, she stood and slid her way along to the cave.

He stepped back as she ducked in.

Sweat dripped off both sides of her jaw, and her clothes were splotched with dirt and dust. Her ponytail loose, falling to one side, she said, "Good call. The view was just what you would have hoped."

As though she'd just taken a two-minute stroll to glance over the edge of a mountain into a valley for the spectacular view.

If he'd been anyone else, and not on the job, he'd have hauled her up against him and the baby and kissed her right then. Right there.

Danger looming and all.

He handed her the juice bottle. She took it, but said, "I had juice up there while I lay watching."

Of course, she had. Dorian, always the doctor, could be counted on to tend to the needs at hand.

The circumstance might have put Scott off, threatened his masculinity even, if he wasn't finding the woman's abilities so incredibly attractive.

If he hadn't been smart enough to recognize their value and be thankful for them.

He saw her taking in the baby's face, and his breathing and posture, too, he figured. "I managed not to upset him," he told her.

"You'd have managed to take care of his needs if he woke up, too," she shot back, sitting down.

With the baby still attached to him, finding himself comfortable enough moving around with the small body tied to his chest, Scott went for the first aid kit.

Not the one they'd taken from the four-wheeler, but the much larger, stocked one he'd found at the mission. A soft-sided canvas zipper bag that had slid naturally into the leather satchel. Grabbing antibiotic cleaning wipes and salve, he approached Dorian.

She reached for them. "I can do that."

"You can't even see them all," he told her, sitting down directly in front of her. "I don't have a medical degree, but I think I can manage this," he held up his little stash. "Did you see anything?"

He couldn't just hang out in a cave like a sitting duck. He had lives to save.

Had to get moving.

Needed information to determine their next steps.

Dorian watched as he took first one arm, and then the other, cleaning every abrasion carefully. He didn't worry about passing muster under the supervision of a medical professional. He might not be versed on removing bullets from flesh, but he knew how to clean a wound.

After a couple of minutes, she seemed to be satisfied on that point and said, "I could see the compound where the mission was. Better with the phone camera. Took a bunch of shots for you. I think those two vehicles are the only two there. I saw two guys, didn't recognize either, have pictures of them for you, as well, walking up higher than our cave. I'm hoping that means that they didn't realize we were there."

"Or they knew we were but figure we're trying to get back out the way we came. Over the mountain. Better the evil you know, and all." He uncapped the salve, focusing on her words, not on how soft the skin was beneath his fingers. "Anything else?"

He needed more. What, he didn't know. Just didn't like the idea of having sent her up into danger only to bring back what they'd basically already known.

Other than a lack of any other obvious vehicles in the compound. That was good news.

And Lord knew, they could use some.

"I saw a place, a mile or two south of here...there were animals. Cattle, or something. A couple of roofs. And just looking out east, toward Globe, there were a few other scattered roofs, probably half a mile apart or more. Not in any kind of settlement or configuration. Just randomly stuck in the mountains."

He stopped, salve-dipped cotton round in hand, and looked at her. Filling with a much-needed burst of adrenaline.

"Did they look occupied?"

Her shrug didn't deter him much. "I couldn't really tell. But even if they're not, if we can get into any one of them, we might find more supplies. Or even some running water, assuming there's a working well…"

"And if they are, we have to be cognizant of the fact that any one of them could be employed by the general."

She nodded, without any hint of surprise.

As usual, they appeared to be already on the same page.

He kept thinking at some point there'd be a fork in their road. That their ideas and opinions would diverge.

"I zoomed in with the phone and checked every inch of land south of here," she said then, naming the direction they'd been traveling that day. "I saw no sign of any life at all. I'm really thinking those two guys earlier…they might be the only two."

He nodded, stood, satisfied. With the work he'd just completed on Dorian's raw skin, but also with his own ability to assess and guess with accuracy. As much as he didn't feel at all like the agent who'd shown up at the birthing clinic a couple of nights ago, he was glad to know he hadn't lost his job skills.

"They're figuring I'm like them, a criminal willing to do what it took to make the big money. They know they'd get rid of you, and so they'll figure I did. My guess is, they've been sent to wait for me to approach with the baby, wanting to make a deal." He put away the remainder of the supplies and felt a jab to his gut.

A foot.

And then another.

Shocked for a second, glancing down, he took in the downy bald head, the puffy cheeks and fully closed eyes.

And, with a jolt, told himself to get back on track.

To stay on track.

He wasn't playing a little "oh, look, I can hold a baby" game. He was dealing with life and death.

Making sure that the infant had a chance at the first.

Untying the sling from around him, he held it in place as Dorian had. She stood as he approached her and pressed against her, and she wordlessly completed the pass off as successfully as they'd accomplished it the first time.

"I'm guessing he's going to need to eat soon," he told her. Not mentioning the couple of foot jabs. They were in no way pertinent to the tasks at hand.

The woman, with all her lack of toiletries, looked…surreal to him…otherworldly…pure beauty.

He shook his head. Hoped he wasn't heading back to the lack of clarity he'd had during those last few yards up the mountain in the early hours of that morning.

"He's waking up now," Dorian said.

She might have shared more, but he stepped away from them, standing guard at the opening of the cave.

Just in case the two hunters came back down the mountain closely enough to discover the cave.

"You have my gun?" he asked then, and when Dorian nodded toward her waistband, he walked right over, all business. He saw her lift her shirt, and slid the gun from her side.

His knuckles against her side were just a hazard of the job, he decided firmly, shoving the gun into the holster he'd helped himself to the night before.

Holster and bullets…no gun that he could find.

He'd cataloged the information.

"As soon as he's fed and settled, we need to head out," he said then, back on lookout. "If those two really are the only searchers, and they're expecting me to show up, this is our best chance to get out of here undetected. And hopefully make it to a homestead before dark."

He wasn't sure how he'd approach that one.

They couldn't walk right up and knock on the door, for sure.

But knew he'd have to make that choice when he came to it. When he could assess the surroundings.

"They aren't going to wait around for me forever. They could feasibly still sell the baby, if they have another buyer ready. And even if they don't, they need me dead. My take right now is that they're betting on my need to blackmail them being the stronger one."

She had the little guy out of the sling. Had changed him. The pack of wipes he'd found with the supplies in the cupboard wasn't going to last forever.

As he'd done while he'd dismantled their cave abode that morning, he dug a hole with his knife, a rock and his fingers, and buried the used diaper. He left it open for the bottle she was about to empty into the baby's stomach.

"Do you think we can make it to the paved road yet today?"

Having to stay clear of the dirt road—McKellips's men were using it—meant the trek would be much longer.

And they had a baby in tow.

"I doubt it," he told her the truth. His leg was hurting like hell, but it would not slow him down. He'd find a crutch if he had to. Learn to run with it.

He asked for the burner phone. Looked through the plethora of pictures she'd taken.

Made a choice. Handed the phone back to her.

"I think we should head here," he told her. One roof. Smallish. Less chance of having to face a squadron running out the door. Hopefully, like many people in the Nevada desert, there were good people who were tired of the lies and rat race in the world, just wanting to live naturally off the land, with only natural dangers facing them.

She glanced up at him, babe contentedly sucking in her arms, and for a second there, Scott saw a wife. His child. And immediately turned his back.

Chapter 16

Scott clearly wasn't doing well. They'd been on the move for hours, stopping only to feed and change the baby, to eat cactus fruit and power bars and drink more juice. And while the FBI agent didn't slow down, he wasn't meeting her gaze anymore.

At all.

Like if he didn't look at her, she couldn't see his pale skin?

Wouldn't know that something was wrong?

Her check of his face and neck earlier, in the cave, had indicated that he wasn't running a fever. The flush was gone. His lack of color came with its own information.

They were still traveling in the mountains, not always in sight of the miles-long road that led out of the mountain range, but parallel to it—their route much longer, more circuitous, due to the peaks they had to climb, or circle around. The need to keep cover—and to hike in the shade for the baby's sake—all played a part as well.

What had looked to her as a day trip from zoomed-in photos and aerial views from above was turning into something far more onerous.

And with Scott clearly fading, the journey felt almost impossible.

Would her team work their miracles and find them somehow? Was it ludicrous to hope for a helicopter overhead, sent by Sierra's Web to save them?

She looked for landing spots as she walked. To keep her mind occupied. To keep at bay the emotions that would weaken her.

To keep belief alive.

If she didn't believe in something, she'd be lost.

And she did believe that she'd do all she could to help save lives. So she walked. She assessed. She climbed, and, on occasion, slid. Insisting, when Scott offered to take his turn with the sling, that she needed him to be ready with the gun. To use his skills to keep them safe.

He'd insisted on carrying the satchel. No way she was giving the man any more extra weight on that leg.

Dusk hadn't yet fallen, but it was getting closer when Dorian saw Scott stumble. He righted himself immediately. Continued on without losing forward momentum. But she'd seen him wince.

His injured right leg had been the one to misstep.

"The baby needs real time out of this sling," she said to him then, no longer able to hold back. Telling a truth, but not the one that concerned her the most. She'd changed the newborn's positions regularly, and had refashioned the sling periodically, as well, allowing him to move more freely, so that his little body didn't get cramped. "I know it's early, but we should find cover for the night."

It would be their second in the mountains.

Her third away from home.

Seemed incomprehensible. Her life had changed so completely in just a few days' time. Far more than it had during her previous kidnapping, where she'd been largely kept physically comfortable, with enough to eat and drink, and in one place.

Seconds after she'd spoken, Scott spared a quick glance for the bundle covering her chest. Nodded. And continued taking them farther from the previous night's compound. And toward, she hoped, their salvation.

She was beginning to wonder if Scott was pushing himself so hard that the effort was affecting his thought processes.

Did she trust him to know best? Or was he so focused on forcing himself onward, blinded by pain, that he'd lost ability to discern?

He'd passed out almost as soon as he'd reached the culvert the night before. If he lost consciousness out there on a mountain ledge…what in the hell would she do?

He'd be fodder for coyotes…and worse.

She wasn't muscled enough to move him far…and to where?

With a baby strapped to her?

She was strong. Able. She acted rather than reacted. But she was human. Exhausted. Scraped up. And…

Scott had stopped at a little clearing, an inlet between the wall of mountain they'd just rounded and the wall straight ahead, then he walked to the ledge. She came up behind him. Seeing more of the valley they'd been following all day.

"Look, a little to the right." Scott's words held…something more than the deadpan tone from the past several hours…as he pointed.

An old shack—a good-sized structure—stood a quarter of a mile down.

And in front of it…"Is that a stream?" she asked, growing excited in spite of everything.

"Yeah," he told her. "I thought so a while back, but wasn't going to say anything until I knew for sure. We've been following it for the past hour or so. I just had to get close enough to see that it wasn't just a dry bed."

He could have told me.

The thought served no good purpose.

And yet, there it stood.

After pulling out her phone, she zoomed in on the shack. And her fingers started to shake. "I think there's a path leading out to the dirt road," she told him, showing him her phone.

Had the universe heard her call?

Her partner and friend, Kelly, would be more apt to believe such a thing.

"It's fairly grown over." He handed the phone back to her. And met her gaze full on for the first time since he'd turned his back to her in the cave when she'd been feeding the baby.

Not that it had rankled or anything…she gave herself a reality check with a taste of sarcasm thrown in.

He could connect with her or not. Didn't change their course of action. He didn't owe her anything.

To the contrary, she owed him her life.

"You okay?" He was still looking at her. With concern.

Dorian blinked. Nodded by instinct.

And then, meeting his gaze again—able to read from it as she'd been able to do from the first time they met—she nodded for real.

Broken, faded, cracked and askew, private property signs hung on various broken-down wooden fence posts. Scott, keeping himself and Dorian and the baby concealed as best he could in trees, tall desert bushes and brush, walked along the posted area, not ready to breach it until he was certain that the dilapidated gray building in the distance was really abandoned.

He'd seen all kinds of living conditions during his years as an agent, and couldn't afford to assume anything.

It was later than he'd have liked, with the sun having already disappeared behind the mountain, leaving the area in shadows. The baby had been fussy for a bit right after he'd eaten that last time, and while Dorian had been able to soothe him, and eventually get him back to sleep, Scott had been loath to leave their little inlet until he knew for sure that if he saw enemies, they'd be able to hide and have a better chance of remaining undetected.

The brief downtime had helped his leg as well. And had given Dorian a chance to rest. The woman never complained, but he knew her back had to be aching. The hiking they were forced to do was hard all by itself…having to accomplish it with a baby strapped to her…

"We could have to walk another mile or more before we get beyond these property markers to make it over to the stream," Dorian said from just one footstep behind him.

They could see the water in the distance.

Almost as though it was taunting them from the other side of the old, in dire need of repair, cabin.

He'd had a thought or two about lying down in the middle of the bed of water, closing his eyes and letting it soothe him for a while.

With his head propped on the bank, of course. No way was he checking out. But he'd give much for a few minutes of respite from the sharp burning in his leg. The pain was getting so great he was starting to have hot flashes.

"Hey!" A voice sounded out of the distance.

Behind the tall brush separating them from the house in the distance, Scott froze.

Had he actually heard an angel from heaven, calling out to him?

Scott rejected the thought. Took it as a warning that he was going to have to find a place to rest his leg soon. Eat some fruit and not burn it off immediately.

He needed to sleep long enough for his body to start to heal…

Right behind him, Dorian had ceased all movement as well.

"Hey there!" The voice came again.

He wanted to turn, to see if his companion was hearing things as well. But he didn't get a chance to do so before he saw the bent form coming toward them, waving her hand and smiling.

"I saw you out there!" the ancient voice said, with a waver and a crackle. "Figured you were lost."

Dorian's hand closed around Scott's elbow. Just held him lightly. Not squeezing tight.

Telling him that she wasn't afraid?

That maybe they'd found the help they so desperately needed in the form of an old spirit?

"My place is nothing fancy, mind you, and my fixings real basic, now that I'm here by myself with my Fred gone and buried, but I can still offer tea and sandwiches."

A couple of quick squeezes of his elbow prompted Scott to follow his own instincts and step out from behind the brush.

Just him, his forearm pressed against the gun beneath his T-shirt.

Dorian stayed behind cover. As he'd have instructed, given the chance.

"Thank you, ma'am, but we're dirty and shouldn't be coming inside. If you wouldn't mind just allowing us a dip in your stream?"

Standing in the open, he had a much better view of the

premises. Saw that a lot of the foot-high grass disguised the clutter strewn around it. Rusted-out pieces from machinery, broken parts of what looked to have been an old sofa, filled plastic bags.

Trash that the woman had been too frail to dispose of properly?

"Don't be shy, young man," the woman said. "You use my shower, my toilet, not that rock-bottomed river. It's got fish guts in it, you know. It does. Not proper for a little one like yours. I've been watching you with my beenoculars. Hoping you were coming my way. I don't get so many visitors here anymore. Now you all come right on in proper here, and I'll get some food on for you."

When Dorian stepped out into the yard, fully exposing herself and the baby, Scott knew their decision had been made. She was going in, whether he did or not.

Which meant that he was going in.

No way he was leaving her without protection.

The idea that he was thinking that she'd need protection from a little old lady who couldn't weigh more than a hundred pounds, and whose bones were obviously frail, gave Scott further indication of his need to take a breather.

He was human. And couldn't be so filled with his own determination and course, couldn't be so hardheaded that he'd refuse the help that they'd managed to find.

Which had been his goal all along. Finding help.

His plan had worked.

It was time to follow its course.

The structure, which appeared to have been a nice cabin at some point, was one main room with two doors leading to Dorian knew not what. But she was pretty sure she didn't want to know. There were stairs leading upward as well.

But from what she could see of them, she was fairly certain there'd be no point in trying to climb them—except perhaps to take in the enormity of a severe hoarding addiction.

Boxes in all different sizes, piles of shoes, a chandelier, stacks of books, of china dishes, folded clothes and many, many things that were unidentifiable due to the thick coats of dust on them, filled every available space. On what she could see of the stairs, and throughout the entire main room.

"Sorry for the clutter," the old woman said, her voice warbly, as she ushered them down a small aisle to a large table—three-quarters of which was also filled. "I'm in the midst of organizing and getting rid of things. For Fred," she said then. "He's not as much of a collector as I am."

Fred? The man the woman had buried? Dorian glanced at Scott. Recognized his frown of unease. She'd expected, as soon as they'd followed the woman inside, to find out how the woman communicated with the outside world, got her supplies, whatever, so that they could make their call for help.

She'd been hoping for a landline.

"Fred's your husband?" she asked quickly, wanting to keep the woman in conversation long enough, and quickly enough, for Scott to figure out what Dorian was strongly suspecting.

"That's right," the woman said. "Been married ten years now. I was just a teacher when he made me his bride, but I'm the principal now. Right here in the local school."

"In Globe or Miami?" she asked, naming the two closest towns to the east Superstitions.

"Miami, of course. School's just a mile down the road from here. My Fred, he works the mine, you know. Copper. He'll be home anytime now for supper. Always after the sun goes down. But don't you worry any—my Fred's a friendly sort. He likes company as much as I do.

"Have yourselves a seat," the woman continued as Dorian shared a longer glance with Scott.

His brow raised. She nodded.

"Go on now, sit," the woman repeated. There was only one chair, at the end of the table where the woman was standing, that was not piled higher than the table with clutter. "Just move that stuff down to the floor." The woman motioned toward the chairs closest to Dorian and Scott— chairs closest to the door through which they'd come. "I'll get it in a bit."

Other than the one small aisleway through the place, there was no floor space.

And then, before anyone could move, the woman said, "Oh, wait, what am I thinking? You'll need the bathroom first. It's through that door right over there."

Dorian needed a restroom. Just the chance to run water on her hands, wipe it on her face, to do her business without squatting in the dust. Glancing at Scott, who nodded, she walked over to him, untied the sling and, pressing against him, transferred the cloth to him to retie around himself. Trusting him to find out how best to get them out of there.

The baby whimpered as she moved away, and she started to take him back, but Scott shook his head. Motioned her toward the bathroom.

It might not be usable. Her lifted eyes and shrug were meant to tell him so. Whether he got the message or not, she wasn't sure, but she took his nod as affirmation.

"Ohhhh, let me get a look at that little one," the old woman was saying as Dorian got her first glimpse inside the door that had been indicated to her.

Shockingly, the room was…not as horrible as the rest of

the house. The floor, cracked tile, was stacked only along the walls. The countertop was covered with things, but not stacked up the foot or more of the rest of the house, and the sink and toilet areas were clear.

And relatively clean.

There was a washer, too, with the lid open, and a few pieces of clothing inside.

The shower, a stall, while cluttered around the edges, looked usable.

Maybe later, if she and Scott were still in the area, she could actually stand under the spray.

Wait! What was she thinking?

Before bed that night, she should be home and would be spending half an hour under her own rain-style spray.

Hurrying with her business, Dorian did take a few moments after sitting. She quickly washed her hands and face, and used a bit of the toothpaste from the tube standing in a glass to finger brush her teeth.

She'd just opened the door, was stepping back out onto the aisleway in the main room when she heard the woman say, "Oh, you'll have to wait for my Fred to take you to town. I never learned to drive."

And saw her hopes for a hot shower yet that night, fading.

As reality—the kidnapped newborn in her care, Scott's injury and being hunted by the worst kind of criminals—came crashing down on her once again.

Chapter 17

The woman's name was Grace Arnold. She had no phone. She and Fred had had no children.

"Oh, there you are!" the woman exclaimed with obvious pleasure as Dorian returned to Scott, and took the baby from him. The little guy was still mostly asleep, but Scott had been holding him in the crook of one arm, rather than in the sling.

Just felt...better...at the moment.

"I have bologna or peanut butter and jelly for sandwiches," Grace was saying as Dorian took the baby from Scott. "I wish I could do better, but the man who delivers my groceries once a week hasn't come yet. He worked with my Fred at the mine, years ago. Helped him fix the well, too, just right before Fred died."

In the few seconds since Dorian's return, Grace seemed to have regained some of her faculties. Glancing at Dorian for confirmation of the possibility, he took her slight smile as just that.

"Fred's ashes were spread here on the property," Grace was saying. "Which is why I stay here."

Scott didn't find the idea a good one in any way. Even if for none of the obvious reasons, then because staying there alone, with her husband's ashes around the place, probably helped feed the old woman's fall back to earlier days when

Fred was still alive. She knew he was close. Just seemed to slide in out and of the reality of her husband's death.

"Her name is Grace," he said to Dorian then. And added, "Peanut butter for me, please."

He'd gained a good amount of information in a little time.

But unfortunately none of it brought he, Dorian and the baby any closer to being safe.

He had to get them to safety, even if he didn't make it there with them.

No second choice, no compromise on that one.

"She's offered to let us stay here with her until her next grocery delivery," he added, just to catch Dorian up on the fact that Grace had no immediate help to offer them. In terms of getting them out of the mountains.

Getting him on the trail of a killer named McKellips, and a high-powered kidnapping ring.

And away from the influence of a woman he'd hardly known but had never forgotten. One who seemed to speak to him without words.

He most definitely had to rid himself of that complication.

In the meantime, Grace had food and water.

Which, at the moment, was a good bit of help.

And she had kindness.

As the woman gathered sandwich fixings, asking about the baby, Scott excused himself to the bathroom, using every ounce of willpower he had not to limp on the way.

Grace landed a quarter of a loaf of bread, a knife and peanut butter and jelly on the table. Dorian, a big salad eater, was surprised to find her mouth watering for that bread.

Solid food. Wheat based.

Reaching down to start emptying a chair as best she could, with the baby strapped to her chest, she looked up as Grace said, "Oh look at these. Aren't they pretty now? The flowers on them!"

The woman was holding two plates that Dorian wasn't sure were clean.

"They're beautiful," she said, setting a shoe-sized plastic container on top of a pile of boxes.

"They're just lovely," Grace repeated, and then asked, "Are they yours? Did you bring these for me?"

And Dorian made another decision. As soon as she was out of the mountains, she was going to send someone up to help Grace. Assess her, at the very least. Depending on the woman's finances, maybe she could hire someone to stay with her. Or at least drive up from Miami once a day to check on her. Dorian would donate the money to pay for that if that's what it took.

The respite Grace was so kindly offering to complete strangers was worth that and more.

She'd just cleared a chair at the table, was sitting down, when Grace came over without the plates. "Your baby is just precious. Let me hold him while you make your sandwich." The tone had changed.

She sounded more like a principal in charge.

But that didn't make Dorian any more comfortable giving the baby to her. Most particularly not unless Grace was sitting down and would have her lap to help support the seven-or-so-pound bundle.

It was just occurring to her that Grace had said *him*, as though she knew the baby in the mixed-pastel-covered blanket was a boy, when the bathroom door flew open and Scott strode across the room, his gun in hand.

One look at him, his sharp gaze meeting hers, and Dorian was up and rushing out the back door behind him.

At first, she was thinking she should remind Scott that in Grace's day, it was common to refer to anyone whose gender wasn't certain as "him."

Until her mind caught up with the gun, and Scott's hurried, solid movements in spite of the pain they had to be causing him. The way he remained stooped, constantly surveying the shadows all around them, lit only by the window at the back of the house, commanding her to "stay low" as he jogged her swiftly from hiding place to hiding place, taking cover, even in the darkness, behind junk in Grace's yard.

Until she was reckoning with the pounding of her own heart.

The strike of fear tangling through her stomach.

Whatever Scott knew that she didn't, one thing was for sure, they were in immediate danger again.

And she trusted him enough to do exactly as he ordered.

Adrenaline helped him push through the pain, helped camouflage it, giving Scott almost normal abilities as he headed his small clan back north, toward the compound they'd left behind the night before. Hoping to throw off McKellips, or whoever else had been driving the truck that had turned onto the overgrown long dirt driveway leading up to Grace Arnold's place from the south.

He'd half thought himself paranoid when he'd taken a look out the bathroom window, just checking that there wasn't any sign of anything amiss on the side of the house he hadn't been able to see or evaluate before entering the building.

"Something wasn't sitting right with my gut," he told

Dorian as soon as they were far enough away for him to make a loud whisper without fear of being heard. "She called someone before she brought us into the house."

He'd figured that had to be the case as soon as he'd seen the headlights.

"Maybe she was playing us with the dementia crap."

"She's on the payroll of these guys?" Dorian's horror was evident even in an almost whisper.

He shook his head. He had no way of knowing why Grace had made the call. Could have been that she'd been told a couple had stolen a baby from the mission, that they were the bad guys. For all he knew, the old woman could be thinking she was helping to catch criminals.

Or she could be on the payroll.

Either way, by falling for her subterfuge, he'd almost gotten Dorian killed. And the baby back on the selling block.

"I told her our first names," he said then, blanching again at what had to have been the stupidest mistake of his entire career. Trusting that woman, even for a second.

Putting them all in immediately life-threatening danger...

"I'm sure mine's been on the news anyway," Dorian told him. "And yours, Scott...that's common enough to be anyone from anywhere."

He didn't respond, just continued pushing through brush in the darkness. Staying close to trees big enough to be shields from bullets if necessary as they started the climb back up into the mountain peak they'd left earlier, before heading south again. He didn't slow, even a little bit, for the first hour. Headed south down lower than they'd been earlier, but still a good way up. Got them past the coordinates at which they'd headed down to what they'd thought was the abandoned shack.

And then, in another inlet, similar to the last one they'd been in that afternoon, he stopped to give Dorian a chance to rest. "We have to assume that they know now that I didn't kill you. That you're still a threat. I'm planning to keep going for as long as humanly possible," he warned, as, moving away from her, toward the ledge of the clearing, he used his phone's Zoom function to survey the landscape below.

What he could see of it.

Grace's home, slightly to the north now, was lit. He saw no sign of headlights.

Anywhere.

Could only hope that she'd called one of the two men who'd been after them earlier in the day. That there weren't more men, a boatload of them, hunting the mountains for them.

"Hey, here, look," Dorian's voice, soft still, but insistent, called out to him. Turning, his entire being froze for a second, when he didn't see Dorian. Anywhere.

Adrenaline pumping anew, he strode toward where he thought the sound of her voice had come from.

Around the mountain?

She wouldn't have gone without him. Not even to pee, unless she'd told him so.

Reaching for his knife with one hand, and pulling his gun with the other, Scott rounded the steep jutting rock, expecting to see Dorian held at gunpoint.

Or worse.

Only to find…nothing.

"Keep coming," her voice called to him softly.

Without fear.

"You alone?" he asked. Knowing that she'd find a way to let him know if she wasn't. He couldn't help her by walking into a bullet.

"Fourteen years ago, the word I wanted so badly to say, I couldn't."

The response weakened his knees.

Doubly so.

That word had been *yes*. When she'd been walking out of his sight for the last time. With tears in her eyes. After having first kissed him, and then pulled away in the middle of it. He'd never forget her last words to him. "If I wasn't engaged, and you asked me to go to bed with you, my answer would be…"

She'd never finished the sentence.

And he didn't allow himself more than a brief memory of the past to come forth as he allowed present-day relief to flood him. *Yes*. She was alone.

"Can I come forward?"

She'd called him. But could still be relieving herself. Had just wanted him to know she'd slipped around the corner. Wanted him to keep watch.

"Yes, please."

Another couple of steps, and Scott saw why.

Dorian had stumbled upon a small cave. A real one that curved back into the mountain enough to allow them to turn on a phone's flashlight, however briefly, to survey their surroundings. To see each other.

To set up camp.

In a place far enough into the mountain that the temperature was at least ten degrees cooler than the heat outside.

The baby should sleep well.

They were on the south side of the mountain, rather than east, with no view of the area they'd come from or were traveling toward. But with a bit of finesse with rocks at the corner of that peak, he'd have fair warning before anyone even got close to them.

And with more brush and natural sources of noise—cracking sticks, rocks hidden under brush as Dorian suggested from a previous case her firm had handled—at the entrance to the cave, he'd be able to get a shot off if anyone breached the cave entrance.

With both of them working, it took another hour to get them settled inside. With a cradle for the baby and a sleeping pallet similar to the one Dorian had made the night before.

It was then that she told him what she'd shoved into the sling, at the baby's feet, when she'd run out of Grace's home.

The loaf of bread she'd had in hand as he'd come out of the bathroom.

Pulling out their filled bottle of cactus juice, she offered up that bread like a three-course meal.

They were in darkness again, to preserve phone battery, but with eyes adjusted to the dark, he could see her in shadows and wanted so badly to kiss her, to let good feeling take away the raging pain in his leg.

He cut off the thought as soon as it hit.

But still admired the hell out of her.

For the night, she'd found them a little home.

After dinner, while Scott did a perimeter check, Dorian fed the baby. Welling up with feeling as she listened to the rhythm of his breathing and swallows. He was such a little trooper.

Content just having his needs met.

And she couldn't help but fall in love a little bit.

The child wasn't hers.

Somewhere a mother who'd just gone through nine months of nurturing had given birth only to have her son snatched from the one place he should have been safest. She had to be grieving beyond what Dorian could imagine.

She glanced up when she heard Scott's two light foot taps after stepping over the rock crunch—which looked like river rock left over from rain and snow flowing off the mountain—at the corner before their cave.

Before he'd left, he'd handed her his gun and told her that if she heard approach without those two foot taps, she was to aim to shoot.

He was just a shadow as he rounded the inside turn to the back of their cave.

And her throat tightened. Tears had been pushing at her most of the night. Stress, she knew. And exhaustion.

And she wasn't done working yet.

But first… "Grace asked his name." While she'd been escorting them up to her house.

Scott had been right there. Had heard. She knew because he'd distracted Grace from the question.

"It's odd, caring for him, not calling him anything." Her words sounded pitiful to her. As though that newborn cared if he was called or not. He needed exactly what they were giving him. And nothing more.

The name calling…that was for her.

And not admirable. "I know his mother has named him," she added then, as Scott lowered himself down, sliding his back along the cave wall not far from the pallet she'd built for him.

Only one again.

This time because the back portion of the cave only had space wide enough for one. It narrowed considerably farther in where she'd put the baby's bed.

She wasn't allowing herself to think about that pallet. Or how she'd slept the night before. He'd been unconscious then.

That night, she'd figured they'd take turns sleeping, with someone awake to keep watch. Just as they'd slept the first afternoon they'd been in the mountains.

"It wouldn't hurt to call him something, just while he's with us." Scott's voice filled the cave so full her chest tightened up. "It's not like he'll remember."

He was right.

And his words brought a bit of a smile to her face. Gave her something positive to think about. "So, what should we call him?"

"I've always liked the name Scott." His words held a definite drawl. And they still didn't hold his normal decisive tone. As soon as the baby was in his cradle asleep, she had to get to work on Scott's leg.

Had purposely been conserving phone battery because she was going to need the flashlight…

"Might be a little confusing," she told him. "Scott here, Scott over there…who am I calling or talking about?" She smiled again. It felt good.

"So how about Michael?"

His last name.

Funny how the man who was never going to marry or have children was wanting a namesake.

But because it kept the smile on her face, she agreed with his choice.

Chapter 18

He couldn't remain standing for wound treatment. Had Dorian's life been at stake, maybe, but over the last couple of hours, every time he even brushed the leg against a twig, he felt tremors up to his hip and down to his ankle.

Even if Dorian just added salve to the wound before rebandaging it—and he suspected the bullet hole was going to need more than that—he'd risk losing his footing and falling on her.

He'd seen some oozing on the bandage when he'd used the restroom at Grace's place.

Which likely meant infection.

So when she told him to give her access to the wound, and to lie down, he didn't argue.

He did wait until she'd turned her back to get supplies before pulling down his pants, lying back and making damned sure his shirt covered every part of his groin area.

Just to be certain, he grabbed the dirty T-shirt he'd worn on the first day of hiking and laid that across him, too.

If she found him prudish, he didn't give a damn.

And if, as he suspected, she figured out that he was finding her more woman than doctor, then at least she wouldn't know for sure.

Even with the throbbing he felt lying down, he was still

getting hard, just being in his underwear, knowing she was going to be bending over him.

Touching him.

Feeling like some kind of sick jerk, he swallowed. Hard.

"I know this is going to seem cliché, but I want you to bite down on this…" She'd brought the burner phone with her, had the light shining on what looked like a stripped clean stick that had been soaked in something at some point.

But was currently dry.

He took the stick. Stared at it.

Did not put it in his mouth.

"I made it last night," she said. "Just in case you woke up before I got the bullet out. And it's not just a movie thing. It'll help protect your teeth from gritting them too hard, which can cause damage to the teeth. More than that, it engages the thalamus, your pain receptor, with more than one message at the same time, which distracts some…"

She'd been talking while she unbandaged his wound. Ripping quickly enough that he barely had to bite as tape left hair. The intense focus with which she studied his leg, the interruption to her conversation told him what he'd feared.

He put the stick in his mouth.

Held it lightly between his teeth. Leaving more intense biting in case he needed it later. Noted the cactus juice taste.

Prickly pear again.

He'd told her that of the four juices they'd had the day before, he'd preferred the pear.

Could be why she'd chosen that particular fruit.

Could also have been that the prickly pear was all that had been easily and readily available to her the night before.

Dorian's gaze had never looked more serious as she moved the flashlight around, moving her head with it, as though some different angle was going to change what she was seeing.

More likely, she was taking in every single speck of the wound, determining just how bad a problem he presented.

He started to get tense. He knew that his muscles tightening wasn't going to help the process for either of them, and took the stick out of his mouth long enough to say, "You said it was just a flesh wound, Doc."

Her nod showed zero lightening of mood. "It's infected," she told him. "It went too long with that bullet in it, raw and open, with the dirt…"

"I'm not blaming your skills, Doc," he said then, caring more about her mental state at the moment than his own. If she was going to start blaming herself…

He put the stick back in his mouth.

"Bite down."

He did so. Without pause.

Felt light pressure on his thigh, around the wound.

Nothing that needed a stick in his mouth to endure. Unless that stick was going to lessen the pressure heading to another male stick in her near vicinity.

What the…

"The pus seems to be all at the surface," she said then, shrinking his male member right down. He missed the distraction, most particularly when she continued. "There's no apparent abscess, yet, which is huge. No sign of need to be overly concerned about tetanus."

Until that moment, he'd never considered that possibility. "I'm current on my shots," he let her know then. Wanting to reach up and wipe the frown from her brow.

Not sexually. Just…because she looked so worried, and he wasn't worth that. He'd be fine. He always was.

"I'm going to have to drain the wound," she told him,

gathering up something from beside her and positioning the light on some rocks she'd brought with her. One taller, one smaller to hold up the phone. Obviously, something she'd figured out the night before.

"It's going to hurt like hell."

He nodded. Figuring nothing was going to be much worse than what he'd endured the previous night, climbing up that mountain with the bullet in an open wound that was rubbing on his pant leg every step of the way.

"Counting down from three," she said, and then, "Three, two, one…"

It took every ounce of everything in him to keep Scott from yelling as the burning, shooting pain went up and down his leg. His fingers dug into the pallet beneath him. He was biting for all he was worth.

And her fingers seemed intent on killing him.

For a time there, as she let up while wiping the area and changing position slightly before applying pressure again, he wished he was already in his grave.

Or that he'd at least pass out.

One thing kept him there with her. The concern on her face.

That, way more than the stick, distracted him enough to keep him conscious.

"You okay?" she asked at one point, glancing over at him.

He might have nodded. He meant to.

He was certain he met her gaze full on. Trying to tell her that she was doing a great job. And that he was going to be just fine.

And then, as quickly as the debilitating pain had started, it was done. She was reaching beside her again. He braced himself for more.

"This salve will not only help prevent any further infection, it's also got some lidocaine in it. It will help with the pain. We're going to need to tend to this every four hours, for the next day at least, whether you like it or not."

He wasn't arguing.

Almost jerked upright when he first felt the solution being spread over his wound, but quickly relaxed as Dorian's tender touch soothed more than it hurt.

The bandage was more than it had been. Thicker.

It was going to hurt like hell, ripping all that tape off the hair on his leg. But…damn…he was already feeling less pain. If that was even possible.

Or maybe his thalamus was just too busy taking other messages. Like what a relief it was to see the lines leaving Dorian's forehead.

To notice the way her chin and cheeks had relaxed back to their normal positions, making her easily one of the most beautiful women he'd ever known.

Red hair, no freckles. Brown eyes, not green. Everything about Dorian Lowell was unusual. Different. Setting her apart in his mind.

Making her one of a kind to him.

He couldn't be blamed for noticing…

Good Lord, she was pulling his pants off over his shoe. The shackle he'd purposely left in place.

"I'm going to lift your leg."

What the…

He glanced down. She was holding gauze. Intended to wrap it around his thigh. He started to raise his foot.

"No, let me do it. I don't want that muscle flexed right now."

Yeah, well, he didn't want other things. And muscles couldn't always be fully controlled.

She'd already lifted. Used her shoulder to help bear some

weight, and there was her face, almost right smack in front of his newly exposed and very tender manly parts, only partially covered by his borrowed briefs.

There'd only been one size. He'd grabbed a few pairs. Had shared them with Dorian. There hadn't been any feminine undergarments.

Was she wearing a pair of the briefs, too?

The thought was the absolute wrong one, bringing him into complete, full on, ready mode.

No way she didn't know, with her hands down there, her gaze still focused, his region under that damned mobile spotlight…

"I apologize," he said, quite seriously. "With everything in me, I'm sorry…"

She shook her head, seemingly not in the least bit fazed. "It's a perfectly normal reaction. Don't worry about it."

The words should have shrunk him right up.

Might have done so if he hadn't, at that moment, glanced at Dorian's breasts—because…he was a normal healthy guy who was turned on and there they were, also in the spotlight as she bent over him—only they weren't just breasts in a bra and shirt. She wasn't wearing a bra. And her shirt was stretched tight as she reached back for scissors to cut the gauze.

Letting him see, with way too much clarity, that her nipples were hard as rocks.

And it wasn't the least bit cold in that cave.

He's a patient. He's a patient. He's a patient.

As Dorian opened yet another of the precious antiseptic wipes to clean her hands after taping off Scott's gauze, she continued the litany in her head.

He's a patient.

Except that—he wasn't.

He hadn't come to her for her professional services.

And she wasn't at work.

He wasn't a patient.

He was Scott Michaels. The man who'd upended her early adult life and shaped the rest of it.

The man who'd just saved her life.

And she was doing what she could to save his.

The fact that she was attracted to him didn't have anything to do with his bullet wound. Fourteen years before, she'd been turned on to the point of changing her entire future, disappointing so many, hurting people she loved, without seeing the man's hard-on.

But seeing it there…so many years later…after two days of fighting to stay alive with him, being hunted with him, caring for a baby with him…

Well, that was a cruel twist of fate.

She had to quit looking at it.

"You said it was a perfectly normal reaction."

Turning her back on *it*, she gathered up her supplies. Telling herself to take a sip of juice for her dry throat.

Returned the medical paraphernalia to the zippered kit. Put that back in the satchel. Just as she'd done the night before. If they had to leave on the run, things had to be packed and ready.

She heard movement behind her. A quick glance showed her Scott trying to work the jeans up over his bandage.

He needed to be dressed. Ready to run.

She didn't want the pants up.

But she needed them up.

In a sitting position, with his leg straight out in front of him, he was struggling. She'd told him no weight bearing for at least a couple of hours as she'd applied the last piece of surgical tape. She only had two more sets of closure strips and didn't want to risk having to go into the wound a third time.

Satchel zipped, she moved back over to her worst temptation. Focusing on the medical knowledge filling her mind. Back in complete, professional control. "Let me help with that."

And…slide.

The pants were up over the gauze. Her hand on one side, his on the other. Joint effort. He lifted his hips. She pulled before he did. Hard enough to get the job done quickly. As his left hand faltered, her bit of a tug ended up with a hand slipping from the jeans, her fist grazing…

Scott's enlarged penis.

Their eyes met. Held. She knew what hers were saying, traitors that they were. And even her mind, that which she could always rely upon to save her from emotional disaster, let her down. Played tricks on her.

Telling her that his gaze was communicating a mutual fire that was about to burn out of control.

If they let it.

Were they going to let it?

She continued to lock gazes with him. Silently. Unable to commit. Or to save herself.

She thought.

Until her mind presented words and she spoke them aloud. "I feel like I owe you one. For the past. Coming on to you like I did. And then stopping so abruptly…"

What was she saying? Her hand was there. Was she seriously considering…

"I don't do one-ways." His low, sexy drawl brought her gaze from his crotch back to his eyes. "Either we both go or no go," he said then, completely serious.

Fire burned within her. Through her. Lighting places she hadn't known she had. Her temporal lobe, her amygdala, was acting out. Having a hell of a tantrum. Careening out of control.

She tried to think. To reason. To think medical thoughts.

To bring herself back from the brink of sure disaster once again.

And said, "I thought I was going to die last year when I was kidnapped. My childhood best friend nearly did. And this week…it's like being in a die-fest…a messed-up world where roulette isn't a game. It's a reality."

The thoughts were clear.

And very clearly emotion based.

But rational, too.

More, they were stronger than anything else she had out there on the mountain, perhaps on her deathbed. "There's something about you," she said then, sitting there beside the man, his pants stuck just below the engorged proof neither of them was denying. "Before, and now. Maybe I need to do this. There's something I need to know. Something only you can teach me."

And knowing was the key to acting, rather than being acted upon.

"Are you saying it's a two-way, then? Because, I have to tell you, Doc, this is getting a little painful here."

The words could have filled her with guilt, her there, hovering over a bullet-wounded thigh. But his eyes, smoldering, without a hint of discomfort from his injury in their dimly lit depths, were showing her how very much he wanted what she'd started.

Years before, and then, too.

"I want it as badly as you do." She was honest with him. "Maybe worse."

"Not possible." His chuckle held little humor, and a whole lot of hunger that sent pangs resounding through her.

And still she sat there. Fighting to save herself. And him, too. Without coming up with any way having sex that night would hurt either one of them.

It wasn't like it would affect anyone else.

And in her life, there was no one who would even care.

"I have no desire to marry or be in a permanent relationship." She blurted the words.

"Already figured that one," he gave right back. "And ditto."

She could do it. There was nothing stopping her. And still, "I'm a total failure when it comes to emotional stuff. I get it wrong. And those close to me suffer."

The words might be all wrong. They felt right.

"Warning received." He chuckled again. Slid his hands up under her shirt, finding her hardened nipples. Sending wild sensations through her. Wiping away the world. Making her want to spread her legs and do things.

To do, and be done upon.

Not a one or the other situation.

Standing, her gaze locked with his again, pinpoint to pinpoint in the near darkness, she pulled down her pants. Stepped out of them. Feeling…powerful…in her borrowed underwear rather than embarrassed by them. She and Scott were in their crashed world together.

Sharing everything.

Relying on each other for life itself.

"You're killing me here."

"You have a condom?"

"In my wallet."

He couldn't get up. She'd forbidden it. After taking off her odd underwear she knelt down on the pallet beside him. Reached under his butt, taking her time at it, to get the wallet out.

Retrieved protection, was ripping into it when he said, "Shirt off, please." His tone was strangled sounding. And lest he suffocate, she complied. Feeling more powerful than ever as her breasts hung free before him.

His hands slid up her stomach, sending delicious chills through her. She reached for his briefs. Pulled down as he lifted his hips.

And within a minute, careful not to put any pressure on his thigh, had impaled herself on him.

She rode him, losing all thought, exploding, feeling him explode.

And then, still awash in residual sensation, she sat there, holding him within her.

Chapter 19

Scott was getting hard again. Normally a one and done, head to the shower kind of guy, he couldn't believe himself.

He was injured. Exhausted.

And ready to go again?

Dorian pulled off from him slowly, taking the condom with her. And when she returned to the pallet, she'd donned her clothes again.

He got the message.

Didn't want it.

He'd been able to flip his briefs back in place without lifting. Had done so as he'd realized she wasn't coming back for seconds.

Wondered if he'd ever left a woman lying in bed after sex, wanting more. Hoped not.

It didn't feel good.

Dorian knelt beside him. Grabbed hold of one side of his jeans with one hand, and gently lifted his thigh with the other. "Let me help with these," she said, softly, calmly.

Professional-like.

The doctor had returned. He didn't want her. In that moment, he didn't need her. He wasn't helpless. And while it might be best for his wound if he lay still for hours, the reality was, they could be up and on the run in minutes.

And he'd perform just fine. Get the job done.

He might pay later. Might have an abscess or some other physical price to pay for not babying his injury. And that was his choice to make.

He brushed her hand aside and got his pants up by himself.

And was thankful that her support under his leg made the process a little less uncomfortable.

"And now we rest," he told her, taking command of the operation because the case was his.

She started to pull away. "I'll take first watch."

He caught her arm. "We both need sleep. There's less chance of someone discovering us here tonight than one or the other of us failing tomorrow due to lack of sleep. We have no idea what's ahead of us, but we can count on it being arduous. We've got alarms set outside—I'm a light sleeper and have my gun ready in the event anyone invades."

She didn't pull away. Just glanced at him, not quite meeting his eyes, and said, "I need to feed the baby. He's starting to wake up."

Scott let go of her. But said, "I'm staying awake until you get back here. I need to know you're going to sleep, too."

He heard her rustling behind him. "I can sleep back here."

"Not comfortably." He leaned up on one elbow, saw her head turn in his direction. "You sorry?" he asked.

When she didn't reply, he had his answer.

He lay back down, trying to convince himself that her withdrawal was for the best.

The baby responded to stimuli as Dorian changed him. He ate well, burped, fell asleep right on target. And Dorian was too exhausted to fight with herself.

The back of the cave…too narrow. Since her kidnapping the year before, claustrophobia had been an issue. Therapy had helped. And her therapist had diagnosed that she might have the condition for life, too.

Wondering, in a half-aware kind of way, what type of long-term mental residue she'd develop due to her current situation, Dorian walked the few steps into wider ground. Thought about heading around the small curve and outdoors. Just for some air.

And a glimpse of a clear night sky with shining stars.

She glanced down at the pallet as she passed. Noted Scott's even breathing and, she was pretty sure, closed eyes. And just stopped walking.

He was right. They both needed rest.

And his chest was the only pillow that seemed to do the trick for her, out there in a world where they were being hunted by devils.

He'd offered it the first day. She'd helped herself to it the night before.

But couldn't seem to do it again. Afraid of what she'd be losing, what she'd be giving up, if she did so.

Instead, she stretched out on the cave floor, laying her head on the side of the pallet, almost touching Scott's shoulder, and promised herself that she wasn't getting weak.

She dozed, didn't think she'd sleep much, but came fully awake as strong arms pulled her up on the pallet.

He didn't speak. She didn't even open her eyes.

But fell asleep almost immediately.

Scott awoke, wide awake, each time Dorian got up to feed the baby. And stayed awake until she was back on the pallet with him.

He didn't welcome her back. Didn't hold her. He served his pillow duties and went back to sleep.

Three times.

Before sitting up straight as a gun blast sounded.

Echoing through the canyon beneath them. And then another. And the third, he was fairly certain he heard hit rock.

Which meant it had to have been aimed close enough to them for him to have done so.

Dorian, up beside him, jumped to her feet. Grabbed the baby, gently enough that if he awoke, he didn't cry, then tying her sling as she kicked aside brush and stepped into her shoes at the base of the cradle.

By the time she'd rejoined him, Scott had the satchel on his back and, gun in hand, had rounded the slight turn in the cave and was approaching the outdoors.

The baby was whimpering. They couldn't afford that, let alone a full-out cry. After reaching into the satchel, he handed Dorian a bottle. They had enough for one more day's feedings. He knew she'd have already counted.

Time was closing in on them. If they didn't make it out of the mountains that day, they might not make it out.

Not a usual thought for him. Yet, there it was, as he slid on his belly toward the ledge outside the cave, peering over, while Dorian stood around the cave side of the peak, feeding the newborn.

First glance from north to south showed him nothing but quiet mountain. Surreal beauty. The occasional roof he knew was there.

South to north, the same.

And then…a flash. Color. Phone out, he zoomed in. One man, slightly north of him, halfway down to the valley. Running south. In his direction.

Further along that coordinate above sea level was another man. Holding up something with both hands. Scott couldn't make out the body, his zoom was too blurred, but he figured it for some kind of animal.

They'd been awoken by hunters?

Legal hunters. Or at least ones hunting for prey that was most likely legal.

Or, as he told Dorian minutes later as they started their third day of hiking, "They could easily have been squatters, hunting illegally, but animal prey. Not human."

"You didn't recognize them, then?"

He shook his head. But had to add, "They were too far away. Too blurry." And also confessed, "My phone's back down to fifty percent battery."

"Mine's at thirty."

They were definitely running out of time.

The claustrophobia was getting worse. Dorian fought it with fact. With logic. Telling her brain what was happening to it, in a scientific sense, so that she could combat it.

Mind over matter.

And the matter was, she was trapped in the mountains, with guns at her back, and a babe in arms.

She was confined with a man she couldn't reason out of her.

Maybe because she didn't know him well enough? If she knew what he needed—as she'd known how badly Brent had needed to be the only man who'd ever strummed her strings—she'd know specifically how she'd be at risk of hurting him. And use that knowledge to stop the desire from flowing through again.

If the knowledge could also interrupt whatever strange nonverbal communication that had seemed to thrum through them from the first day they'd met, that would be a wonderful bonus.

With a solid goal, and a specific way to meet it, she had more energy in her step as she followed Scott along a mountain ridge, into another slight valley between two peaks. He'd said, with the hunters down below, they had stay up high for a while, which made for more strenuous hiking, but when they headed down again, they'd be much closer to the road than they'd been the day before. The paved road.

The good thing about the little valleys, besides easier trekking, was the natural cover the peaks surrounding them provided. They couldn't be seen from down below.

Stopping to change and feed the baby, to eat and replenish their juice supply—Scott feeding while Dorian insisted that he rest his leg, while she hunted and cut cactus—she welcomed the respite.

Along with the hope that resurged at the thought that the blacktop road had become the current goal, rather than a future one.

The journey was taking much longer than she'd thought it would, but they were alive. Relatively okay. And making progress.

She was feeling so much better she'd almost convinced herself that she'd overcome the earlier panic, until she returned to see Scott with little Michael in his arms and yearned to walk up and give them both a thankful hug.

They weren't hers to be thankful for.

And if they were, she wouldn't trust herself around them. How did one see they were blinded by emotion if they were blinded and couldn't see?

Somehow, from their very first meeting she'd romanticized Scott Michaels. Because she didn't know him well enough.

The thought came stronger than ever. So much so that as they started out again, with the easier walk ahead of them for a bit, she pressed forward verbally, too.

"When did you know that you didn't ever want to marry?"

She just put it right out there. A person's life choices were generally based on life lessons. The combination made them who they were.

"The first time, I was six, in first grade. The second, a year after I got engaged when she still didn't want to set the date."

Whoa. She stepped and restepped. Moving only about half a step. "You were engaged?"

"For a year."

Yes, they'd established that. But… "When?"

For two days she'd been looking at the back of the man's head for most of their time moving forward. That moment was the first time she was frustrated by that fact.

She was desperately in need of the information that he was only partially imparting. Without access to his eyes, how could she fill in the blanks?

And that, right there, was the reason she had to get him out of her. To find the key to expelling him. No way she could really read a man's mind through his eyes.

She of all people—a scientist, an expert in her field—knew that.

His answer was a long time coming. She was working on a repeat question when he said, "A year before you and I met."

"What happened?" Could it be that easy? She'd find her answers in one of his?

And…what woman in her right mind wouldn't set the first date possible to join herself to him? If she was the marrying kind.

"I pushed. She cried."

She waited for more. Tense to the point of irritability in her need to know. The valley's verdant brush was pulling at her ankles, she was sweaty, starting to stink, and the baby's sling was putting a permanent crick in her neck. "And?"

Tell me you got impatient with her. Gave her an ultimatum. Maybe she'd wanted to finish college first. Maybe she'd needed to get through medical school before being a wife.

"She told me that she couldn't marry me."

Now that, she hadn't expected. Brent had been in a hurry to marry, too. But when Dorian had told him it would have to wait until after she'd completed her residency, he'd been as supportive as always.

"Why not?"

Her need to know was all-encompassing now. Without justification to egg it along.

"Because she didn't want to risk having children with bad blood."

She stopped walking. Stared at his retreating back when he didn't even slow down. "Scott," she said as she caught up to him. He didn't turn.

"Why would she say a thing like that?"

It wasn't about her need to protect him from herself anymore. She'd never met a man with "better blood" in her life. Unless, "Does leukemia or something run in your family?" But even then...

"Nope, we're healthy as can be."

She scrambled to keep up with him then, as he seemed to find new sources of energy, propelling him faster forward. But she was just as fast.

And without a bum leg, she could keep up the pace longer. Caught up to him. "Why did she say that?" she asked, side by side with him. Glancing over.

His gaze remained steadily straight ahead.

"Because it's true."

No. No. No. No. No. Not good enough. She'd…they'd… he was attached to her somehow, by a string she couldn't identify. For his own good, she had to cut the thread.

"What makes it true?"

He still didn't stop. But Scott slowed to a more reasonable pace for both of them, considering the distance they had yet to travel, the climbing ahead of them, as he said, "My paternal grandfather died in prison. My maternal grandfather, best we can tell, dealt drugs to hippies back in the late sixties. My father is currently serving a life sentence for murder. My paternal grandmother had a substance abuse problem that eventually killed her. My maternal grandmother liked men and spent most of her life running off with one or another of them. And my mother is also in prison. She has quite the rap sheet for small crimes but is serving life as an accomplice to my father."

Her justification for questioning him disappeared as Dorian listened, her heart flooding with pain for his pain, and with an admiration she couldn't quell if she'd given her life to do so.

Pulling on his arm, she yanked him to a stop. Looked him in the eye, and, with all the command of an expert scientist in her voice, said, "You couldn't possibly have bad blood, Scott. You were born to people who obviously made very poor choices but look at you. With that start, with that baggage, with that example, you still managed to make the right ones."

Chapter 20

The woman was just being kind.

He'd saved her life. Of course, she'd spin him in the best light.

No need to convince her otherwise. It wasn't like they were going to see each other again once they got to safety. She'd be whisked off; he'd have to endure a quick medical check, and then he was going to be right back on the case.

Saving one baby was great. But there were too many more out there. Needing to be found. And needing to be protected from future kidnappings, too.

And, maybe Dorian had needed to paint him in colors she could look at more easily since she'd had sex with him, wham bam though it had been.

They'd reached the far end of the valley, which precluded further conversation at that point, anyway. Back to the hide and seek form of travel, sticking close together, speaking in whispers and moving from natural barrier to natural barrier, spending as much time out of sight as they could.

Always scoping out potential hiding places, just in case.

They'd been hiking since just after dawn—before six—and by noon he knew they had to start heading down. Much farther and they'd be circling around too far and would begin heading southwest. Farther away from the couple of small towns toward which they'd been heading.

Finding one last cave, to cool off and feed and change the baby, they rested for a couple of hours. Sitting upright, eyes closed, heads against opposite walls. She might have dozed. He doubted it. He planned.

The hours ahead. Anticipating ways a hunter could prevent them from reaching town. Planning solutions for each obstacle.

And moving on toward finding the general, too. The man was going down. Whether Scott was dead, or alive to participate. No way Sierra's Web or the FBI were going to let this one go. If nothing else, Scott had exposed the operation. Many of his colleagues, and, he assumed, all of the Sierra's Web experts, were more than qualified to finish the job.

He jerked upright.

What in the hell was he doing? Writing himself off?

No way in hell.

Standing, his leg stiff, but not throbbing nearly as badly as it had the day before, Scott grabbed the satchel, moved out of the last mountain domicile he'd share with Dorian and the baby and scoped out the safest route to head down the mountain.

Safe from physical harm, a landslide or slick rock that could send them catapulting. And safe from discovery, or capture, too.

By the time Dorian joined him, the baby once again changed and fed, he pointed out a jagged trail winding sideways at times, but that would get them down the mountain. He wanted her to know the route, just in case.

Told her so.

And at her nod, set off.

* * *

She missed Scott. Longed for the camaraderie of their first two days on the run. Recognized the futility of longing for anything, pursuant to her current reality.

Warned herself against any form of Stockholm syndrome—not relating to her captor, but to the captivity itself. And made it down the mountain without embarrassing herself further with phobia-induced chatter.

She did let Scott know that she'd filled a couple of formula bottles with cactus juice and was switching them out, two formulas to one juice. Just in case something happened to her and he was left to care for the baby.

Michael.

She'd denied herself the right to call him that. It wasn't professional.

Didn't seem to stop her thinking of him as such, though. Hard as she tried not to do so.

Scott was so worried about passing on his genes when, in fact, he was doing the world a disservice by not having a little Michael of his own. With Scott as a father, that human being would be pretty much guaranteed to make the world a better place.

When the man she wasn't supposed to be thinking about on a personal level came to a sudden stop, Dorian was so lost in her thoughts of Scott that she almost bowled right into him.

And then saw why.

"All points down seemed to lead me here," Scott said. "Now I know why."

They'd run into a rudimentary dam. Built who knew how many decades before. A cement wall taller than both of them put together. It ran from a wall of mountain to a huge swamp area.

"A retaining wall," she said. "To keep the snow and rain

rushing down the mountain from flooding something on the other side."

He nodded. Turned, and pointed to the north of the huge swamp. A huge drainage ditch ran along the mountain wall. "We'll have to head back this way," he told her, pointing in the opposite direction. "The brush is thick enough to give us some cover, but I have to tell you, I don't like it so stay close. At the first sign of trouble, head down into the ditch and into the tunnel."

He'd given her a hiding place, she knew. And, for the baby's sake, she also knew she'd use it if she had to.

And didn't ask if he'd be using it with her.

Keeping right behind him, she covered the top of the baby's head with the sling, using both arms to ward off branches as they walked through them. Avoiding prickers in some, and just more scratches along her arms in others. Scott did the same, holding branches for her as he could. Cutting through the thickest points.

They moved slowly, stopping often for Scott to use his phone to snap photos and enlarge them for both of them to study for any sign of a trap on the other side of the brush.

By the time she could see the end of the brush, and flat land, ahead of them, she was starting to believe, for the first time, that they had a better chance of getting home than she'd let herself imagine.

Mostly thoughts of being free had been suspended. They brought emotion that would get in the way, cloud her mind to what had to be done in the moment.

But as they drew closer to sunshine in the distance, she let hope flourish. The first ray of brightness nearly blinded her because she'd been looking upward, wanting the sense of freedom that blue sky up above used to give her from ground level.

Scott was the one who'd stopped.

It took her only a second to realize that his focus was on the ground.

At first, she just saw darker-than-dirt color in places. Some kind of plant life. But when one, and then another part of the small field started to move—to slither—she gasped.

"Rattlesnakes," she hissed on her last bit of air. Backing up. Scott did as well.

Far enough away for them to determine that the snakes weren't looking to follow them.

"It's a trap," he said. "Those hunters I thought I saw… one was carrying a snake. I realize that now. The gunfire was aimed up into the mountains, as I first thought. I only heard one hit because they were probably shooting at different areas. Trying to lure us out, a warning to us that they knew we were up there. And the snakes…the men knew the direction we were moving. Knew, with the retaining wall blocking us on the other side, our route would would lead us here…"

"So we go back," Dorian said, as though the thought of it didn't take every bit of strength she'd ever dreamed of having. And she was healthy. Scott, with his leg…another trek all the way up…he might make that. And then what? The baby wasn't going to be well on a cactus juice diet for long. The diapers were only going to last for another day or two, if there were no major loose stool episodes, which the cactus juice would likely cause.

"We can't go back up," Scott said then, his voice barely above a whisper. "They've chased us down to this. They're fully prepared for us to retrace our steps. I can pretty much guarantee you someone is at the retaining wall right now, waiting for us. Or above it, waiting to shoot us from above. They still want the baby."

It was the thought of the killer ever touching little Michael, ever even looking at him again, that cleared Dorian's mind.

"Then we go forward," she said, and grabbed hold of Scott's hand.

Scott stood his ground. They'd had a rough three days. He could understand Dorian's panic. But there was no way he was going to walk them into…

"Rattlesnakes are by nature solitary creatures. They'd only be there if someone had planted them as you say," she said, looking him straight in the eye. "The only time they gather is during mating season, which doesn't start until late July."

She continued to hold his gaze. "They aren't an aggressive snake," she told him. "Unless they feel cornered. And from what I could tell there were fewer than twenty of them immediately at the entrance." He saw a shudder pass through her, or thought he did, but she continued. "And they seemed to be moving on their way. McKellips might have planted them there to stop us, but they don't know that and certainly don't have a share in his plan."

She still didn't look away. At which point, Scott laced his fingers through hers. He knew a bit about snakes, too. "You're suggesting that we step carefully, walk through them slowly, and…"

He'd seen what had looked like a wheat field just beyond the end of the forest of brush they'd come through. They could lay low in that long enough to plan from there, if they made it that far.

"Worst case is we get bit," she told him. "You might not have noticed antivenom in that kit you stole, but I saw it there. And I'm fully trained in treating snake bites. Beyond that, I'd much rather risk the mouth of a rattler than a killer's bullet."

They could end up with both. He didn't bother saying so.

Nor did he tell her, when they made it back to the edge of the brush, facing the small clearing, that he was going to pick her up—baby and all.

He just did so and started walking.

"What the hell!" Dorian unleashed her fury on Scott the second he put her down, on her butt, in the wheat field. "Let me look at your legs," she said in the same breath, her gaze trying to take in every inch of both legs from the knee down at once.

"I'm fine," he repeated for she'd lost count of how many times. Once for each step he'd taken in that quagmire. "Look, see?" He lifted his pants legs. "You get bit by a rattlesnake, you know it." When the man had the audacity to put his finger under her chin, lift her gaze to his and then grin, she almost bit him herself. "I'm feeling better right now than I have since I was shot," he told her. "What a rush…something like out of *Indiana Jones*, wouldn't you say?"

He was sweating. Carrying her and the baby had taken too much toll on his leg. But it was hard for her to stay angry with a man who was feeling so good about himself.

Most particularly one who didn't find himself worthy of fathering kids.

"We need to keep moving," he said then. "They're only going to wait so long for us on the other side. And a snake or two could have followed us."

"One could have come in ahead of us, too," she pointed out, irritably, but with a keener eye on the ground around them. "And McKellips, or whoever is in charge, has to have planned for the chance that we'd have continued forward through the snakes."

"Not necessarily," Scott said, sounding sure as he crawled

along in front of her. "He's going to assess from his own perspective, figuring out what he'd do. I was ready to turn around."

"No way you would have walked back there into a barrage of bullets."

"No, I was going to get you safely ensconced, and then go hunting. In either case, we're going to hang out in this wheat field until we find a way out of it without being exposed. And pray that it isn't watering day. If this field is watered normally, we have a one in fifteen chance of getting drenched, but since it's past late afternoon, I'm giving us a fairly good shot."

She crawled silently for what seemed like hours, but was probably only thirty minutes. Watching the ground, and Scott. Keeping her movements as small as possible so if someone was watching the hay, any movement would seem normal with the slight wind that was blowing.

They'd lucked out on that one.

But then a valley, at the mountains…most days there was at least a breeze. Hot as it might be.

After a while, the snakes weren't such a concern anymore. And Dorian found herself staring at Scott's butt in front of her.

Remembering sitting on the front side of that body…

And forced her thoughts to the baby tied to her chest. He was going to need to eat again soon. Glancing down at him, she was surprised to see him wide awake. Watching her. It was the first time she'd seen his eyes fully open.

She smiled at him. And continued to crawl.

A few minutes later, as dusk was falling, Scott stopped. They were in a middle of a row, where a couple of plants didn't mature, giving them some space, but one that wasn't obvious to anyone looking out over the field.

"You plan to wait right here until dark," she guessed, what she should have already figured.

"It's about time for Michael to eat."

He was right. She took the diaper he handed her, before passing off the dirty to Scott and then took the bottle. From the outside looking in, one could be forgiven for thinking they were seasoned parents.

At the thought, a longing hit Dorian. Hard. One she'd never let past her defenses in the past.

"As long as we're surrounded here, anyone coming after us is going to be detected before they get to us," Scott said, his timing perfect for getting her out of a hell of her own making, and back into the one they had a hope of escaping. "If that happens, you head away as quickly and low to the ground as possible," the FBI agent continued. "And I engage with however many bullets it takes."

There were holes in the plan. If he was hit…

Silently, she stared at him.

"We're in a pickle here, Doc," Scott said then. "You got a better plan?"

She tried to find a plan. Any plan at all.

And only came up with one.

Leaning forward, she pulled him over, leaned forward and kissed him full on the lips.

Long and hard.

Like she'd wanted to do in the past—had started to do, before she'd come to her senses, shocked at herself—and had pulled away.

That late afternoon, with no easy way out, she didn't pull away.

She held on.

And on. And on.

Chapter 21

Scott broke the kiss, but he didn't move away from Dorian. Sitting side by side—him facing one side of the row, her the other—their thighs almost touching, they could each keep an eye on an opposite side of the row, maintaining cover of all four directions.

He remembered the night before, instead. The way she'd frozen him out after they'd had sex. As though he'd taken advantage.

When she'd made the first move.

And beyond that, their situation absolutely did not support any activity that took energy away from that which they were going to need to save their lives.

Nor could he afford the distraction.

They'd both stipulated, openly, that they weren't looking for, or even open to, any kind of relationship flourishing between them or with anyone else, so there should be no hurt feelings.

And yet…the way she'd turned from him the night before…had rankled.

Not hurt exactly. You couldn't hurt when your heart wasn't involved. But…he'd admit it. To himself. He'd been put out.

And told himself, as he prepared to pose a question to

her, that he was going to ask just to pass the time until it was dark enough for them to make a run for their lives.

He queried, "I know why I'm doing life alone, not shared, so...why are you?" Not quite the words he'd intended, but they sufficed.

With a sigh, she looked down at little Michael, sleeping as though he hadn't a care in the world. Scott was pretty sure he'd never been that peaceful. Not even in the womb.

Almost as though she could read his thoughts, Dorian looked up at him. "You want the short version?"

"Is there a long one?"

Her shrug said little.

"The long version," he opted. With nothing but stalks of hay and hard dirt to look at, he figured he could use the diversion.

"My parents were both gifted in their fields," she told him, and he got that he was getting a longer version than he'd envisioned. Way longer. But with nothing better to do, wasn't averse to listening. "I was an only child, born to them in their early forties. They taught me from my first memory that I was to use my mind to better the world. Didn't matter what I was good at, just be my best at it. I was to do, not be done upon. To act, not react. To keep my head about me."

From what he could tell, the woman she'd turned out to be must have pleased them immensely.

"I met Brent when I was two and he was four. Our parents were all members of a local group sponsored by an international organization for people with higher-than-average IQs. The group's quest was to use their minds to serve others. As Brent and I grew up, we also became members of the group..."

Brent, her fiancé. He wasn't sure, suddenly, how much more he wanted to hear.

He didn't stop her, though.

"We started dating, officially, our freshman year of high school, though we'd been telling each other since we were five that we were going to get married someday."

Yep, he should have stopped her. Thoughts of Lily came pouring back. The only child with a close-knit family with close-knit friends. Scott's advent into her life in high school had messed everything up. Until, ultimately, she'd chosen to dump Scott and marry the family friend...

When Scott realized his thoughts had had time to spiral on him because Dorian had quit talking, he looked over at her. Prompting, "And?"

When her eyes pinned his, he swallowed hard, but didn't turn away.

"We were engaged when I met you."

That was it. As though that explained everything. It didn't.

"And?"

Dorian glanced away, shook her head. He thought she was done talking, until she burst out with, "My emotions are not in sync with my mind. They're... I don't know... immature...is the best way I can think of to describe them. I ended up not only breaking Brent's heart, but hurting his parents, and mine, too."

"How? What did you do?"

"The things I felt around you...they were based on nothing. We weren't even friends. They made no sense."

She'd felt things, too. He'd wondered. So many times.

Knowing that it made no difference to the outcome. She'd done the right thing, getting away from him.

She'd fallen silent again. He offered no prompts.

The conversation had grown...difficult.

He left it there.

* * *

She couldn't just leave him hanging there. It wasn't fair. Not after he'd explained his own life choices. She'd yet to fully explain hers.

Not in any way that would lead him to her reality.

Glancing off, down her end of the row, seeing again that there was no light, no movement, coming at them in the near darkness, she glanced back to see the baby still asleep and said, "I'd never felt anything like it for Brent. I told him so, hoping that we could work on it, do something to, I don't know, spruce things up. We'd known each other forever. We just needed to see each other in different ways…" She'd done her research before having the conversation. Had a list of possible actions to take.

Hadn't even made it to number one.

"He said that if I felt that way about another man, and not for him, then our relationship was doomed before it began. Feeling horrible about myself and my wayward emotions, I offered his ring back. He took it. And when my parents still supported me, and his did him, sides were taken, and a lifetime of friendship slowly eroded."

"So, you didn't love him…"

Her gaze shot back to Scott when she heard his words. "I did love him!"

"As a very good friend." His gaze was barely visible and seemed to glint truths.

"A brother, even," she admitted. "Not quite, but pretty close."

"You were ripe for any guy who paid attention to you, or you found good-looking and had cause to contact you physically, to show you that. It's certainly no reason not to trust…"

Shaking her head adamantly, Dorian cut him off before he could finish.

"He wasn't the first person I hurt," she told him, ready to get it all out so they could move on away from her, with her choices firmly established, just as his were, between them. "The first was Faith, the woman who was with me when we were kidnapped last year. I was her soul mate. Her rock. She had a really rough life, to the point that we had rescue codes. And when she was ultimately taken away from her mother to live in another state, I just let her go. Never tried to find her. To let her know that I was still there for her..."

"Childhood friends slip away, Dorian. You have to know that. It's a natural part of life when families move."

Pressing her lips together, she told herself to just rip off the bandage. "Sierra was my best friend. I knew something wasn't right with her, but because she was a private person, because I needed her friendship and was afraid I'd piss her off, I didn't push. Had I done so, she wouldn't have been murdered. My emotions steer me wrong, Scott. They're unreliable. Immature. I can't trust them. And I won't let my lack hurt anyone else. End of story."

"Sierra?" His tone had changed. Softened. Like he was on her side.

Which was ridiculous as there were no sides.

"Sierra's Web," she said. He'd said he was familiar with the firm. The story of Sierra was right on their website. And often mentioned in news stories.

"You named your firm after your friend whose murder you blame yourself for?"

She'd hoped to be done. It was getting dark. The baby would need to eat again, and then they had to be off. Hopefully to the blacktop, a passing car and maybe even home before dawn.

It was either that, or not make it.

To get things moving, she gave him the quick rundown she'd thought he already knew. "We were all friends with her. All had noticed things, different things, and when she went missing, we took our collective thoughts to the authorities. Our information led police to her rapist and his bookie killer."

"So you aren't the only one who noticed things..."

"No, but if I had followed my professional code, pursued the facts sooner, I could have saved her life." She couldn't say more about Sierra's clinic visits. But there was no doubting the facts.

And the fact was, it was time for them to move on.

From the conversation.

And the hay field.

The perimeter of the hay field was being guarded. They'd almost reached a clearing and Scott couldn't lead them out of there.

With his head flat on the ground, he'd seen the lights shining into the growth. The first time had come just a few minutes after they'd started the last leg of crawling themselves out.

And now, with the clearing in view, he caught the taillights of a running, but stationary vehicle. He had to assume that McKellips's team had guns posted on all perimeters.

There was only one chance of getting Dorian and the baby out of there alive.

He was prepared.

Reversing course, motioning for Dorian to do the same, he backtracked far enough into the hay to be able to speak softly without fear of immediate discovery.

Whether or not McKellips knew they were in the field

was immaterial. The killer knew they were somewhere within his mountain or in hiding on the ground. He wasn't going to quit looking. He had time on his side, as he didn't have a baby to feed, and he apparently had the manpower to pretty much guarantee his success. Scott wasn't willing to risk Dorian's or the newborn's life by trying to retrace and get back up the mountain.

He'd led them right into a well-laid trap.

With adrenaline pumping through him, his gut filled with certainty.

But he had something to do first.

"What did you see back there?" Dorian asked as soon as they were once again sitting as they'd been earlier. Side by side, facing opposite directions. Albeit in far tighter quarters. No dead stalks to give them more space.

"A flash of light," he told her. The truth. Not all of it. Not the worst of it. Not until she listened to him about something else that had to matter. That *would* matter if she made it out alive. "In the meantime, since we're back here waiting again, let's get back to that conversation…"

"What conversation?" Her tone remained low, as it had been all the while they'd been hiding out in the hay, and yet it sent a certain warning with it.

The same freeze he'd been met with the night before?

He didn't have time to take the hint.

"Yep, that's the one. I've been thinking about what you said—I think you're wrong, Doc." Never, in a regular day of his regular life, would he have said such a thing. Regular life was a thing of the past.

"Excuse me? You think my life choices are wrong? What gives you the right to judge?"

Good. She had anger left in her. The will to fight.

And he didn't have a lot of time to defend himself. The

longer it took McKellips to find them, the more troops he'd call. The writing was on the wall.

They'd done their regular checks for phone service all day. Still had none.

He could no longer rely on any hope that his team or Sierra's Web was going to find them.

"I think your assessment of circumstances is skewed by personal involvement and preconceived notions about yourself. Or an inability to see outside yourself."

Her glance in his direction was sharp. When she didn't argue, he pressed forward. "I've been thinking about what you said. Your reasonings. And it sounds to me to be more of a case of you not being able to understand or explain your emotions in a way that makes logical sense to you, so you see them as a flaw."

What, he'd become some kind of psychiatrist now in the waning hours of life?

Or something more was guiding him. Mixed in with behavioral analysis training. He chose to go that route. What did it hurt at that late stage?

"The instances you use as proof… Brent, Faith, Sierra… all circumstantial, Doc. You were engaged to a man you loved but weren't in love with. Those were the circumstances. Faith's childhood…circumstances. Sierra…a set of tragic circumstances. Those lives came into close contact with you, but you didn't cause the circumstances."

He could go do his job much more easily if he could do so with the assurance that he'd be leaving Dorian with a new lease on life.

With the hope of having a personal partner, a child, of her own.

Of having the things he'd never had.

Of having it all.

He could go feeling good about himself.

"I'm guessing Brent took his ring back, not because you were attracted to someone else, but because he knew you weren't in love with him. I can pretty much guarantee that any man you're in love with, who loves you in return, will love you for your mind and your heart and will eagerly welcome the occasional loss of cerebral response, take on the risk that you might miss a fact now and then, when you're caught up in the emotion of the moment. That's what love is, and does, Doc. And the lack of perfection you seem to find as a fault…it's called being human."

She sat there. Staring straight ahead at the hay just a foot from her face. The baby asleep against her.

He couldn't look at the little one, again.

In his mind, he'd already passed the newborn over. He was trusting Dorian to get him back to his parents.

"Any man?"

Dorian's softly spoken words had his head swinging in her direction. Her gaze caught his before he could stop it from happening. Moments careened down upon him.

That first kiss all those years ago. Seeing her again, scraped up, in the interview room at the clinic. Her feet kicking in the barn with moves he'd taught her. The sex. The kiss she'd planted on him earlier, just before they'd headed out to the clearing…

"But not you." She wasn't asking.

His eyes had adjusted to the darkness. He'd seen the question there, when she'd first turned toward him, through the shadows. That was his take on it. And the question wasn't there any longer.

Taking a breath, he finished the job he'd crawled back to do. "Not me."

He had to convince her. To set her free.

"I'm as selfish as they come, Dorian. Every single thing I do, I do for myself. With myself in mind." Total, undeniable, ugly truth. One he'd never have admitted under any other circumstance.

"I visit my parents in prison, flying to two different states, several times a year. They live for those visits. And I don't give a damn about that. I don't go for them. Ever. I go for me. To remind myself of who I will never be. Every choice I make, it's with one thought in mind. Me. Being the me I can live with."

He stopped, evaluating the solid truth in his words, coming up with total certainty. And then finished his task with, "My whole life has been about me taking care of me. I'm not capable of loving others."

He might have faltered on that last bit. He didn't test himself again. Didn't have time. "Let's head out," he said, last task done, ready to implement his final plan.

Without waiting for her agreement, he turned and started to crawl.

Chapter 22

Dorian wasn't ready to move forward. With every knee and hand moving forward, she grew angrier at the man whose butt was less than a foot in front of her.

The idea had been to appear as one movement, not two. A deer, not human. She couldn't think about what the day's turmoil had done to Scott's leg. There'd be time later to examine that.

In the meantime, how dare the man sit and tell her that she'd misjudged herself, but think he saw himself clearly?

How dare he offer the possibility of more to her, and then retreat, taking the one thing she might want?

She wasn't saying she did, but…what the hell?

The anger buoyed her. Made her a little less aware of the sharp ache in her neck, and the stinging in her hands.

Who cared about an irritant like physical discomfort when one had more important things to consider—like ripping into a man for…what?

Hurting her feelings?

For his own lack of clarity?

Or…or…pretending he didn't want her?

They were yards away from the clearing. As Scott lowered down to his belly again to scout, she remained completely still, ready to put a knuckle into Michael's mouth if he started to stir, just in case. She would need to pacify him so he didn't give them away to anyone who could be close by, until they knew the person was a friendly.

Or, at least, someone not out looking for them.

How would they know?

Grace had been a hard-learned eye opener.

Still down on the ground, Scott scooted around toward her, motioning her down to him.

Leaning forward, so that her ear was close enough to hear his whisper, she thought she heard him say, "I need you to listen. To do. Period."

Pulling back, she stared at him in the darkness. Saw pinprick glints in his eyes. And nodded.

"The stream we were following from up above is through this row to your left. You are to leave now, take the first row break you come to. It's about ten yards back. Follow the break, crawling as we've been doing, down to the water. And then, staying low, and along the bank, step in and move at the pace of the water, no slower, no faster, to keep the rush of water from sounding against your legs. If someone comes, you go under, baby and all, and stay down as long as you can without risking the child's life. While you're under, you move, in various directions, coming up for air, and going under again…"

While her heart thundered and her mouth hung open, she saw him move again, fidget some, and then he was handing her his knife. "Strap this to your ankle. And don't hesitate for one second to use it."

She who hesitates could lose her life.

His words from self-defense class so long ago came flooding back to her.

As she had back then, she nodded. Took the knife. Moved little Michael as little as possible as she strapped the weapon on. Trusting Scott fully to have her future safety in mind. To teach her how to protect herself.

"If you can swim across the river, underwater, do so as soon as possible. About half a mile back, the river butted right up to the mountain. Get there. Find a place to hide. And keep hiding until you're rescued."

Reaching into the satchel, he then pulled out the last bottles of formula. "I can't help you with diapers, they'll be soaked, but stick these in your waistband, and pockets."

He waited while, with trembling hands, she did so. She had questions. But she needed all the information first.

With his whisper turning urgent, he said, "Good, now go. Stay in your head, Doc. Do." He didn't wait for a response, just turned around and started to crawl away.

"Scott!" she hissed, going after him. "Scott."

He didn't slow down. Didn't even glance back.

And she got the message. Whatever he was doing, he had to do it alone. She and the baby would hamper him. Slow him down. Get him killed.

Just as he had that first night at the mission, he was trusting her to stay safe until he came back to them.

She had her instructions.

Turn around. Stay low.

Get to the water.

And with her heart in throat, and also with Scott, she did as he'd ordered.

Scott had nothing but the plan on his mind. Getting it right. The test of his life was ahead and there'd be no room for error of any kind.

As he crawled, his mind went over the plan.

Create every distraction he could. Make it appear as though there were two adult bodies in the field. Draw all manpower in the hunt to the hay field. Have all eyes on the continued ruckus he created. Attack, move through the hay, attack. He'd recorded the sound of the baby crying the night before. Had about 20 percent battery. He would have to make certain that he utilized the limited capacity of his ace in the hole in the most effective way.

The baby was McKellips's guarantee of a paycheck. Getting the kid back would likely save his team.

Certainly, that baby would be the killer's only hope of saving his own ass. And if McKellips made good, his team would likely be protected as well.

McKellips wasn't going to have anyone fire at any target that couldn't be clearly seen, lest the baby get hurt.

All Scott needed was enough diversion to get all eyes off the water, away from the mountain, long enough for Dorian to get to safety.

From there, his plan was, ultimately, to set the field on fire. Drawing first responders. A load of them. With the water source right on the edge of the field, preventing the flames from jumping up the mountain, a perimeter could be dug around the field, preventing spread in the valley.

A burn off not completely unlike ones that farmers did sometimes to refertilize their ground.

The fire was his last act. When Dorian had had ample time to escape. And he was staring death in the face.

Scott didn't hope to save himself. Didn't have any plan to do so.

If he made it out, he'd be thankful as hell. If he didn't… he couldn't waste a second worrying about it.

He was the bait. The sacrifice.

It had come down to Dorian's and the baby's lives. Or his. He'd made his choice. Felt right, knowing that he'd have lived his entire life, and gone out, a good man.

Beyond that, he wouldn't—couldn't—go. Just as when he'd been overseas, a young soldier sent to battle enemies that went beyond the scope of any training he'd had, he focused on what had to be done.

Not on what would happen to him.

He would not die as his parents and grandparents had lived. Breaking laws and oaths, sacrificing others, to live.

Nor would he cling to those in his life, as his parents had also done. If they'd been willing to sign away their rights to him, he could have been adopted out.

They'd been more interested in the welfare money received on his behalf. And maybe of their own selfish love for him.

And he was not going out with them on his mind.

Figuring, based on her earlier progress, he'd given Dorian enough time to reach the water—thinking of her and Michael swimming away to safety—Scott lay on his belly, aimed low.

Ready to slither like a snake to his next location.

And shot.

She was in the water, wading slower than she'd ever walked, hugging the bank when she heard the first shot. Freezing in place, Dorian listened. A couple of long minutes later, she heard another shot.

And then, only yards away from her, the click and static of a radio.

Dear God, was she being rescued? Had Scott known?

Too frightened to show herself just yet, she held the baby's head to her chest, ready to duck underwater, and hardly breathed as the river flowed slowly by her.

"All, I repeat all, hands to base. Just heard the baby cry in the hay field. I want all eyes in there finding the merchandise. And if the woman happens to be alive, get rid of her. That's an order."

McKellips's voice sent chills through her. Followed by nausea.

And reality crashed down on her.

Scott had set a trap for them, more ingenious than the one they'd set for him. He must have recorded the baby crying. It was the only way McKellips could have just heard…

Tears flooded her eyes, and she stymied them. She couldn't afford so much as a sniffle. Stood still, praying Michael stayed asleep, ready to slide them both underwater if he so much as twitched, as brush moved, twigs broke and the sound of more than one big body moved farther away from her.

All sound ceased, other than a barrage of gunfire in the distance, and still, she remained still. There'd been at least two men in the mountains. For all she knew, there could be a dozen or more by then.

Another gunshot, she heard a masculine note barely floating to her through the air. McKellips sounding victory?

Scott hit? Giving her some last warning?

About to move, she stopped when she heard the rhythm of the water change to her left. Something clearly in the water. More than one something. For a few seconds, it sounded like a waterfall over there. Or a dam burst.

Preparing herself for an onslaught of water, she was left staring as only calm waters came at her.

The last of the hunters, those in the mountains, had crossed the stream.

She'd bet on it.

They were the last of the bunch.

At their backs.

She was free to run. To head into the mountains and hide. To wait for rescue.

And there was no way in hell she was going to just slink away and let Scott Michaels die like trash.

They were closing in on him. Floodlights had flipped on after his first shot. He'd seen poles, had expected as much. Just kept moving. Detonating.

During the time he'd allotted for Dorian to make it to the water, he'd watched the flashlights and crawled around inside and outside the field, planting bullets in hills of dirt in various locations.

He'd shot two of them. The first had brought the floodlights, and two sets of footsteps running.

That's when he played the recording of the baby crying. Using an app that amplified it, but made it sound like it was coming a distance away from him.

By the second shot, there were four sets of feet on the ground.

He was now counting six. All teams of two. Like the hunters that morning.

He believed that, with McKellips, there were seven. And was fairly certain the killer had assembled his entire team. At least the parts of it that knew about the foiled kidnapping.

If the operation was as large as Scott suspected, and as was indicated by the website and the ledger he'd copied the other night, the general in charge had to be someone with clout, somewhere. Someone with a load of money by this point, too.

Someone in a position to have made certain that McKellips would disappear if he found out the man had been compromised.

So…the six-member team…someone, probably McKel-lips, was keeping the news small. Mitigating fallout.

At that point, they'd have all hands on deck to search for that baby. It was the only thing that made sense. The woman who'd been kidnapped… McKellips could have been saving her life for all anyone knew. Seeing a woman in distress, shooting to protect her.

Then some wild man comes out of nowhere and takes her again. McKellips's only crimes would be not reporting the murder, tampering with a corpse, with a crime scene, and not reporting the second kidnapping.

Nothing that would lead to a newborn kidnapping ring. Or illegal adoptions.

The hunters were systematically combing the hay field, circling in closer, leaving him less and less wiggle room. His only chance of escape was to get by one of them.

The floodlights limited possibilities.

His best bet was the same way he'd sent Dorian. The river. It was dark, with trees hanging over much of the bank, blocking any hint of moonlight. He could disappear underwater in the event of flashlights.

But he didn't want to risk leading McKellips to her.

He had to travel upstream. Meant swimming underwater until he got far enough out of earshot that his body against the current didn't create a surge.

He could do that.

And go in farther upstream, too.

He continued to move slowly. Had one more bullet he needed to shoot. The one farthest from the water. But foot-steps were getting so close, he couldn't shoot without giv-ing away the location of his gun.

He could shoot the leg. Then the next, and the next.

Which would definitely give up his location and bring

a barrage of bullets down upon him. They wouldn't shoot to kill, though.

Not until he gave up the baby.

Which he wasn't going to do.

Damn sure they weren't ever going to let him walk out of there. Baby or no.

"I think I got something here…"

Scott heard the voice. Continued to belly crawl. Pulling with his elbows, pushing with his feet. Staying in shadow, beneath blades of plants, as much as possible.

A radio crackled, and then, another voice, "I've got something over here, man…a diaper, and it wasn't here five minutes ago…"

The feet coming at Scott ran down the row next to him, so close he could have tripped the guy. Was just passing on the option, when he froze again.

"Attention!" The female voice commanded what she'd demanded. Loudly. Clearly. Through a megaphone?

"This is Captain Michaels with the Phoenix police. The FBI is here as well. You're surrounded. Come out with…"

"Scott!" Dorian was there beside him, on her hands and knees, with the baby strapped to her chest, looking…just as he'd last seen her, though wetter. "Come on!"

He didn't question, didn't need to know at that moment. With the satchel still on his back, he followed the woman and child to the river.

Chapter 23

As soon as they were in the water, Dorian took her place behind Scott, not even pretending she knew what to do next.

She'd saved him.

That had been the end of her plan.

He took them upriver, mostly swimming.

With the summer heat, the water was like a tepid bath and little Michael woke up but didn't cry. She fed him as soon as they were on dry land in a low mountain cave. And found some dry diapers in the satchel, too.

She wanted to wait for his sleeper to dry before moving, but Scott had said they didn't have time. He wasn't meeting her gaze.

Hadn't talked to her, other than to give directions or check in on how she was doing, since she'd found him.

"We've got to go back up tonight," he told her, standing at the base of the mountain. "And head down on the other side of the dam."

She didn't see how he was going to make it. Not with the way he'd been dragging his leg around on the ground for hours. Wasn't sure she would, either. But didn't say so.

"Following the dirt road out is no longer an option. We'll head out farther west instead. And run into the north-south blacktop at some point."

It could take days. He didn't say so. Neither did she.

She just started hiking when he did. Watching the baby. Watching him.

And trying to believe that as long as they were still alive, they had hope.

Scott realized the futility of pushing too hard when he heard Dorian's foot slip behind him. She was a doctor, not a triathlon athlete. And she'd been carrying the extra weight of a newborn for days. With nothing to eat but cactus fruit.

Granted, their supply was plentiful. They'd been switching between the four different kinds of plants that Dorian knew for certain were healthy and safe. And had different health benefits.

But as the moon reached its peak and headed downward, and he and Dorian were only halfway up the mountain, he knew he had to call a halt.

He needed intel. And then they both needed sleep. One thing was certain, McKellips wasn't going to just give up.

He might be calling in backup. Or, if his supposition was spot-on and the man didn't want to alert anyone else of his kidnapper's major screw up, he and his men would sleep some.

Which gave him and Dorian a little more time.

Just depended who all was on McKellips's payroll. And who he might call on in an emergency.

The hunt for the man and baby was clearly a crisis. A life-and-death one.

As an inlet came into view, leading back into a smaller cave, one that was deep enough to provide decent protection, he called a halt.

Built a cradle and pallet as though he'd been doing so for years, as Dorian fed and changed the baby with their last dry diaper. And he arranged the unused, river-soaked diapers on warm rocks along the wall for drying.

Their own clothes had been dry within half an hour of leaving the river. Arizona's dry summer heat was a real thing.

The first aid kit they'd taken from the four-wheeler hadn't fared well. The one he'd stolen from the mission was waterproof. He hadn't known. But was thankful as, dropping his pants, he got a look at the stained off-color gauze around his thigh.

The fresh blood didn't please Dorian.

He'd figured it was there. Had felt the injury open a time or two.

Lying on the pallet, too tired to care whether or not his shirt covered limp parts, he didn't speak as Dorian tended to the wound.

But was thankful when she announced, "There's no sign of infection right now."

It could come. The river water would have been on every doctor's list of things to avoid. He felt her reapply salve. And strips. Before beginning the bandaging process. They'd be out of gauze, too. If not in the next seconds, then by the next bandage change.

Just as they'd run out of formula sometime the next day. Even switching it out with cactus juice, the baby milk was running out.

As were the diapers. "Good call, leaving a dirty diaper…" he said then, sounding woozy, even to himself. But only because he was allowing himself to relax for a minute or two.

The second he heard any sound of approach, he'd have his gun out and be ready.

He'd rather have his pants pulled back up first.

"But the Captain Michaels thing?" He had to ask. The question was there…

"I heard a radio transmission, that the baby had been crying in the wheat field." She'd finished with his leg. Helped him get his pants up.

Neither one of them so much as paused as they went over his penis and he zipped them closed.

"You recorded him on your phone, right?"

Looking up at her in the shadows, with eyes adjusted to the darkness, he realized, "You just did all of that wound cleaning without your phone."

"I didn't know if I'd find you, so used the name Michaels, as a clue to you. Turned out, watching the circle of men closing in, finding you wasn't the issue. Getting them away from you was."

He could see that. Still didn't…

"I used palm leaves to make a megaphone," she told him. "Set them, with the burner phone, and my recording timed to start, far enough from you to give us a chance, and then hightailed it, at a crawl, over to you…"

She'd saved his life.

Good. They were even.

Holding out an arm, Scott waited until Dorian had settled down beside him, her head on his chest, and then let himself sleep.

Dorian didn't wake up in fear. She awoke slowly, with a sense of relaxation, and as consciousness descended more completely, didn't move right away. The steady rise and fall of Scott's chest, the strong, healthy heartbeat were…nice.

More than nice.

She'd been up every two hours in what was left of the night. Could see bright sun shining in a small corner of rock around the small cave's bend.

Didn't even think about the day bringing rescue. Instead,

she got up, used the quiet time to carefully check her surroundings and then tend to her own ablutions and returned to see Scott changing the baby.

She squeezed fresh juice into an empty formula bottle, rinsed out with juice, and then fed little Michael while Scott tended to himself, and then cut up breakfast for them.

It was routine. And a sense of well-being settled upon her. For the moment, only, she knew. Her life had begun to consist of only the current moment. They couldn't live as they were for long. She only had one more bottle of formula. And three dried disposable diapers that she'd have thrown away if she hadn't been desperate.

A diet of only fruit wasn't good for her or Scott, either. They'd finished off the power bars the day before. It wouldn't be long before their digestive systems reacted to the fruit overload.

All stuff she knew. Just didn't worry about on that early morning. After days of the same, she'd grown weary of the effort it took to be bothered by things over which she had no control, things she couldn't change.

While Scott went back out to investigate their surroundings in daylight, to determine their next moves, Dorian dismantled their pallet and the baby's cradle. Rearranged the satchel some. Holding out the medical supplies she'd need to change Scott's dressing before they headed out.

She was tying the little one to her chest, ready to go find Scott when he came back in. Handing her his phone. "Look," was all he said, but his demeanor, the tone of voice, all different. Stronger.

One glance and her pulse picked up.

"A road," she said, glancing from the phone to his face, and right back to the phone again.

"Paved and about a mile down the mountain," he told

her. "It could mean cell service. But even if we're too far out for that, I've seen two cars pass over the stretch already, and it's early yet."

"What about trucks?" she asked. Every vehicle they'd seen since they'd been in hiding, all driven by their hunters, had been trucks.

"Not so far," he said. "But it's not like we're going to head down there and just stick our thumbs out at the first passing vehicle," he added. "We find a hiding place with a good view of what's coming up the road. We observe. And then we pick a vehicle that is most likely to carry law-abiding people and we flag them down."

"How do we know who's law-abiding?" Thinking of Grace, in particular, she had to ask.

"We don't." His statement, so matter-of-fact, sent the day's first tremors through her. "It's all guesswork."

He thumbed through his phone again, then, held another photo up to her. It was blurry. Beyond blurry. But she made out enough. "A police car," she said, recognizing the aerial-view number displayed on roof.

"If we can, we wait for another one to pass by. If not, we look for a woman with children, for instance. Or, better yet, women with children. Maybe four women, heading out to lunch. Young couples. A vehicle full of young dudes, with at least one of them holding a basketball..."

He grinned at that one, and she smiled back. Silence fell as they watched each other. Until she broke contact and said, "I get it."

There were no guarantees.

And the only things certain were that they weren't safe and could die.

Sobering, she straightened her shoulders. "I need to tend to your wound." There were no guesses about that one. Her tone of voice must have communicated as much because Scott immediately dropped his pants but remained upright. "My muscles hurt like hell, but the wound itself feels less tender today," he told her, while he stood, looking at his phone.

With the baby strapped to her chest, maintaining professionalism was a given. Helped by the fact that Scott couldn't have been less interested in her kneeling beside him with her head at crotch height. He didn't care. She didn't look.

The wound appeared better than it had to date. Some of the coloring was still concerning, but the skin was already pulling together. She applied antibiotic cream, rebandaged and wrapped and stood. "I'm ready when you are," she told the man she still trusted with her life.

Her attraction to the man, and any feelings she might have for him, were what couldn't be trusted. Whether she believed what he'd said about her past being circumstantial, not a deficiency in her, or didn't believe him. One thing was clear to her. Aside from feeling drawn to Scott in the past, her current situation could clearly be the result of a form of Stockholm syndrome.

She almost said as much. Just to make things clear between them. With words, not just looks and actions.

But when he set off without looking at her, she followed behind him silently, thankful that she could.

The woman's touch was an addiction that he had to avoid at all costs. Scott told himself he was just reacting to days in hiding, living with death on their doorsteps every minute of the day, being responsible for two very precious lives, while still aware of all the other babies in danger. And all the babies in misplaced homes whose biological parents were grieving them.

An hour had passed since he'd avoided embarrassing himself by staring at a blank phone screen so his gaze didn't wander, reminding himself of the danger they were in. Reliving the night before, planning for the day ahead, Scott was still thrumming with an awareness of the woman walking the path with him.

She was everything he'd ever admired in a person, all in one. To the point that her physical beauty, which was definitely noteworthy, took a third-row seat to everything else.

He wanted to believe that once Dorian and the baby were safe, he'd be back to normal. His desire to be close to her, to hear her voice and see her face, would fade. His gut wasn't convinced on that one. But the possibility hung there.

Heading back down the mountain was much quicker than climbing up. Doing so on an angle made it easier on his leg. The vegetation was different on the western peak, thicker, with more leaves. By midafternoon, Scott was finding a total influx of adrenaline again.

He was going to get Dorian and the baby to safety. Nothing else mattered.

They'd made it to mostly level ground, were close enough to the road to find a hiding place. He'd seen no sign of hunters.

And he had bullets in his gun.

"Do you have phone service?" Dorian's question sounded with a note of the hope he'd been trying to keep in check. So he didn't make a mistake.

She glanced over his shoulder, so close he could feel her sweet warmth, as he turned on his phone. "You do!" She exclaimed, right there, next to his cheek, and he wanted to turn his head and kiss her.

The desire plummeted as his phone screen went blank.

"Your battery's dead," she stated the obvious. "And I left the burner phone in the hay field."

What kind of fate did that? Got them right to the winner's circle, only to make them stand outside it? The part of the plan where they had service and called for help was deceased.

It was a setback, not a fail. Scott shook his head, pocketing the evidence.

He was too close to believe that they wouldn't make it.

Warding off a strength-sucking downward cycle, wanting to hold Dorian up, too, he focused on the good. They'd made it out of the mountain alive.

"We see a paved road. Another hour and we'll be in hiding someplace close to it," he stated the plan again. A reminder to her, and to him. And then, when he started to reach for her, to pull her against him, as though to make some silent open-ended promise that he'd get her home yet that day, he shook his head and headed toward the closest cluster of desert brush.

Good intentions or not, he had no business making promises he wasn't sure he could keep.

With a nagging pain in her shoulder blade, a crick in her neck, Dorian put one foot in front of the other. And, when necessary, one hand and knee in front of another. The farther out from the mountain they traveled, the more important it became for them to stay low. Out of sight. For their movements to appear animal like to anyone up on the mountain looking for them.

Michael was moving more, crying some.

"He's got to be tired of that sling," Scott said, as they sat within a cluster of flowering bushes.

Rocking the newborn, trying to quiet him, Dorian, who'd

just fed and changed him, nodded. And then added, "It's also the cactus juice in his tummy. I knew it was going to affect his stool, but that's better than no nourishment." It was all a matter of choices.

You made the ones that kept you and others alive, first. And then?

Any man. Scott's words from the night before in the hay field had been rankling for most of their travel time that day. In spite of her best intentions. He'd said any man who loved her in return. But not him.

It looked like they were at the end of their journey. Scott had picked out another cluster of flowering brush, much like the one they were currently in, nearer the road as their final destination. From there, they'd pick the vehicle that would, in all likelihood, get them back to their teams. And then home.

She wanted that. So badly. Home. For all three of them.

But she didn't want to never see Scott Michaels again. And with him in Vegas, and her in Phoenix, that likelihood loomed.

The baby's discomfort seemed to have passed. His eyes closed, he gave an occasional dry sob in his sleep.

Another second or two and Scott would be announcing that it was time to head out.

As he studied the landscape, she studied him. She might not get another chance. Was incredibly saddened by that thought. "Why not you?" The words pushed up out of her.

He turned. Met her gaze for maybe a second before returning toward the road. "Why not me what?"

She had a feeling he knew. And knew to leave it at that. Pressure built in her. "Why any man, but not you?"

"It's time to head out."

Dorian put a hand on Scott's arm. "Not you because you

couldn't love me? Or not you because you could, but think you're not good enough?"

He turned to her then, his gaze professional. Sharp. "Really, Doc? Now?"

His demeanor changed hers. Made her more determined. "Can you think of a better time?"

Moving slowly, carefully, Scott resumed his crawling position, the satchel balanced in the middle of his back, instead of swinging under his stomach as he sometimes wore it. And Dorian slid into acceptance mode. Blinking. Refusing to allow tears to flood her eyes, as she, too, got back up on hands and knees.

Scott glanced back, checking to see that she was ready, she knew, as he always did. "I personally can't imagine any man that had your love, not loving you back," he said, and then, without waiting for a response, turned around and started to move.

"Just for the record, I can't imagine any woman who loved you ever thinking you weren't good enough."

Had they just issued declarations of love?

For a second, Dorian got all giddy and shaky. Open to the possibility that her life choices could change. But the larger part of her, the woman who knew all the things that she knew, figured there'd been no intent to admit to loving each other. Whether emotions had grown between them or not.

They'd been thrown together, with a bit of past connection between them, and were merely clinging to each other because of circumstances.

They were simply two like-minded, savvy, independent professionals who'd just issued their parting shots.

And her heart was going to have to accept that.

Chapter 24

The second he saw the police car, with the familiar emblem on the side, Scott's adrenaline surged with such force he said, "That's the one," and went immediately into action.

He'd worked with Creekville law enforcement on a case a couple of years ago. A larger municipality in the Phoenix valley, Creekville had a thriving diverse population with a low crime rate.

"Why would someone from Creekville be up here?" Dorian's question reached him as she followed him into the culvert at the side of the road, staying by the drainage ditch as he'd instructed while they'd been waiting for what he'd determined as the best vehicle.

"Best guess, looking for us," Scott said, and stepped out of the culvert and up to the road. Raising his hand with his official ID wallet displayed across the palm.

Police would likely stop for anyone flagging down help. He was hoping his insignia would give the officer some warning that, with an agent in trouble, there could be imminent gunfire.

As he'd expected, the car, still an eighth of a mile away, slowed and pulled to the shoulder of the road.

The officer, Sharon Luthrie, her name badge read, was already out of her car, and reaching to help, as Dorian stepped up to the road with the baby.

"Let me take him for you," the dark-haired, slim woman said.

Scott had already pulled open the back door of the car. "That's okay," Dorian smiled at the officer as she quickly ducked under the roof. "He's asleep," she added, sliding over so Scott could jump in beside her.

With an intent, assessing look, the officer shut the door behind Scott, climbed back into the driver's seat and sped off, sending an alert of their rescue out over her radio. Seemed to be listening to a reply through an earbud. Gave a response.

And Scott's entire system froze. Recalibrated. Shifted to a higher gear than he'd ever known before.

Looking at Scott in the mirror, the young officer, clearly unaware of what she'd just revealed, said, "Agents and officers all over the state have been looking for you two. I can't believe I just drove right up to you."

She signaled a turn with confidence. As though she knew exactly where she was going.

"I've been on vacation out of state. Was just called back this morning to help with the search."

Scott felt Dorian's fingers touch his arm behind the sling.

He'd captured a Creekville car via his phone just after dawn. When he'd seen the road. Large ID number clearly on the roof—462. Luthrie, as an obvious reply to a question on the earbud, had just identified her vehicle as 462.

Keeping his expression bland and facing the officer, Scott pushed against Dorian's knee. From the rearview mirror things had to appear as though he was exhausted and relieved.

The woman had just signaled a southeast turn. Not north,

or west. Either of which would have taken them away from the compound. To a city and safety.

"I'm assuming there's some kind of substation set up?" Scott asked, sounding as friendly as he could get under the circumstances, keeping his knee pressed against Dorian's.

Knowing in his gut that something was horribly wrong.

She hadn't been called in until that morning?

"There is," she said. Making the turn, still on blacktop. But Scott had a sick feeling they'd just turned onto the blacktop toward which he'd originally been headed. The road that connected with the dirt road out of the compound. The direction fit.

"Any sign of McKellips or his crew?" he asked, purposely letting her know he had some information about the case. Whether Scott died in the next minutes or not, the jig was up. His agents, Dorian's partners, were not going to just let them disappear.

He had no immediate plan, except to keep Sharon talking. Unaware that he was onto her.

What he needed was a miracle.

"McKellips?" the woman asked, shaking her head. "I just know about some guy named Conrad Boring. The kidnapper who had Dr. Lowell. Until now, no one even knows for sure you two are together, or if either of you is still alive. But like I said, I just called in this morning. Am just arriving in the area. I'm not even officially on duty yet. I was just heading to temporary mountain headquarters when I saw you. That's where we're heading now."

She sounded friendly. Reassuring. Calm. Professional, even.

She knew facts about the case. Was, in all likelihood, a working officer in good standing.

Completely unaware that she'd just cooked herself. Car

462 had been the zoomed, very blurred photo he'd shot that morning.

He had to stop the car. Get them out of it. Killing the young woman seemed like the only way. But he risked the car wrecking and killing them all.

A glint in the distance, half a mile or so up the long straight road, caught his attention. A bumper. High up.

On a dark vehicle.

The black truck? Filled with McKellips and his six goons?

Scott had no time left.

Dorian hadn't been sure she'd made out the 462 on the photo that morning. She'd thought 482. And had known that was too close for comfort.

Scott's pressure against her knee confirmed her fears. And sent alarm shooting through her in waves too sharp for her to calm.

She had to think. To do. Holding Michael close, her heart was breaking. For him. For all three of them. Their little family.

Scott was going into battle against those killers…fear engulfed her.

She started to shake. Couldn't figure out a plan. Or how she could help. She focused on Scott. Afraid he was going to jump into action at any second.

Tried to be aware.

To catch any clues he sent her.

To help him.

He tapped her arm. And then pointed to the floor. Still looking straight ahead. He held three fingers out, down low. Pretending to check on the baby, she watched them count down. Three. Then only two.

Then one.

Shielding Michael, Dorian dove for the floor as Scott, reaching for his knife, slid forward in a one-second, fluid motion.

"We all die here and now, or you have a chance to live." She knew she was listening to Scott. But could hardly recognize the steady, menacing, determined tone of voice. Glancing up, she caught a glimpse of his arm reaching around the driver's headrest.

Around the officer's neck? Had to be the knife in that hand, because the hand she could see had a gun buried in the dark hair that was all that was visible to Dorian.

"You're going to stop this car, open the back door, and then, with hands up by your head, lie flat and kiss the ground, or you're dead," Scott said then. "Reach for your gun and you're dead. Are we clear?"

"Yes, sir. Please… I didn't mean to… I fell in love. Was used. And then threatened…"

"Now!" Scott hollered the word so loud that Michael jumped. Started to cry.

Before Dorian even had a chance to kiss the baby, to try to soothe him, the car jerked to a halt. The door opened next to her head; Scott slid out. She felt the car dip slightly, heard a door slam and with a sharp turn—to avoid a body?—the vehicle sped out so fast her scalp slammed into the door.

"Scott?"

Was she with him? Or had the cop managed to cut him off somehow? Was she about to be turned over to killers?

Michael's cries grew. But she couldn't help him.

Not until she knew…she leaned forward, had to get at least a glimpse.

"Stay low." The command was loud. But no longer filled with death threats. And all Scott. Dorian's eyes flooded with tears. She let them.

Didn't know how to stop them.

"If you can, slide up and buckle in, but keep your head below the window." He was yelling, over the sound of the baby's frantic cries. The car bumped and hurtled. As though Scott had gone off road.

Before he'd even finished talking, Dorian, with one arm propped on the seat, was sliding her butt and the baby up to the fabric of the front seat. Lay there for a second, with backside up against the satchel Scott had left on the seat. And very clearly, knew one thing she could do to help him. Pulling the last bottle of formula out of the satchel, she quickly affixed the attached nipple and quieted the infant.

Scott drove like a bat out of hell. The words of a song flashed along with the cactus he barely missed as he turned yet again, keeping the car behind trees and tall brush as much as possible. Knowing his chances of escape, of getting out of the day alive, were growing slimmer by the second.

His only hope was to find a spot to stash Dorian and the baby, without McKellips knowing that they were no longer in the car with him.

And to drive long enough, keep McKellips and his men on his tail long enough, that Dorian got herself to a hiding spot. And eventually to the road.

To flag down a car that fit the parameters he'd already given her.

A bullet sounded in the distance. He didn't bother shooting back. Not until someone was close enough to him that he could actually take out a windshield.

Or more.

There was a chance, depending on how many were after

him, that he could take them down one by one. He had five bullets in his gun.

Last he knew, there were seven of them.

As the baby's cries quieted, and an eerie silence seemed louder than the road noise in the car, Scott stabbed his blade into the headrest next to him.

"Take the blade," he told Dorian.

And in his peripheral vision, saw the blade disappear.

The woman was a godsend. Followed all instructions. Kept her cool. Did all anyone could ever expect of her and then some.

She'd be alright. A sense of peace infiltrated the tension pushing through his skin.

He'd taught her all he knew, and she had a mind that would not only remember every bit of it, but one that could figure out how to adapt, to adjust, as she used the information. If it was possible for anyone to get that baby safely home, she was the one who could do so.

He was nearing the mountain, but the trucks—he'd counted at least three—were gaining on him. He had to get around a couple of peaks at least to be out of sight long enough to dump Dorian.

The car's undercarriage hit an object. He was pretty sure he'd put a hole in something. Could be draining fluid that, when gone, would stall the car.

He swerved. Scraped the side of the car against rock.

Swerved again, sliding in the dust, and saw a six-foot rock abutment.

"On the count of three, open the door, and run as fast you can. Behind the rock. You know what to do from there."

Scott's throat thickened. So much he couldn't say other things.

"One. Two... Three." Stabbing his foot on the brake, he

heard the door open, then close, and shoved his foot to the gas, getting the hell out of there before anyone knew he'd driven into the range.

As he peeled out from behind the peak, Scott knew he'd just committed suicide. His detour had given McKellips time to catch up to him enough that the truck, with its four-wheel drive and bigger wheels, was going to overtake him sooner rather than later. But Scott didn't give up.

He wasn't going down a loser.

With his foot pressed to the floor, and sweating two ton, he turned, and swerved, turned and peeled out straight ahead.

For ten minutes.

Twenty.

Watched his mirrors as he careened over rocky desert ground. Saw the convoy getting closer.

Within shooting range.

Heard the shot. Glass breaking.

Felt fire in his left shoulder.

Kept driving.

Thought he heard sirens. Knew he was hallucinating. That he'd likely triggered the police car's warning sounds. Was blaring his whereabouts…

And just kept driving.

Trembling, hunched over the baby, Dorian sat in a small indenture in the mountain, just beyond the six-foot boulder where Scott had dropped her. Knife at the ready. She'd only ever cut a person for surgical purposes, to save lives, but sat there reminding herself that she knew exactly where to slice to do the opposite.

As minutes ticked by, her own life didn't matter. She wasn't sure she could take another life to preserve her own. But for tiny Michael…

The silence became a roar in her ears, as she wiped away tears she couldn't afford to shed. They'd lead to dehydration in the ninety-degree temperature. Sounds of the police car's engine had long since faded into the distance. And then, the louder roar of multiple engines had, too.

Dare she venture out?

Aim for the culvert by the road where she and Scott had hidden to watch for vehicles? Did she trust herself to choose one that wouldn't get her and the baby killed?

Or that would return the baby to hands of traffickers?

It's what Scott would advise. She had one dry diaper. No formula. And a horde of men who'd be hunting her when they didn't find the baby with Scott. Her options were to try to get back over the mountain—with the baby at least a two-day hike—and then out of it along a miles-long stretch of dirt road. Or flag down a car for help.

He'd told her what to look for.

First responders were off the list.

She had to get to that culvert. The choice was clear.

And so, after a quick meal of cactus, cut from a plant at her foot, and filling a second bottle with juice, she held the newborn close to her chest with one arm, settled the satchel in the middle of her back and set off on a three limbed crawl. No reason she couldn't use her fourth. She'd been doing so while wearing the sling for days. It would make balancing the satchel easier.

But holding on to that warm little body gave her a strength beyond anything physical. Or logical. And so she drew on it. Filling herself even while she further depleted what energy she had left.

She would get to the culvert. One bush, one cluster of bushes, one bruised knee at a time. Scraping her already raw palm. Switching hands, and doing it some more. She didn't rest much. She couldn't bear to sit out there alone, without Scott. Was afraid that if she stopped, panic would take over and she wouldn't start up again.

And then, reaching the last cluster of six-foot-tall flowering plants, Dorian crawled inside, huddled in the branches Scott had broken to fit them earlier, closed her eyes and breathed. Shaking, she held Michael, felt him stir. Knew that he'd be waking soon.

Knew, too, that she needed to have a bottle ready to put in his mouth, to keep him quiet, when he awoke. It was a given, already established routine. She knew what to do and she did it.

Do, don't be done to. Act so you aren't acted upon. Act rather than react.

Her parents' words were like a litany to her as she sat there with branches poking at her hair, her back, feeding the baby. Trying to decide if she should change his diaper or save the last one in case of a cactus juice stool situation.

She could fashion diapers out of the scrubs she'd stashed at the bottom of the satchel the day Scott had brought her pants and a shirt to change into. Out of her underwear, even.

Laying her head against the branches sticking into her, allowing them to hold her tired weight, she held the bottle for the healthily sucking baby and closed her eyes.

Longed for…escape.

For Scott.

Was he even still alive?

He'd have come back if he could.

Tears trickled from the corners of her closed lids. She didn't care enough to wipe them away. She should have told Scott that she loved him.

Stockholm syndrome aside, she'd been drawn to the man fourteen years before with such undeniable power that she'd broken off her engagement over it. He'd thought himself forever marred by biology, and she'd failed to prove to him that he wasn't.

She'd failed to do. To show him how very valuable, how wonderful and worthy, he was to her. She'd told him he was a good man.

He'd told her he was selfish.

And…she'd done nothing. Just let things linger unsaid.

She could make diapers out of her sweats.

Or take a nap, first.

The baby's sucking stopped.

Eyelids popping wide, immediately, Dorian saw him lying there in her arms, sound asleep, tiny toothless mouth open, with the nipple still touching his lip.

He was content. Secure.

He trusted her.

As Scott had.

Do.

She had to go choose a car.

Do.

The word wouldn't let go of her. Wouldn't let her give up. Or wallow.

There were things she hadn't done. In the faraway past and in the recent past, too. Because she wasn't superhuman. She was one woman. Who couldn't do it all.

Who did a lot.

And could do more.

She had to go choose a car.

Up on all fours, Dorian settled the satchel on her back, kissed the top of Michael's head, and…

Was that a siren?

A *rash* of them?

Remaining in position to move, she peered out from between the branches camouflaging her. Saw the vehicles, some unmarked, pulling up at all angles along the road.

Froze.

Had McKellips found Scott? Knew that he didn't have the baby? Called in more troops? Did he have an entire police force on the payroll?

Was he that desperate to save himself with the general?

Or was the general in charge now? With powerful people behind him?

Was their operation that lucrative?

Pulse jumping through her skin, her thoughts flew while she remained completely motionless. Listening to the high-pitched warnings piercing the air.

She was one woman with only a knife. Didn't matter how well she knew the human body, or where and how to slice...she couldn't take down multiple attackers at once.

She had to retreat.

Get back into the mountains. Live on fruit and juice and diapers made out of leaves if it came to that.

Raise a caveman.

They'd grown up strong in the past...

"Dorian Lowell, Doctor, this is the FBI—if you're out there, let us help you. You're safe." They had a real megaphone. Were approaching from the road.

She didn't budge. Was afraid to blink lest she alert someone to her presence.

No way they were getting Michael. She couldn't lose another loved one on her watch.

"Dorian?" She heard Scott's voice. It didn't sound right. "We got them."

No. They had him.

"It's Hud, Dorian..." They had a recording?

"And Win..."

"Savannah, too…"

"And Kel… You're safe, honey. The baby is safe."

"And Glen…"

"And Mariah, sweetie…you know you can trust me with Michael…"

Michael.

Only one other person knew that's what she was calling the baby.

Only one other person knew it had been her way to let him know she was there.

Scott Michaels.

With tears streaming unchecked down her cheeks, and the newborn strapped to her chest, Dorian crawled out of the brush, leaving smudges of blood in the dirt.

Chapter 25

The paramedic wouldn't leave Scott's side. "We need to go, sir. You've lost a lot of blood and the hospital's an hour away…"

Scott didn't care if he lost the use of his left arm, he wasn't leaving the site until he saw Dorian and the baby. Knew they were safe.

His own team had already tried to convince him.

And had accepted that they weren't going to get him to budge from the case until he'd led them to Dorian.

It was good to be known that well.

It was family.

They'd pulled a car up as close to the culvert on the side of the road as they could get. He'd had to stay seated. Had nearly lost consciousness when he'd tried to walk.

But he wasn't going anywhere with his charges still out on the run. He was the only one who knew where Dorian would go. How she'd hide.

And how she'd survive.

He'd called out to her. Her partners had.

If they had to go farther into the mountain to reach her, he was the only one who…

"We've got her!"

He heard a voice before noticing the commotion. All six of the Sierra's Web partners took off at a run across the desert. Followed closely by members of Scott's team, and paramedics.

"Now, sir?" The uniformed medical man beside him didn't touch him. Didn't attempt to take a hold of his arm and guide him away. He'd done that once. Earlier.

It hadn't gone over well.

"Not yet." His throat was dry. He ached...everywhere. But he hadn't seen proof.

Motioning someone to stand by Scott, the paramedic—Bruce, he thought—walked away to talk on his radio. And was back a minute or so later, while Scott continued to stare in the direction everyone had run.

"Here, Agent Michaels, does this do it?" The man was holding out a phone.

Scott reached for it. Nearly passed out from the pain. Glanced at the screen.

Dorian, with the baby still strapped to her, in the arms of her partners. A big, family circle of arms, all wrapped around each other.

And baby Michael. He looked again at the sling. And the tangled ponytail of red hair.

"That does it," he said, stood, intent to go under his own cognizance.

And felt himself floating away.

"Is Scott okay?" Walking slowly, with Win's and Hud's arms around her for support, Dorian approached the road-blocking barrage of law enforcement vehicles. She'd already given up the newborn. Kelly was ahead of them, walking faster than Dorian could, to get the baby to the ambulance waiting to take him back to Phoenix. To the birthing center where he'd been born.

Where his mother, who was having preeclampsia issues, was still a patient. Hunter's return—Hunter, not Michael—was expected to help her recovery in a major way.

None of her partners, those holding her up, literally, and those walking behind her, had answered her question.

"I heard his voice," she said then, feeling confused. Unsure of herself.

Had she heard him?

Or had she just imagined him calling out to her?

She stopped walking. Looked to the two sets of concerned eyes on either side of her, and then, glanced over her shoulder, too.

"Agent Michaels," she said, finding strength from somewhere to give the tone that would let them know she meant business. "Is he okay?"

"We don't know." Kelly their psychiatry expert came up to stand in front of her. Making eye contact. And Dorian's bravado slid away.

Along with the strength in her legs. She felt the grips from the men beside her as they stabilized her.

"Tell me," she said.

"He's been shot, Dor. Through the back, left shoulder area. No indication yet on internal damage. He's lost a lot of blood. Was breathing on his own, but clearly struggling to stay conscious. And refused to leave the site until you were found. They're on their way to meet a CareFlight copter to get him to Phoenix."

Her knees strengthened then. Enough to allow her to keep walking. Albeit slowly.

Scott was alive.

He'd brought his mountain mission to a successful conclusion.

The baby, Hunter, was on his way home.

She'd done what she could do.

And that would have to be enough.

Scott's entire body hurt too much to move. He was…
somewhere. Felt like he was encased in something. Tied
up maybe?

He had to open his eyes. Figure it out.

Didn't want to alert anyone that he was awake until he
knew who would benefit from the knowledge. His side or
the other.

If only the annoying beeping would stop, maybe he could
gather more clues.

And the stench. Like someone overdosed on Dorian's
antiseptic…

Dorian!

His eyes shot open.

And saw all three members of his team, along with his
unit chief, standing around him.

He was in a bed. Strapped down?

What the hell?

Glancing into four concerned gazes, he looked down instead of dealing with them. Saw the white gauze tying his
left arm to his chest. Wrapped all the way around him. Not
just taped there.

And frowned.

"My leg was shot," he said, remembering. So why was
his torso tied up?

Where was Dorian?

And Michael?

"There's a little muscle damage there, but not much,"
Tommy, his second-in-command, said. "The wound had
already healed too much to stitch. Leave it up to you to get

trapped with a gorgeous doctor." The man's grin was familiar. Scott relaxed a tad.

"Dorian?" he asked then, eyeing his unit chief.

"She's fine," Bonita Holmes assured him, with her no-
bullshit voice. "Scraped and bruised, but already back at
the office, from what I've been told."

Back at the office?

"How long have I been out?"

"Two days."

Two days? He'd lost two days of his life and didn't even
know it?

And Dorian was back at the office.

Not at the hospital.

That felt all wrong.

Yet, it was right, right?

His head throbbed. And he was tired.

Exhausted.

"Where am I?" he asked, to make certain he had some
bearings next time he awoke.

"Once you were stabilized, we had you flown back to
Vegas," Bonita said, as Ashley, Henry and Tommy all looked
like they were about to do something asinine, like cry.

And he figured he might as well know. "Am I dying?"

"No, sir, you most absolutely are not," Ashley spoke up.
"The bullet was lodged in the outer lining of your lung. It
was touch and go at first, but Sierra's Web called in an expert who was able to extract it without puncturing the lung.
You're going to be just fine."

The bullet from his leg traveled up to his lung? Didn't
make sense.

He shook his head. Big mistake. "Dorian got...bullet..."
He heard his voice. But wasn't sure he was still awake.

And, surrounded by his family, let himself fade off.

* * *

Dorian had thought, when she was rescued, that she was free. Instead, there she sat, with a bodyguard, McKenna Meredith, in her office. McKenna had retired from field work the year before, ran their bodyguard unit, but had insisted on taking Dorian's case herself.

Which was really Scott's case.

And now Sierra's Web's.

On the morning of the third day since her rescue, Glen Rivers, forensics expert, partner and friend, walked into her office. Nodded at McKenna before looking straight at Dorian, and said, "Ballistics have come back on the bullet that killed Chuck McKellips."

"And?" she asked, knowing that him telling her was only a courtesy. At the moment, with Scott unconscious, she was the only viable witness to a high-powered national case—not an expert working the job.

"It's a match for Scott's service revolver. He managed to get the fiend."

"And he didn't remember that?" Scott had been conscious when she'd been rescued. She knew now that she *had* heard his voice call out to her. That he'd insisted on being at the scene, in case he had to help find her. He'd know where she'd hide.

"He didn't mention the shooting, if he did remember. He was in bad shape," Glen repeated what she'd already been told. Sending another weight to the growing pile in the pit of her stomach. "The man was hell bent on using what strength he had to find you."

She'd heard that before, too.

Glen's sympathetic look flashed briefly as he turned and left her office.

From the second she'd crawled out from under the brush,

Dorian had been under the concerned and watchful gazes of the six people who knew her better than anyone ever had.

Her Sierra's Web partners.

They had questions about Scott Michaels. About her and Scott. About what had happened between them during their days on the run. Personal questions. She could almost feel the queries on the tips of their tongues.

But no one asked them.

And she had no answers for them.

She was pretty sure that she was in love with the man. Didn't completely trust herself to be discerning. And was absolutely not going to talk to anyone else about what had happened between her and the FBI agent in the mountains until she had a chance to speak to Scott.

If she *was* really in love, he should be the first to know that that little complication had arisen.

At the moment, they had a bigger problem to contend with. A killer dead. His henchmen unidentified.

An old woman with dementia who kept confusing Chuck McKellips, who'd helped her out ever since her husband died, with said husband.

And no idea as to the identity of the general.

By the time the FBI had gotten to the mission, it had been bulldozed, with a perimeter dug around it filled with water, and torched. Clearly part of a well-thought-out exit plan. They'd found the officer Sharon Luthrie dead from a single gunshot wound to the chest, tossed in the debris.

What they did know was that Dorian's and Scott's identities had been all over the news in missing persons reports, as part of what everyone had assumed was a manhunt for Dorian's kidnapper, with them as his victims. They'd originally assumed, when they found McKellips's dead body, that Chuck McKellips was the kidnapper. Dorian had quickly set them straight on that. Her kidnapper's body had yet to be found. Until Dorian had mentioned the general to her partners on the way to the hospital, everyone had thought the case had been solved.

And because she and Scott had been in the news, they had to assume the general knew who they were.

No one was sure whether the general knew if McKellips had mentioned his existence within earshot of them. No way to tell if the general knew Scott and Dorian were aware of his existence. But after the terror of the previous days, no one was willing to risk that he didn't know.

The joint FBI and Sierra's Web team working the case had determined, unequivocally, that she and Scott could not be in the same place at the same time until the general was identified and locked up. They weren't going to give the unnamed leader a chance to take them both out.

They'd further proclaimed that having the two of them even in the same state was too close.

Luckily, by the time the experts had reached that conclusion, she'd already brought in the surgeon who'd operated on Scott, and had been a microphoned observer of the surgery itself.

Since then, she and Scott had both been placed in protective custody. Separately. In two different states.

Made a troublesome thing like a pretty strong possibility of a declaration of love a moot point.

And it wasn't like anything was going to come of her feelings, real or not, anyway. Scott was firmly ensconced in Las Vegas. His team was his family. Her home, her firm, her partners, and now her childhood best friend, Faith, were all based out of Phoenix.

And he'd said, *any man,* but not him.

He'd made his feelings clear on the matter.

Besides, love or not, she was not at all ready to seriously consider the idea that she might change her own life choices as far as her future was concerned.

In spite of emotional involvement, she'd managed to help Scott keep the baby safe. And…maybe…emotions could be dealt with to the point of—if not exactly relying on them for guidance, then at least learning to accept and live with them…but…

"You ready to do another cognitive interview?" Kelly popped her head around the corner of Dorian's office. "They want me to take you back to that officer whose body they found this morning. Luthrie."

"Of course," she said. Her steady gaze indicated her need to communicate her willingness to do whatever it took to find the man who'd ruined so many lives for his own financial gain.

To save any babies in current danger, and to recover those who'd already been taken.

To help Scott finish the job.

Even if that meant relieving the terror a thousand more times.

Chapter 26

For all his physical trauma, Scott was working from a chair in his hospital room by the afternoon of the third day after he'd been shot. With officers stationed at his door, he listened through headphones as he watched a series of cognitive interviews with Dorian. The most recent had been recorded that morning.

Focus on the words, the information, came naturally. He'd been absorbing her insights and impressions for days. Relying on them. Working together, they'd saved at least one baby's life.

A time or two, as there'd been a pause in information, moments of silence, he'd experienced an uncomfortable lurch. She was looking at the camera, at him, answering questions as they were posed to her. Was reliving time spent with him.

And yet, she was so far out of reach.

Agonizingly so.

As she started speaking again, and he immediately tuned in to every nuance, every word, he brushed aside the sense of longing as nonessential. A residual feeling from being shot.

He'd be himself once the case was solved. The general caught. And the babies all accounted for.

Some of the earlier interviews he'd listened to that afternoon had been reminders of what he'd already noted in his reports. Accounts of things accounted for. Validation of his information.

But the current one—regarding Sharon Luthrie…he hardly remembered the woman. She'd been the officer on McKellips's payroll. Scott remembered threatening her, leaving her face-planted on the ground. Stealing her car and careening off into the desert.

He hadn't remembered her telling Dorian she'd take the baby, as Dorian got into the car. He did as she said so, kind of, peripherally, but not clearly.

Because of his blood loss, he knew. There were definite holes in that afternoon. Doctors had said he might never remember all of it.

He'd remembered shooting McKellips, as the man had pointed a gun through his truck window. He'd fired, not so much to save himself from a kill shot—he'd figured he'd already had that—but so that the killer couldn't escape. He'd needed his team to find out who McKellips was. And more importantly, had needed the killer to lead them to the general.

He remembered being in mind-numbing pain, fighting to remain conscious, as he waited to hear that Dorian had been found.

"So, you're on the floor of the backseat with the baby, and Agent Michaels, Scott as you call him, is leaning through the open partition, with his arm around the officer's neck—you think, he has a knife, you think to her throat, and he gives the officer an order to stop the car, threatening her life if she doesn't comply?" Scott recognized the voice coming from somewhere off camera. He'd been listening to it all afternoon. Kelly Chase, Dorian's psychiatry partner, he'd been told.

"Yes." Dorian's eyes were closed, but she sounded strong. Sure. "That's right."

"What does she say?"

She didn't say anything. The thought popped into Scott's head, as he watched Dorian frown. "Yes, sir."

What? Leaning forward, Scott froze for a second as his bandaged chest and arm rebelled against the movement, and, staring at Dorian's face, watched her mouth move as she said, "He asked, *Are we clear?* She said, *Yes, sir.*"

"And then what?" The offscreen voice came again.

"She says, *I didn't mean to… I fell in love. Was used.*" Dorian's lids flew open and she was staring right at Scott. "I think. I'm pretty sure that's what she said. She was saying something about being threatened but Scott yelled *Now!* and the car lurched to a stop…"

Holy hell. Staring at the screen, Scott rewound. Needed to watch every nuance of Dorian Lowell's face. To hear her words, in context, again.

And then stopped the tape. Reached for his phone. Pushed Speed Dial.

Sharon Luthrie hadn't been in it for the money. She'd been in love.

"Hudson? I need a deep dive on Luthrie's personal life. Yesterday."

Still watching Dorian, feeling her, growing more confident as he studied her stilled expression, he felt the familiar adrenaline coursing through him.

They were closing in.

His gut told him so.

And what it was telling him about his chemistry with the doc?

That was going to have to wait.

Dorian heard from her IT expert partner, Hudson Warner, late that day that the intricate look into every aspect

of Sharon Luthrie's life had turned up a couple of prior re-
lationships, but nothing in the past couple of years. At all.

Disturbingly so.

Along with weekends where she seemed not to exist. No
texts, no phone calls, no streaming services or credit cards
used. Once in a while, that would make sense. But for almost a year, it was two or three weekends a month. Even
her car's GPS system showed up empty.

The woman had been in love. And then threatened?

The likely conclusion, apparently drawn by Scott and
passed on and agreed upon by the team, was that she'd been
having a secret affair.

With a married man?

A woman?

Two members of Scott's team were on the ground in Arizona, talking to everyone who'd known Sharon. Hud's team
was tracing her steps immediately before she'd started disappearing for weekends at a time. Glen's forensics experts
were going over McKellips's home with a fine-tooth comb.

Law enforcement was combing the mountains and surrounding areas, on all sides of the range, for any sign of
McKellips's team members. The blurred photos on Scott's
phone were all they had to go on, but they at least gave an
estimation of skin color, body shape and a decent approxi-
mation of weight and height.

And for all anyone knew, another baby was being stolen, while they all sat in their offices, or worked the field,
in relative comfort.

Eating healthy meals. On time. Sleeping on mattresses
in air-conditioned comfort.

As Dorian ate a late supper of cobb salad and homemade
wheat bread in her office with three of her partners—and a

police officer stationed at the door while McKenna grabbed a nap across the hall—she kept thinking about Scott.

Her time with him.

Nights lying on rock and brush, with her head on his chest. She'd slept better those nights than any since her return.

All the conveniences of normal life had been stripped away, and she'd found…more.

Something that lasted when everything else was gone.

When all that existed was the moment between life and death.

Certainly, she would have bonded with whoever had saved her. But she hadn't just connected with Scott over their fight for survival.

She'd found parts of herself through him.

Her phone beeped as Kelly and Mariah discussed a shared client and Dorian glanced down to see the Text icon showing.

Tapped and opened the message.

A picture of Hunter, eyes open, looking up at his mother, with his father sitting on the bed with them, his arm around them both.

Blinking back tears, she smiled.

And knew there was no one else in the world who'd understand the mixture of joy and grief washing through her, except Scott.

She had his cell number. Not only from remembering it during her times with his phone during their fight for life. But because it had been included on the interoffice memo delivered to every Sierra's Web partner when the firm had partnered with the FBI on Scott's baby kidnapping ring case.

Quietly pushing the contact information she'd entered for him, she forwarded the picture.

And tried to be content with his returning message.

Job well done.

As in, over.
He'd moved on.

Scott's team got a lead regarding a political rally Sharon Luthrie had worked a couple of years before, right around the time she'd started mysteriously disappearing for weekends.

Hudson's tech gurus followed up with multiple internet searches, including social media services, collecting hundreds of photos from the event.

They scanned them for facial recognition of Luthrie, and assigned others to go through them one by one with the naked eye, on a physical hunt for any hint of the fallen dirty officer.

By the time Scott was discharged from the hospital the next morning, and, at his insistence, was taken to the office rather than heading to a hotel with his protection duty, a man had been identified as someone of interest. Several people had turned up photos that contained Luthrie in the background, talking to the man. A political donor, Colin Evart, who'd been known to back several major candidates.

Judging by some of the expressions on Luthrie's face, they hadn't just been discussing business. The way she'd been looking at the unmarried entrepreneur, the smiles in some of the photos, made it pretty clear that she was, at the very least, enjoying their conversations.

While Scott hadn't officially been cleared for duty, his unit chief was allowing him to call shots from his desk, as long as Scott agreed to head to his hotel with his detail at lunchtime for a rest.

Scott sent one of the Bureau's Arizona agents helping with the case to find Colin Evart and bring him in for questioning. He'd watch, and participate if the need arose, via teleconference.

Winchester, Dorian's financial expert partner, had his people looking into money trails. Starting with any monies other than her regular pay that might have been deposited into Sharon Luthrie's account in the past eighteen months. And following out from there.

They'd be delving into Colin Evart's finances, too, as soon as they had legal access to them.

And then, since Dorian had initiated contact between them, he texted and asked if she'd be up for an interview with Grace Arnold. He knew the expert physician had been in the office every day since her release, working steadily to help find the general.

Before heading with her detail to whatever hotel they had her stashed in at night. The exact location of her temporary lodging was need to know only, and he had no need to know.

Not professionally at any rate.

His phone vibrated in his hand, signaling an incoming text, less than a minute after he'd hit Send.

Of course, he read.

Two words. No lines to read between.

The answer he'd sought.

And it wasn't enough. He needed more from her.

You sure? He thumbed the response back. He was asking a lot—for a victim to face one of her attacker's known consorts.

Absolutely.

I'd like the interview to take place at the Sierra's Web offices. With Kelly Chase. His thumbs flew quickly from letter to letter. Using Autocomplete whenever possible. As though, if he didn't get things out with speed and alacrity, he'd lose her. Maybe lifting her out of her environment, and away from McKellips's influence, will help free up something more.

He couldn't ignore the sense of a weight easing away from his chest as he connected with the doc.

But moved through it.

Until he saw Dorian's response. Seeing me might help, too.

He'd had the exact thought. Had left it unexpressed so as not to put undue pressure on Dorian.

The way she'd seemed to read his mind, or at least to be on the same thought wavelength as he was, had followed them out of the mountains.

His relief, though illogical, was palpable.

And he typed one more time.

I miss you.

Dorian read and reread the text what seemed like a hundred times, as she waited for Grace Arnold to arrive.

She responded in kind. And deleted.

Typed that she hoped he was okay, and deleted that, too.

As she ate lunch with the partners in the office, brought in by their receptionist who'd been with the firm since its inception, and caught up on the case, she heard that Scott had been sent to his hotel to rest.

And left her phone alone.

But when word arrived that he was back at the office, and doing well, she picked up her cell again.

I miss you, too. She hit Send without a second's hesitation. She was done fighting with herself about it.

He'd been brave enough to put it out there.

She couldn't ignore the gesture.

And she couldn't lie to him.

Nor could she get him out of her mind as she listened to Kelly interview Grace Arnold late that afternoon. The woman recognized Dorian. Called her *dear*. Asked why she hadn't been in church on Sunday. And how her little girl was feeling after that cold.

She remembered seeing someone in the brush at the edge of her property, after Kelly prompted her with a description of the incident. Said that she'd fed *those folks*.

Spaghetti and meatballs. Fred's favorite.

Dorian knew the questions were establishing a groundwork for Kelly to work from—a level of lucidity—as the psychiatrist determined the best way to proceed to extract the information the team so desperately needed from her.

Grace was the only person they knew of who'd had dealings with Chuck McKellips. The only one who could lead them closer to the killer's crew.

Other homesteads interspersed throughout the area, roofs Scott and Dorian had seen on camera from atop the mountain, had either been vacant, or the owners had claimed ignorance of the mission and its work. The agents had not been completely convinced that no one knew anything, but it had been very clear that no one was going to say a word.

Could be they were all on McKellips's payroll.

"How did you meet Chuck?" Kelly's question came casually, without a word of warning to Dorian.

"Chuck is a nice boy. He helps me." Grace, sounding as kind as Dorian remembered, smiled.

"How long have you known him?"

"I'm sorry, honey, known who?"

"Chuck."

"Oh, Chuck…such a nice boy."

"Have you known him since he was a boy?" Kelly wasn't lightening up on the woman at all. Maybe not her usual method, but this time, a member of her family, her firm was involved.

"A boy, yes. Such a nice boy."

And on it went. Kelly let Grace guide the conversation to a point. Following the woman's mental wanderings. But always bringing them back to Chuck McKellips.

Half an hour into the conversation, Grace said, "This is fun, and so nice of you all to invite me for tea. And… I'm afraid I have to excuse myself. I need to go."

"Go?"

"To the ladies' room," the woman said, wiggling in her seat, clearly agitated.

Understanding how quickly the need to pee could hit, particularly at Grace's age, with lessened ability to hold on, Dorian stood. "I'll take you."

They'd had no tea. Had been sitting on couches in Kelly's office, with McKenna just outside the door, and as Dorian headed down the hall to the single-use bathroom reserved for clients, the bodyguard followed just a step behind her. Waiting with Dorian as the older woman disappeared inside.

Before there'd been any chance for the confused old woman to have completed her business, the door opened. "I'm sorry, dear, my zip is stuck. Can you help me please?"

With a glance at McKenna, Dorian reached for the front closure on the woman's pants.

"Oh, my, missy, we can't do that here. Not with gentlemen in the house…"

Afraid the woman was going to wet herself, Dorian stepped inside and closed the door, with the hope that, with them alone, she could get Grace to chat more freely. Scott was counting on her to make the difference. Nothing the woman said would be admissible, but once Scott got the "in," he'd find whatever proof he needed. She had no doubt about that.

And Sierra's Web would be right there with him, delivering whatever he asked of them.

Grace walked to the sink, not the toilet, leaning against it to turn on the water.

"Let me help with your zipper," Dorian suggested gently, from just behind the woman, preparing for a flood on the floor.

Tile, that would be more easily cleaned than the carpeted hallway and offices.

Grace turned, slowly, revealing the revolver, with a silencer, held steadily in her grip. "It's all your fault. Stealing that kid. I'm old. It's my time. I'll die, all roads point to me, and they'll never know what's still going on right under their noses."

For a split second, Dorian was working, a doctor with a patient having a psychotic break.

Until she saw the steely, hate-filled look in Grace Arnold's eyes.

Chapter 27

Scott was sitting at his desk when his cell phone rang. A second later, his desk phone pealed, as did those of his team members just outside his office.

Adrenaline pumping, he answered the cell. He'd seen the screen. Sierra's Web. His link to Dorian.

And was standing before he even saw every one of his team members up and rushing toward him.

Tommy got to him first. "I've just arranged a private jet for you," he told Scott, who was nodding, his one usable, free arm holding his phone. Whether the Bureau picked up the tab, or Scott would be billed for it, didn't matter a whit to him.

With the call ended, he dropped his cell into his left hand inside the sling and loosened his tie. Feeling the air cutting off at his throat.

"She's expected to be fine," Tommy said, hurrying beside him as his detail, getting briefed, followed closely behind.

"She has a bullet in her leg." He bit the words out. Could hardly sustain the fury—and panic—racing through him.

He'd lost friends. Comrades. Both soldier and agent. He'd lost Lily in a different way. And nothing compared to the despair roiling through him.

"I talked to Glen," Tommy was saying as they rode down

in the elevator. From what Scott had gleaned, as soon as they'd heard shots, every partner in Sierra's Web, as well Dorian's bodyguard, had rushed the bathroom to find Dorian bleeding and semiconscious, and the old woman, Grace Arnold, dead.

Kelly had been climbing into the ambulance with Dorian, when Hudson and the others had all called every number Scott had given them as contacts.

"He said the woman, Grace, was faking senility. She'd left a note on the toilet, detailing her deeds."

Chin tight, Scott nodded. Watched the floor number lights move, counting down. And was through the door the second that it popped open.

Protective team be damned.

The perp was dead.

His team, Sierra's Web, would be ripping apart Arnold's life to find the money trail. The connections. And hope to God, the babies.

He had to get to Dorian.

Men were after her. Dozens of them. All wearing handkerchiefs over their faces so she couldn't identify them.

They had guns.

Bullets flew through the air.

Dorian turned her head from side to side, trying to deflect the spray, to protect her head. As long as they missed her head, she had a chance to tell Scott she loved him.

And was carrying his baby.

Wait. No, she couldn't be pregnant, could she?

A bullet was coming straight at her. In slow motion.

She kicked up her leg, sharply, just like Scott had taught her and screamed for him.

"Dorian…ssshhh… I'm right here…"

She heard the voice. Felt a soft touch on her face instead of the bullet. But her leg wasn't right. Numb. Something tight was around it.

"You're safe." Scott's voice again. And then, "Thank God. Is she alright?"

"Her vitals are fine, sir."

She recognized the beeping then. The tone of voice coming from a woman.

And memory flooded back.

Grace. She'd kicked the gun. Knocked the silencer. And fire had rent through her.

She opened her eyes.

Was laying with her leg propped up above her heart. In a hospital bed.

And...there was Scott. Standing beside the bed. His hand gently rubbing her cheek. Pushing hair away from her forehead.

Was she still dreaming then?

But no, her mind was clear.

"Scott?"

"Yeah." He grinned. "You're back with me."

"I didn't know I'd left. And what are you doing here? How're your chest and shoulder?" He shouldn't be standing there tending to her.

"You were in surgery for half an hour, and I've been waiting for you to wake up. I'm sore as hell. As you will be soon enough."

She frowned. "No, Scott, you shouldn't be here. It wasn't her. She was in on it, somehow, the fall guy, I think. They're still out there..."

"Hudson's already found the money trail," Scott told her, sitting on the edge of the bed as the nurse checked various readings, typed on the computer and left the room. "Millions of dollars, all moving through Grace to offshore accounts. He's been able to trace various deposits to twenty-three illegal adoptions in the past six months…"

Scott was talking faster than normal. Hardly took a breath. Or let her get a word in. "Scott…" She tried to sit up. To get him to listen.

"All of the babies were taken right after birth, all from birthing centers not hospitals, and all but three of the children were being adopted legally, through another, legitimate source unrelated to this ring. My team's in the process of coordinating the rescue of the babies, the arrests of the illegal adoptees, and contacting the proposed adoptive families to see if they still want the infants."

"Scott!" Dorian spoke sharply. Needing him to listen to her.

And heard commotion in the hallway. Shards of fear shooting through her, she grabbed Scott's one good arm, clutched him tightly with both hands. "Duck!" she said, and then saw Hudson and a man wearing an FBI identification badge rush into the room.

"Another baby's been kidnapped," Hudson said, looking right at Dorian. "When they were wheeling you out, you were trying to tell us something…"

Another baby! Despair fought with anger. "Yes!" She gave Scott's arm a squeeze. "She intended all along to kill herself if anyone got close. There's someone else out there, someone running things. Someone close enough to Grace Arnold that she was willing to die for him…"

She'd barely gotten the words out before Scott's arm tensed in her fingers and, jerking away from her, he turned to the two men.

"Evart." He bit the word. "It just hit me. In Grace's house, I had to move things from a chair…" He swung back to look at Dorian, and then faced the men again. "There was a frame with a newspaper clipping. About a woman. Miranda Evart. It had been signed. 'Love, Mama.'"

Dorian stared at Scott. "In the fray... I totally forgot about it," he said urgently, looking at Hudson. "Check birth records. A mother would die for her child. What if Grace had a son before she married Fred Arnold?"

"Evart," Hudson said, rushing from the room, with Tommy right behind him.

Scott took a step toward them, glanced back at her and stopped.

"Go," she told him.

And smiled a little as he rushed from the room.

Even as uncontainable tears started to fall.

Colin Evart was adopted out as a child to a prominent family who raised him to understand the influence gained by being rich, and the personal power one carried to shape the world as they wished it to be if they were in possession of enough money.

He'd inherited several million dollars, but it had never been enough. There'd always been more to do, apparently. More lives to control through political endorsements. More money to be gained.

The political donor had been involved in all kinds of schemes during his nearly sixty years of living. The adoption scheme being just the latest.

He'd come up with the idea after Grace had reconnected with him when Fred died. He'd played on her guilt for abandoning him to earn her everlasting loyalty.

And the rest, he'd confessed to Scott and those watching the interview, had been almost too easy.

Until Chuck McKellips, a man who'd owed Fred and

Grace his life, had enlisted his deadbeat brother to make that last kidnapping, with the idea that they'd keep double the money in the family.

Even in handcuffs and chains, Colin Evart had been cocky. Seeming to think he had enough money to buy his way out of any legal problems that came his way. He'd declined to wait for his lawyer, as though there was nothing he could say that would keep him locked up. The man expressed no remorse. Not even a hint of grief at the loss of his mother.

And didn't remember Sharon Luthrie's last name. Saying only that the cop had come in handy.

It was the most nauseating interview Scott had ever conducted. He strode from the room, turned the case over to his team and left the Phoenix FBI building without slowing down.

Dorian had been discharged from the hospital, had been planning to head home with Kelly Chase keeping watch over her, and Scott couldn't get to her fast enough.

Over the past twenty-four hours, he'd spent what little time he had after work to rest, napping on and off in a chair in Dorian's hospital room. And had found more respite just having her close, than in any sleep he might have managed to get.

She'd become home to him.

He had no idea what that meant, in a real-world sense. They were independent loners. Both better suited to single life. She was here; he was there.

But when he saw her on crutches, through her front window as he took the walkway up to the front door in the gated community he'd been buzzed into, he finally had a moment of total clarity.

"I don't have to have all the answers," he told her as she

opened the door. "I've got some—you've got some—some we both have. Any way you look at it, between the two of us, we stand a good chance at figuring things out."

Mouth hanging open, Dorian stood there, speechless as the blonde psychiatrist he'd met a couple of times over the past few days stepped into view.

"I…think I'll be heading out," Kelly Chase announced to no one in particular. Grabbing her purse from someplace behind the door Dorian still held, she leaned in to give Dorian a kiss on the cheek and smiled at Scott as she brushed past him.

Dorian still stood there. Staring at Scott.

"You want me to go, too?" Scott asked. Because…he was who he was.

"No!" Stepping back, a little awkwardly with the crutches, Dorian made more room for him. "Of course not. I'm just…"

She stood there, leaning on crutches, and gave him a once-over, sling and all. Medically, more than in a man-woman way. As though to reassure herself, once again, that he'd gotten lucky and all vital organs were just fine.

"I'm in better shape than you are, Doc," he told her, shoving his good hand in his pocket. It was either that or attempt to pick her up with his one free arm, letting her crutches fall where they may.

She nodded. And then, her eyes getting that adamant look he'd grown to watch for over their days in the mountains, she said, "I love you, Scott. That's the answer I have. I debated about telling you. But when I was looking down the barrel of Grace's gun, and your face flashed before my eyes, along with words from long ago, telling me how to do that kick… I did it exactly as you'd taught me, lean and punch, knowing that if I survived, I had to tell you I love you."

Her stance, even on crutches, was filled with authority. Mixed with a bit of defensiveness. She most definitely wasn't going to apologize for crossing into territory he'd clearly marked with no-trespassing signs.

And all he could do was laugh. Out loud. Heartily.

Before he pulled his hand out of his pocket, lifted her up over his right shoulder as she squealed, and carried her toward the stairs.

Luckily, he'd fallen for a super smart woman. She was already directing him toward a bed before he'd made it halfway up the steps. He got there without mishap, but his chest was screaming at him, and his leg was throbbing a lot.

They fell to the bed together, Dorian leaning to use her hands to bear some of the weight, and then, with her still half sitting on his good leg, he kissed her. Full on. Long and hard.

Not caring a whit that his engorged penis was pressing up against her hip. He had it for her. Bad.

"I love you, too," he finally said when they came up for air. And then sat there, looking at each other.

A necessary break due to the fact that they were both in various stages of recovery from gunshot wounds.

"I don't want a long-distance thing," she told him, her face just inches from his.

"Me, either. I can put in for a transfer to the Phoenix office." Her firm didn't have another office. And her private practice office was there, too.

He'd miss his team. But they'd be in touch. And…they all had their own families.

Finally, he did, too.

"So…we're going to do this?" Dorian asked. "Be a couple?" She didn't look like she'd fall apart if he said no. But he could read the hope in her gaze.

"Yeah," he told her. "We're going to do it. And, federal lawman that I am, if I have my way, we'll tie it all up, nice and legal."

She threw her arms around his neck, managing, doctor that she was, to miss his shoulder, and followed him gently down as he lay back.

Her mattress seemed to be an extension of her. Welcoming him, harboring his aches and pains. Safeguarding their hearts.

Dorian's head planted gently on the right side of his chest. He heard her let out a deep breath. Scott lifted himself, taking her with him, just long enough to prop a pillow under her wounded leg. And settled back with an exhausted, grateful sigh. The last thing he remembered, as he started to drift off, was her saying something about starting a family someday.

And he fell asleep with a smile on his face.

* * * * *